AFFECTIONATELY YOURS

September
Alverston Hall

Dearest Anna,

The fields are full to bursting, the meadows are green and lush, the sky here is so brilliantly clear that yesterday I spotted a hawk flying over the Mill Pond ten miles distant—it is a glorious summer in our corner of England. I have always loved this land the most of all my father's properties, and am so glad to imagine that I will now never have to leave it. I am learning to make this my home, and it has welcomed me. Indeed, I have never felt so welcome before. I hope someday that you may share its glorious summer too.

Here the writer's pen retraced its script and crossed out the last sentence on the page.

An invitation to visit, however indirect, could not be tendered. It was, the earl pondered, an unfortunate truth, made necessary by the deception being practiced, the deception that seemed so essential for her satisfaction, and for his, as she had put it, "peace of heart." Something that had been done as an act of sympathy had become for him a certain lifeline.

BOOK YOUR PLACE ON OUR WEBSITE AND MAKE THE READING CONNECTION!

We've created a customized website just for our very special readers, where you can get the inside scoop on everything that's going on with Zebra, Pinnacle and Kensington books.

When you come online, you'll have the exciting opportunity to:

- View covers of upcoming books
- Read sample chapters
- Learn about our future publishing schedule (listed by publication month *and author*)
- Find out when your favorite authors will be visiting a city near you
- Search for and order backlist books from our online catalog
- Check out author bios and background information
- Send e-mail to your favorite authors
- Meet the Kensington staff online
- Join us in weekly chats with authors, readers and other guests
- Get writing guidelines
- AND MUCH MORE!

**Visit our website at
http://www.zebrabooks.com**

AFFECTIONATELY YOURS

KATHRYN JUNE

Zebra Books
Kensington Publishing Corp.

http://www.zebrabooks.com

ZEBRA BOOKS are published by

Kensington Publishing Corp.
850 Third Avenue
New York, NY 10022

First Printing: February, 2000
10 9 8 7 6 5 4 3 2 1

Printed in the United States of America

*Thank you, Mom, Dad, Anne, Tom, Mary and Meg—
for your enthusiasm and encouragement.
And thank you, Georgie—for always reading the
pages as soon as I could write them.
I love you guys.*

ONE

The lines of careful script crossed and recrossed the single sheet of crisp linen paper.

July
Hedgecliff, ＿＿shire

My dearest Valerie,

How I have missed you! It has been now almost three months since I have heard from you, and I am so anxious to hear you are well and happy. How I miss our summers in your grandmother's gardens, strolling along the pathways of my uncle's land, getting into mischief that no "well-bred" young ladies, as Lady Greenwich would call us, should ever consider getting into! I am so looking forward to hearing about your Season—my forehead is getting practically wrinkled with squinting into the afternoon sunlight looking for the post every day, awaiting a letter from you—although my Aunt Louisa says on alternate days that the wrinkles are either the imagination of an eighteen-year-old innocent with no idea of what real wrinkles look like, or are caused by all the brownings my face suffered in your company, traipsing about the country-side unbonneted and unattended! Whatever the truth

*of the matter, I am indeed winding myself up into such
a ball of anticipation that I am not quite sure if I will
ever be able to unroll when I finally do hear from you!*

*My dearest, I fully understand that life in town is
terribly busy, a whirlwind of activity and entertainment, and while the weeks stretched by here in
_____shire they must have flown by for you in London.
I imagine you had little time for writing, but did think
of me as I think of you.*

*How was your time in London, my dearest friend?
I know you must have "taken," as they say, right away,
with your curls and (despite our sunny summer
jaunts!) cream-white skin, and especially your warm
smile. Those London gentlemen hadn't a chance, I
merit. You were probably the belle of every ball, your
dance card filled from the moment you stepped into a
ballroom. Oh, I am eager to hear how it all was. Tell
me all about the soirées, the musicales, the balls, driving in the Park, the theater... Almack's! And how did
your Audience go off? Quite splendidly, I am sure. You
always have been so very much more poised than I,
haven't you, my friend? I would have been quaking in
my slippers! I would probably have fallen over on Her
Highness's lap or something dreadful like that. You, I
do not doubt, were all poise and ladylike comportment—at least, that is, for the minutes you were expected to be so!*

*My precious Valerie, I must tell you something I have
discovered this last ha'year. It is simply this: Imagining
you among the* ton, *making friends with the most
charming (and loveliest, of course!) girls and flirting
outrageously with the most handsome men, dancing
and sparkling your way through every* fête, *I have felt
so satisfied simply knowing you are happy and finally,
after this sad year of mourning your dear, dear grandmother, enjoying the life of guiety that you are meant
to enjoy. Because of this, I have felt less and less the*

*bitterness and more and more the sweetness of losing
your company this last spring and summer. Knowing
you were having your Season for both of us, I have
almost felt as if I were having one too. Simply imagining it all has been so pleasurable an activity for me.
I thank you for that vicarious enjoyment.*

*Now, however, I will scold you and tell you that in
not writing and describing every single tiny detail you
have deprived me of more than your share of the Season; you have deprived me of my share too! I do hope
to hear from you soon, with all of your news and all
of your stories. Do not forget a one, please, as I will
not be satisfied with partial histories. And because I
know writing is not your particularly favorite activity,
I implore you to imagine that we are together in Lady
Greenwich's garden, on the oak bench under the peach
tree, and that you are telling me everything face to
face. The writing will go swiftly that way, and I will
that much more quickly have the immeasurable pleasure
of sharing your memories with you.*

*With all of my affection,
Anna*

* * *

*August
Hedgecliff, ____shire*

Dearest Valerie,

*How I have looked forward to hearing from you. I
hoped that the quiet warm months of the summer would
provide you with sufficient time to write and tell me
of yourself, and especially your come-out in London last
spring. I have never known you to be a reluctant correspondent, (although indeed you have always been a
brief one, as you would be the first to admit!) or an*

inconstant friend. I have not expected tomes, *but have desired only to hear news of you. I remain here at the home of my uncle and aunt, as always, looking forward to your company, if not in person anymore then at least in letters. Since your grandmother's passing you have no reason to come to our sleepy corner of England, but you should always know that your friend here hopes not to be lost from your memory. Valerie dear, new friends and experiences could not have caused you to forget your devoted companion, the devoted "sister" that you have had, can they? I have, on account of my uncle's infirmity, as you know, no news from outside of ____shire, and no way of knowing whether this sad possibility has come to pass. I sincerely hope it has not.*

My friend, I have missed your company this summer as acutely as I did last, the first we have not spent together in so many years. This summer, however, I have had the happiness of imagining you deeply engaged in your new life. Please be so kind as to share the excitement with me, my dear! I still await a letter from you, and hope always that you are well, not doubting it for a moment.

*Yours in affection,
Anna*

* * *

*October
Hedgecliff, ____shire*

Dear Valerie,

The fields of Hedgecliff are cleared, the harvest in, the late-summer blooms along the paths we so blithely skipped down through the summers of our girlhood are faded and gone. The winter is hastening in particularly quickly it seems this year. All of these things I have written to you before during other autumns, I know. This one, however, has been the first in which you have not written back. How I have missed your short and thoughtful letters; how I miss your friendship.

I am determined to avoid becoming maudlin. I have passed distress, and even have gotten through a bit of anger; your sweet character does not deserve it, though my less well-tempered heart sometimes produces it. I shall not, however, write again. I am saddened by the loss of your regard, and can only imagine that your new life has introduced to you pleasures of friendship which eclipse my modest offerings.

Yours always,
Anna

TWO

The feet positioned dangerously close to the flames leaping within the huge fireplace were clad in impossibly scuffed and mud-caked yet well-shaped leather hessians of the finest quality. The legs stretched out toward the unfelt heat were long, strong, and far from relaxed. The gold waistcoat and coat of bottle green superfine were creased and travel stained, a far cry from the condition in which they had exited Weston's shop. The broad shoulders were thrown at a careless angle onto the high-winged chair of burgundy leather, belying the trembling tension of their master. Charcoal gray eyes, shaded by dark, thick lashes too long for a man, stared sightlessly beyond the carved marble mantelpiece into the fire reflecting tiny orange-gold flames within their smoky depths.

Captain Valentine Monroe, lately the seventh earl of Alverston, raised his glass to his lips and swallowed the remainder of the fiery liquid. An empty bottle rested on a mahogany table beside him, next to a tray of food he had not looked at. Gray eyes slowly shifted their gaze from the fire to the empty brandy glass, and a slight sneer of self-pity curled around his smooth lips. There wasn't enough brandy in all of England to erase the images that stared back at his lordship from the depths of the library's fire. Carefully, almost too gently, he placed the glass on the table and rested his large, shapely hand on the arm of his chair.

He had tried—Lord, he had tried—to deaden his senses, to exhaust himself, to fill his belly and brain with drink in order to drive the images from his head; but neither body nor mind would respond. Almost two months now he had been back, working himself near to death, seeing to his unexpected, unwanted inheritance as if driven by Beelzebub himself until everything that needed doing was done, then creating even more work for himself. His steward, God bless him, thought the new earl was mad, had never seen his father or even his brother behave with such ruthless disregard for themselves.

Old Tilly had known Master Valentine since he was a child, of course, and when he had heard about the carriage accident, had understood perfectly what the pain of losing both his father and his older brother at once would do to Lord Alverston's second and only surviving son—a man who as a boy even had had more intelligence and sensitivity in him than his father and brother had ever had combined. During the past two months, Tilly had sympathized with Master Valentine, had instructed and guided the young lord into his new and unsought position, and had wisely stayed silent when the earl had demanded more work than he could possibly do.

Of course he had done it; Tilly Brubanks should have known better than to ever think otherwise. But it was not the pain of loss exactly that the old steward saw in his lord's dark eyes when he met him daily to review estate business, a business which the second son had not been trained for, but was quickly learning to understand well. It was the pain of *horror* that glinted in the earl's eyes, that lined his young, serious face, that kept his lithe hands in constant movement whether in the office or in the fields with the laborers, the responsibility for whom was newly his. Lord Valentine Monroe, Earl of Alverston, was suffering the accidental death of his father and brother, no question. More than that, though, he was suffering something even graver: the death of hope that had come with the unspeakable horror of a war that should never have been fought.

Valentine found that he had clenched his hands into fists, and had pressed so strongly that his nails, always short, had dug into the roughened skin of his palms and left deep red marks. He relaxed his fingers and ran one hand through the already tousled sable locks that curled slightly down the nape of his neck. "I shall have to have Baggand cut my hair soon," he muttered to himself in the shadow-darkened room, straightening his shoulders and gathering his legs under him in preparation to rise. Balance was not won so easily, though, and once up he wavered between sitting and standing before he discarded his pride and grasped the back of his chair with one hand. "I suppose," he continued as if to an invisible companion, gesturing with his free hand, "that this lovely potion has had more of an effect on me than I had thought." Glancing over to the sideboard with a none-too-smooth turn of his head, he crooked his lips in what might have been a wry smile. "Those probably didn't have anything to do with it."

Beside the two empty bottles placed more or less next to each other on the sideboard was another of their kind, unopened. Thinking that he might experiment in seeing if in fact the contents of that bottle's companions had given him the wonderfully unexpected wobbliness of his limbs and the almost-dense fog across his vision that he had sought so often and failed to find during the past two months, Valentine began to make his way across the library to make possible the option. He thought fleetingly that perhaps he should not drink sitting down, since he never seemed quite to *feel* the effects of the drink as well when he was still as when he was moving—evidenced by his none-too-straight progress to the sideboard in contrast to his tension-filled near-paralysis sitting before the fire. But before he reached the table, his eyes, nearly closed, fixed on a gleam of white in the fire-lit room.

His father's—indeed, *his*—vast walnut desk inhabited one corner of the spacious book-lined room, and on the edge of it was a stack of three letters, neatly placed between a small pile of invoices and another of old visiting cards. The latter Valentine still had not been able to throw away, though the person whose name graced them in raised gilt script had been dead almost five months now. It was not that he was unable to face the death of his only parent or his brother. From the moment the messenger had arrived to inform him of the accident and to request his return to England to take up his position as head of his family, Valentine had felt loss, but not particularly gross pain. He had respected his father and had cared deeply for his brother, but had seen neither for over four years; and their correspondence had been infrequent and largely impersonal.

The countess had died some four years before that, leaving her sons and only daughter with memories of her loving and joyful warmth, and with a surviving parent who strove—unsuccessfully—to forget her absence by finding alternatives to living alone on his quiet echoing estate all the year long. His sons, both heir and second son, had remained in school, as was expected and natural. Valerie's situation had been less easy to solve, but solutions had been found. She was sent to school from the age of ten, and during the summertime, as on most holidays, had lived in the countryside with her mother's mother, being carefully prepared for the life she was destined to lead as daughter of an earl without troubling the earl himself with any of the details. The sixth earl of Alverston had been a fond but largely disinterested parent where his daughter was concerned. Valerie, with all of the beauty and warmth of her mother, but ten times the spirit, had responded to his practical dismissal by making friends with everyone she met, learning all that was expected of her during her years in school, reveling with fervent joy in the freedom and love found during her summers in the countryside, and defying her father on every minor account possible.

Valentine stopped in his journey to the sideboard and swayed for a moment in indecision, his gaze swiveling across the desk and to the three letters, letters addressed to his sister who had defied her father one last time, but one time too many. Almost gracefully he turned himself about on the thick Aubusson rug, the heel of Hoby's finest digging deeply into the richly colored pile as he tried to maintain an upright stance. Then, in one movement, before he could force his brandy-fogged brain to consider his next action, he crossed to the desk, grasped the tiny stack of papers in his hand and nearly catapulted himself back to the chair before the fire.

The effort was almost too much for him, and the fire blurred before his hazed eyes as he lifted the letters up to the level of his face, holding them with both hands. They were yet unopened, their wax seals still intact and bearing a vaguely familiar stamp, one that he knew from his more sober moments of glancing at them was not of the nobility. Of the author of the letters, too, he had some idea. His vague knowledge of her, as well as the unshakable code of honor

that bound him as a gentleman, had served to pre-
serve them undisturbed on the corner of his desk for
the past two months, until his sister should return.
He knew he should have sent them to her as soon
as he had discovered them in the late earl's belong-
ings; but some vestige of respect for both his father's
wishes and his sister's had stalled him. The old earl
had expressly forbidden his daughter any correspondence with her former life since her disgrace; and in
any case Valerie herself had written to her brother
upon leaving London, telling him in no uncertain
terms that she wished to have no contact with the
beloved world she had had to leave behind, that although she loved him dearly and wished him safe,
any communication from him or otherwise would
likely break her heart.

She had been the first he had written, of course,
upon learning of the accident which had taken their
father's and brother's lives. She had written back immediately, her letter stained with tears, her laments
and sorrow and searing guilt springing forth almost
tangibly from the page. He had entreated her to return to England, to make her home with him, to try
to heal the wounds from which they both suffered,
born of lives that had not gone as they had expected.
Valerie had declined, bitterly rejecting the world she
had once adored but wished never to hear of again,
while ensuring Valentine that he would forever remain in her heart her dearest and most beloved
brother. He had received this last letter from her
upon his return home to Alverston, had written to
tell her the news of his return, and had assured her
that although he would not bother her with news
other than of the most personal family kind, he would
not by any means give up communication with her,
no matter how she went on. He understood her pain
and, he did not write it, her shame, but she was his

only sister and he her only brother; they were all of the family they had left, and he would not stand for her foolishness. He would write to her regularly in America, not expecting replies if she did not wish to write them, but his house would always be open to her should she ever decide that she wished to come home.

It seemed, however, that his sister would never return. This had been the last missive from his cousin Denbridge in Boston, a note that had arrived by post only that morning. She was not happy, but resigned to her life abroad and making the best of it. Valerie was active and gracious to all, reported Denbridge, but her spirit was broken. The death of her father had deprived her of a reconciliation, one which she had imagined for eight years, but which had never come and now never would. She had read Valentine's early letters, his cousin wrote, and had been red-eyed and ashen-faced for days after the arrival of each, but had not otherwise mentioned them to either him or his wife. The most recent letters she had not even opened. Her heart, it appeared, had closed, leaving behind a beautiful young shell which was, needless to say, much adored by all of the local beaux. Apparently she was as unaffected by her American admirers as she was by her brother's entreaties. While unfailingly graceful and kind, the young woman had made no close friends during her half-year stay with her cousins, and Denbridge saw no signs of improvement. Perhaps the coming of spring would see some change.

Valentine drew his muddled thoughts from his sister and gazed once again at the careful writing on the cover of each envelope. The hand was steady, clear, and neat—not the hand of the smiling brown-eyed child whom he had met almost seven years ago, but the hand of a young woman the age of his sister, a young woman who had indeed been a sister in all but blood to Valerie since their girlhoods.

Letting two of the letters fall into his lap, Valentine slid a finger underneath the wax seal of the first and tugged gently until the pale disk snapped in half. Blinking hard to focus his gaze, he carefully unfolded the thick paper and held it up so that he could read by the fire's light.

Sibble, the Alverston head butler for as many years as the young master had been alive, cleared his throat one more time before drawing back the heavy velvet curtains of the library on the thin midday winter sun. The young earl, asleep in his desk chair, slowly opened his eyes, dark lashes flickering as he became accustomed to the light, and his memory of the previous night came back to him. He was sitting at his desk, a scattering of ink-stained papers around him, the fourth and only half-empty brandy bottle close to where his right hand rested on the desk's surface. Next to the bottle, he noticed in a sudden heart-thudding moment, were the three opened letters to his sister, late of Boston. So it had not been a dream.

Sibble cleared his throat again. Valentine responded by clearing his own, and turned gingerly, testing the soundness of his head as he did so, toward the door at which the butler stood, waiting to speak.

"Should my lord wish some breakfast this morning?" The butler's tone was deep and perfectly neutral. Valentine smiled.

"Yes, Sibble, I should like some breakfast this morning." His hand reached behind his neck to rub at the sore spot he had acquired sleeping in the chair since the wee hours of the morning. "And I should like to see Baggand as soon as he has the opportunity, please," he added, deciding it was about time he finally did something about his shaggy appearance.

"And Mr. Brubanks, my lord?" Sibble's face was patient.

"No, I won't want to see Tilly today, thank you, Sibble." Valentine's words were a polite dismissal. He reached for the letters in front of him.

The butler again cleared his throat. "My lord, Mr. Brubanks is waiting for you in the breakfast parlor, as you requested yesterday. Shall I tell him you wish to change your appointment?"

Valentine's eyes reluctantly left the letters as his butler spoke, and he had to repress the sigh that rose in his breast. "No," he said, almost but not quite wearily. "I had forgotten I had made it. I will see him shortly, as soon as I've had time to change. I expect in this case I'll find Baggand myself in my rooms, Sibble." Valentine got to his feet slowly.

"Just so, sir." Sibble backed out of the door and closed it behind him. Valentine cast one last look at the slightly wine-stained letters before he slid them into the top drawer of the massive desk. They had already waited several months and would have to wait longer now, unfortunately, while he attended to more urgent matters. But throughout that day and the next, while he worked with his steward over a problem on his estate that needed immediate attention, he was unable to shake from his mind the image of a memory from years ago: a young girl with tears in her tender doe brown eyes, waving good-bye to her friend as the friend's brother helped his sister into a carriage and drove away with her into the late-summer afternoon.

THREE

Anna could feel the breath coming back to her with a whoosh and her heart beat suddenly with extra vigor. It was almost too wonderful to believe. She stared at the letter in her hand, and a slow smile spread across her pink lips as the pleasure of the moment sunk into her consciousness. Finally Valerie had written to her. Finally her friend had remembered her and had responded to her pleas for news of her closest companion.

Leaning for a moment against the wall at the side of the drive, where she had just received the post from the carrier that morning, Anna Tremain took a careful breath. She must not expect a great deal from this letter. After all, it had been almost an entire year since she had heard from the girl who had once been her near-sister. Even if Valerie did remember her fondly, the earl's daughter had never been much of a letter writer; this letter was not likely to be an improvement in that respect at least.

The best she could expect, Anna thought as she slowly made her way back up the drive to her uncle's house, was an apology and a brief explanation of why Valerie hadn't written, at least a few lines about her come-out almost a year ago now and a few more describing her autumn and early winter activities. Anna supposed, had been supposing all winter, that her old

friend had spent the Christmas holidays at some fes-
tive house party under the supervision of her aunt
and had since then been traveling from one grand
party to another until the time would come when she
would return to Town for the next go-around of Season delights. She supposed, naturally, that Valerie had
met so many new friends in London she now had
little need for the childhood reminiscences of a country-bred girl like herself, one who had no prospect of
ever making her own come-out in Town.

She knew it was unfair to her friend to think this;
Valerie had always been the kindest of girls, ever generous with her love. It did not seem consistent with
what Anna knew of her that Valerie would have de-
serted her so entirely. This letter, hopefully, would
clear her mind of doubts and help her to understand
what it was that had kept her friend silent for so long.

She came in sight of the modest Elizabethan-style
manor house and turned off the drive onto a path
which led her into her aunt's garden at the edge of
the orchard. A carved oaken bench awaited her under
her favorite tree. The early March morning was surprisingly mild and dry, and Anna sat down to enjoy
the pleasure of her friend's letter in the privacy of
nature—the privacy that she and Valerie had since
childhood made their own.

She opened the letter with hands trembling slightly
from anticipation, noting the dark frank of the earl
in the letter's corner and the address printed in a
firm, masculine hand, then unfolded the pages gingerly. Her eyes widened when she took in the pages
of script, each line carefully written in what was to
Anna the clearest hand that her lifelong friend had
ever penned. London, Anna supposed, was more than
dancing and ballroom flirting, it seemed; Valerie had
finally left behind her careless schoolroom ciphering
and had trained her hand to the script of the young

lady she now was. Anna's eyes sought the salutation eagerly.

February
Alverston Hall

My dear Anna,

How to begin a letter which can only be filled with justifications and pleas for forgiveness from my dearest friend? I cannot ask right away for your forgiveness for my negligence, but can only beg you to read my explanations and withhold your final judgment of me until this letter comes to a close. Before I begin, I wish to thank you for your letters—each of which I cherished receiving despite the fact that I responded to none. I hope you will understand why when you have finished reading this. For now, however, I tell you that I hope you are well, happy, and content in the country that I made my own for so many years. ____shire holds treasured memories for me, and I will always imagine you there in my memories and wish for your well-being and happiness.

As for me, I shall begin at the beginning. You are kind to ask of my Season, as you cannot have known it did not turn out as I had expected. I did "take," as you put it, so neatly echoing the expression used by everyone in Town; and my first few weeks in London were all that was wonderful. I should like to tell you more of the particulars sometime, but for now I will tell you only the heart of the story. I was enjoying myself to no end until I met with an unfortunate accident. This accident incapacitated me for an extended time, and when I was able to go about again, I soon saw that the advantage I had won within the ton had all but disappeared. Deeply saddened by this, I decided that I would rather return home than complete the Season in Town. Cousin Margaret agreed with me in my de-

cision, and we repaired to Alverston with Denbridge, my father, and my elder brother, James.

Shortly thereafter another terrible accident occurred. Anna, I cannot expect that you have heard of this; I know your uncle and aunt are so removed from Society that you rarely hear news of the world outside of ____shire, a life which I long for as I know you long for a wider world to live in, so I shall tell you quickly: The Earl and James were overturned in a carriage not far from our estate; neither survived.

Anna's hand flew to her mouth and she gasped in shock. Her uncle and aunt were now the only family she knew, but imagining Valerie's pain was enough to steal her breath and rob her of even the ability to continue reading for a moment. Finally, compassion stirred her to resume.

My brother Valentine, who, you may remember, had been away fighting that dreadful Corsican in the Peninsula, was called home immediately to take up his role as head of our tiny family. We are befuddled by our pain, my friend, and unsure of what to do with our loss. My cousins have returned to America, and I have left Society for a time to try to better understand how to cope with my loss and my changed life. My brother has taken up the reins of the estate, throwing himself into his work in order to be doing something. Secretly I fear that his despair—perhaps I may give such a name to that which we are both suffering—comes not so much from the loss of our family but from something as yet unnamed to me that he experienced in the war; and I am more afraid for him because of it. I am hoping that time will heal these wounds.

Anna, I am glad to finally tell you this news. I think perhaps I did not want to despoil the purity of my memories of you and Grandmother with the reality of this horrid year past. This was the most selfish thing I could have done, I recognize, and I beg you to find it in your gracious heart to forgive me this cruelty I have practiced upon you.

For the present I will not be returning to Town. I spend much time on my own, am industrious and busy, but not going about in Society at all, due to both my disinterest in it and my mourning. This has been best for me, and I hope that you will understand too when I say that I cannot bear too much the talk and company of others. You, however, will always remain in my heart as sister and friend. May God bless you, dear Anna.

Affectionately yours,
Val

* * *

March
Hedgecliff

Dearest Valerie,

My friend! How I have mourned with you this day since reading your letter! I have been about my work and duties, my meals and conversation with sorrow deep in my heart, as if I, too, had lost a father and a brother, had had my world falling down around me.

My precious Valerie, you have suffered so many terrible things these past two years—it is not you who should be asking me for forgiveness but I who should be begging you for yours. I judged you without understanding. I, who knew how terrible your pain was when Lady Greenwich passed away from us to her Maker, was selfish enough to believe that you were too caught up in a whirlwind of Society to remember your humble friend back in the countryside. Never did I imagine the suffering you were going through, the feelings you must have at the loss of your father in such an unexpected way—and your brother! I beg your understanding and forgiveness. But, selfish creature that I am, I do not halt at this demand. I wish with all of my heart that you will let me comfort you in your sadness. Tell me what I can do, let me be of service to you. You are my family, and I suffer with you and your brother both in your loss. You must write to me and give me the chance to serve you in your distress, to comfort you in your time of grief and, hopefully, healing.

Until then, I am

Affectionately yours,
Anna

* * *

March,
Alverston Hall

Dear Anna,

I remember your tenderness well, and I am not surprised at your kind request. I am, as I have told you, not in Society at present, nor am I expecting to return to it soon. My brother's work consumes his time, and we are left with little company or entertainment largely by choice; indeed, we have become quite solitary in our ways.

I would, however, enjoy hearing of you. My days have become of late something of a trial to me; living with my memories seems to be more and more difficult as each day passes, not less so as many say it should be. The images I hold in my heart of ____shire, however, are entirely unassociated with the shadows that I constantly seek to evade. Could you, perhaps, tell

*me something of life in your country, to help me take
my thoughts away from the paths to which they are so
eager to stray? I would be eternally grateful, and remain*

*Affectionately yours,
Val*

* * *

*April
Hedgecliff*

Dearest Valerie,

*I am only too happy to comply with your wishes! It
is something that for me will be too easy to do, to tell
you the stories of how the days pass in my little hamlet.
I will even feel as if you are with me as I write. Indeed,
today as I went about my daily activities I imagined
that you were with me as you used to be every summer.
As I gathered flowers in Aunt Louisa's garden I
thought of how often we had done just that task together. I will not tell you of how I nearly wept at thinking we will never do it again.*

*Oh! I am moved to strike out that last sentence. I
am already making a hash of what was intended to
be my gift to you, the unaffected stories of life in
____shire that you requested, to enable me to fulfill my
need to do something for you in your trying time. But
I shall not strike it out! This perfectly lovely sheet of
paper will not be wasted on such a trivial thing as a
bit of overflowing sentimentality! Aunt Louisa would
understand, but Uncle Robert would be likely to scold
if he found the discarded page (you know how he is
about writing materials, the dear old miser!). To avoid
a scene I would have to burn the page right now. Given
that no fire blazes in the garden under the newly green
peach tree where I sit and write to you now, that task*

*might prove a difficult one to accomplish. Better per-
haps that I simply continue with my description of my
activities of late and warn you that, should a miserably
sentimental statement like the above begin to eke its way
out of the tip of my pen, I will stop it in midword
and not allow it to travel any further onto the innocent
page. This letter will likely end up a bit splotched and
with words struck out as a result, but I am certain
you will understand. You always did say I had a sentimental streak in me as wide as a mile, did you not?
And that was when we were barely out of pinafores.*

*Well, I shall inform you now before I go any further,
in order to leave no secrets between us, dear sister, that
with my maidenly maturity I have become* much
worse! *Indeed, much, much worse. I seem to produce
tears at the drop of a hat. My weeping has become so
pronounced that I feel something like those dreadful
papist saints of years ago who could not control their
crying and lamenting however hard they tried. On any
given day I will reach to a shelf to bring down a pitcher
of lemonade or my sketch pad, and I will find un-
looked-for rivulets of water running down my cheeks
for no apparent reason. It is really quite tiresome.*

*I attribute it to the Approaching Spring and the
Warmer Weather, or some such thing; or perhaps I have
been standing out in the early rains and not noticed
it? Aunt Louisa says it is simply because I have not
had the opportunity that most young women have had
to make my debut in Town, and thus have not had
the requisite number of chances to look coyly down at
my crumpled handkerchief, or the crumpled handkerchief of the fortunate gentleman-of-the-moment, while
forcing droplets of sparkling tear-dew out from under
my innocently lowered eyes and gently insisting that I
really* do not *need that* particular *bonbon or bonnet
or what-have-you after all; thus, my tears are falling
quite unbidden and are lacking all of the discipline to*

which other young ladies of my age would be subjecting them. I told Aunt Louisa I did not quite understand what she meant by this speech. She smiled, of course, in that enigmatic way of hers, and then Uncle Robert said he expects I have rheumatism.

I think, of course, it is simply because I miss you; you may choose your diagnosis according to mood, whim, or proclivity, naturally.

But I digress, do I not? Tell me what you least remember of our tiny hamlet, and these are the portraits I will draw with the most detail. . . .

FOUR

May
Alverston Hall

Dear Anna,

Your letter has left me with aching sides. I have not laughed so since . . . since I cannot well remember! I have sat here in the library all afternoon enjoying your letter again and again, barely able to think of or do anything else.

Do you know, I do not remember your Aunt Louisa quite in the way you describe her. Your anecdote about her meeting with the vicar's wife was quite the most marvelous account of a social faux pas that I have heard in many months. Mrs. Shively sounds like—and I am sorry, in advance, to be so judgmental—a shocking bore! What could she have possibly done or said to arouse such fervor in your aunt's reply? I can only hope, however, that the dear vicar's wife chooses not to wear that particular hat to church again, given its chickenlike qualities. How very, very unfortunate for all involved!

But more seriously, Anna, I am delighting in the stories of your village, and beg of you to continue this service you are rendering. My mind is still daily filled with unbidden memories, like your unbidden tears, but,

I fear, much more a product of reality than imagination, and my nights are unhappily sleepless. The sleep I do find is rarely restful. My brother is much the same, and in this vein our household is often rather dull.

I shall write again soon, but implore you to respond as soon as you are able. I am as always,

Affectionately yours,
Val

* * *

June
Hedgecliff

Dearest Valerie,

My head is full of things to tell you. I could barely finish my aunt's correspondence this morning for wanting to rush to my own. She was suspicious of my fidgets, but when I explained to her that we had this spring resumed our regular communication and that I was looking forward to a long morning of responding to your most recent letter, she quickly asked me to send her warm wishes for your health and that of your brother. She asked especially about him, but I had little to tell her. Please do include some news of his doings in your next message so that I can pass them on to Aunt Louisa; she will be very gratified, I am sure, as she took to him so strongly that year when he traveled to our little hamlet to retrieve you at the end of the summer months. She has never forgotten him.

Do you know, Valerie, I barely remember the new earl. I remember only your father, tall and stern; we must not have been over ten years old at the time I met him. I seem to recall that your brother was very tall as well, although I suppose to a girl of twelve a young man would seem so even if he were not, and very finely dressed. I do remember that he was quite friendly to all of us here at Hedgecliff, and looking back on it, I suppose that a boy of his age should not have been quite as gracious and pleasant with my old aunt and uncle as he was all of that evening and morning before you departed. While we romped about in the fading summer sunshine outside, he and my aunt struck up an unlikely but fast friendship. From what I have seen since of young men of Means and Title (albeit, this has been little!), they seem to be short of patience and wholly interested in themselves. This does not square with my memory of your brother. Doubtless my slight familiarity with him from your letters over the years kindly disposes me toward him, but I suspect he was never the sort that your older brother was. Your stories of James's haughty disapproval of you were always softened by Valentine's kindnesses. I do wish for the present Lord Alverston's happiness and contentment, as I wish the same for you. Since he is your sole companion and friend these days, I also wish him peace of heart and the charity of character that I understand he already possesses.

Now I must tell you of the May Fair we celebrated here last month. It is much the same as it always was when you were here to celebrate it with us, although your absence during the Dance of the Maidens around the pole-tree is still remarked among the villagers. (Never was there so lovely and lively a Spring Maiden as you, dearest Valerie!) Naturally, as we are now Young Ladies with a decorum to follow, and no longer the Innocent Girls we once were, we would be watching the dancing from the sidelines and not partaking of it ourselves; but I will never forget our memories of those years, and I suspect you will not either. How many daughters of earls, do you think, are ever permitted to dance around the maypole of an early summer's night? I expect very few!

But again I digress. I will tell you now—among other things—of how at this year's festival one of the ribbons from the pole-tree became entangled in Squire Freekirk's wig and could only be extracted by first extracting the good squire himself from the disobedient hairpiece. Aunt Louisa vowed she had never seen anything so diverting in her life, but of course I scolded her, telling her not to allow the poor man to see her giggling over his plight. Uncle Robert, standing stone-faced, noted that if the silly man was fool enough to go bewigged in the countryside in this day and age, what else could he expect . . . ?

* * *

July
Alverston Hall

Dearest Anna,

Your most recent letter has once again transported me into fits of uncontrollable laughter as it has simultaneously moved me to tears. Your talent for diversion is extraordinary, dear Anna, but I have long known that, indeed. I am honored and grateful for your continued attention, and for your regard as well. A person could not be more flattered by the regard of so kind a friend.

I am most anxious to hear how the foaling of your aunt's favorite mare went, and hope you will write again very soon with news. I have always been curious to understand how your uncle, who shuns Society so, makes such a fine business of horse-breeding when he barely corresponds with the world outside of ____shire. This is a mystery I have long pondered.

This brings me to another thought, one that has been on my mind of late. Forgive me for being brash, but had we ever (because of your social seclusion) considered somehow allying you to one of his wealthy and dashing customers? If so, I think we must have been mad. *My time in London, however brief, taught me a few things about men of that stamp; I would rather not think that a future with one of them is even a remote possibility for you, dear girl.*

While I am about sharpening my virgin claws on the subject of men of any stamp at all . . . I recall that your aunt has asked to hear of my brother, so I am, although reluctant, bound to respond. As I have mentioned before, he is terribly busy learning the business of the estate. He never expected to inherit, of course, and while not disinterested in the workings of our family lands, he never spent any time thinking of them until he was told they were suddenly his responsibility. He had never considered a reality without James, I suppose, although they were never particularly close, I shall readily admit. You already know, of course, that he is devoted to me, *and would do almost anything to ensure my happiness. He and I are all we have left, dear Anna, and we must not let our troubles drive us apart, but see that they bind us together more firmly.*

Our days pass thusly: Valentine often rides before breakfast, if he has not been abroad late at his various activities, and takes to his office before the morning is well advanced. He spends most of his time there among his ledgers and the hundreds and hundreds of books in the library. (I cannot imagine why the two people I love most in the world—you and my brother—love books *so fondly when I am the unlikeliest reader I know.) Consequently, Valentine has his library to himself when he chooses to be there, which suits me well. Dinner is a quiet affair; we do not entertain, as I have said, and do not accept invitations other than from the vicar and his wife, who are cousins of ours (several times removed) and quite kind. The silences in our home are often long and sometimes almost deafening. Music lifts the spirits when there is energy or inspira-*

tion to play—your last letter, which detailed that amusing dinner party where the delightful Widow Eversham played Scottish reels to her heart's content and Vicar Brown's discontent, provided such inspiration—but laughter rarely finds its way within our walls, and is much missed.

Much more of my brother I cannot say, except to add that his frantic busyness has not served to still his restlessness. As I have said before, I fear that he has not put behind him the things he saw and experienced in battle. I suspect indeed that something of a particular nature occurred during his time in Spain, but he tells me he cannot find the words to speak of it, and I do not press him. Hopefully he will be able to talk about it in time. It has been nearly a year since he left the Peninsula, and still his sleep is troubled with dreams of war and death. Please keep him and me in your prayers, dear Anna.

Valentine sees me writing this letter and entreats me to send to you, your aunt, and uncle his fondest greetings. He remembers you all from that time he came to Hedgecliff at the end of the summer to accompany me back to school, and tells me with sincerity that he has rarely felt so welcomed by strangers before or since.

Please hurry your next letter; I await it with happy anticipation.

Affectionately yours,
Val

* * *

July
Hedgecliff

Dearest Valerie,

How glad *I am that the summer rains have not muddied the highways so badly as to affect the mail coaches this season. Your letters arrive regularly; my days are so happily occupied in responding to your questions that I fear if we ever cease our correspondence I will be unable to remember how I spent my time before this. I hope this will never come to pass.*

I am glad to hear news of your brother, but truly saddened by his continued unhappiness. We cannot understand what he must have experienced in war, that horrible thing that men wage. I understand, dear Valerie, that because of the sacrifice of young men like your brother, and older men too, we in England are still English on this very day. But I cannot like it, I cannot accept it. Our youth have become men under the violent hand of Mars, and they are marked, as is your brother, by a fiery brand that can never be removed from their hearts and minds. I will pray for the earl, because it is the only thing I can do for him and for all of our nation's sons who have lost their innocence upon the fields of human destruction.

You will scold me likely enough for plain speaking such as should not come from the mouth of a gently bred country maid. Well, my friend, I will not apologize. I feel these things as acutely as any man may, and I will not deny the feelings that injustice and hatred arouse in my breast.

You will not like my expression of them; but this may as well serve as an opportunity to show you how much I have been learning during the past two years since we last met. Uncle still refuses to allow us a journal from Town, but I have been meeting regularly with an old scholar who has moved to our little village, and I have learned more from Mr. Thimbly than I did in all of my education from the mumblings of Miss Caruthers, however good-intentioned her governessing was. They are talked about among our neighbors, my visits to Mr. Thimbly's house; but I go with my maid every time, who sits and mends while we discuss the many wonderful things he is teaching me to read, or else Aunt Louisa accompanies me, and the three of us talk until it is nearly dark some days. It is very *exciting, Valerie, to learn of thoughts and ideas that I had never even imagined before.*

To shorten my story—for although your letters are more thoughtful than ever they were before, I suspect that too much talk *still makes your eyes glaze over; never have I known a person of more active spirit and will than you, my dear friend!—I have learned many new ways to* think *about this world and our kingdom, and I am every day filled up with more and more thoughts that bubble to the surface of my brain and beg for escape. Mr. Thimbly was for years at Magdalen, and he tells me my enthusiasm rivals that of his most enterprising former students. Aunt Louisa, whose spirit of discussion he takes more in stride on account of her advanced years, has told me I shock as much as please the old man; he still finds it difficult, she says, to believe that a young* woman *can comprehend matters which in his world have been confined to the company of men alone. I suspect he allows me to see him for diversion's sake; I think, too, that he misses his past and seeks to find some comfort in the present in any way he can. In any case, I am grateful.*

He remembers your brothers well, Valerie. I was forward enough to ask when once he let drop a mention of certain noblemen he had tutored. He had little to say of James but much to share about Valentine, and he drew a truly flattering portrait of the new earl. What a splendid young man your brother must have been— must be! It could not have been many years ago, could it, that James and Valentine were up at Oxford? I do not remember that either of your brothers was so very much older than you. It does not signify, but I thought you would be pleased to hear this news. Please do not tell your brother that I was asking after him; it does not become *my maidenly modesty, after all!*

Oh, how good it feels to giggle with you again like girls, my friend, even if only via the post. Do you remember when . . . ?

* * *

August
Alverston Hall

Dearest Anna,

I have often heard my brother talk of war, and while I do not presume to understand it as he does, I do sympathize with the words you have spoken. I do not *imagine you clad in blue stockings at all, and I encourage you to tell me what it is you have learned in your studies with your tutor. I cannot easily respond, but certainly do not begrudge you your happy activity. After all, how could anyone fail to recognize the gentle lady behind the fiery opinions you have learned to express? You somehow manage to combine the two within your unique character.*

But do tell me more of Mr. Thimbly, for I know much of the old don and would like very much to share with Valentine how he goes on in his country retirement. . . .

* * *

August
Hedgecliff

Dearest Valerie,

How my heart goes out to your poor tenants whose homes were washed away in the flood you experienced so recently! I wish you to tell me what you and your good brother have been able to do to alleviate their suffering and loss. You two, who have lost so much yourselves, must understand them more sincerely than any other masters could. I am certain the two of you are doing everything you can to relieve their discomfort.

We have had nothing here of the weather you have had in the North. The peach trees are dropping their fruit already, but the real harvest has not yet begun. I enjoy the sunshine from the peace and blessed solitude of our beloved hilltop, shifting into the shade under the branches of our broad old oak when it becomes too warm. I cannot, after all, withstand too many lectures from Aunt Louisa over my often-freckled complexion, and so do try on occasion to remove myself at least partially from the danger.

Now, my friend, to comfort your heart and mind from the troubles that beset you and yours these days, I will tell you more of Mr. Thimbly, as you requested. Then I will regale you with the latest on dits (are you terribly impressed with my Town cant?) out of _____shire. The story about the dairy farmer's son and his most recent paramour is, however scandalous, particularly diverting and I just must share it with you or I shall burst with the glee of it . . . !

* * *

September
Alverston Hall

Dearest Anna,

The fields are full to bursting, the meadows are green and lush, the sky here is so brilliantly clear that yesterday I spotted a hawk flying over the Mill Pond ten miles distant—it is a glorious summer in our corner

*of England. I have always loved this land the most of
all of my father's properties, and am so glad to imagine
that I will now never have to leave it. I am learning
to make this my home, and it has welcomed me. Indeed,
I have never felt so welcomed before. I hope someday
that you may share its glorious summer too.*

Here the writer's pen retraced its script and crossed out
the last sentence on the page.

An invitation to visit, however indirect, could not
be tendered. It was, the earl pondered, an unfortunate truth, made necessary by the deception being
practiced, the deception that seemed so essential for
her satisfaction and for his, as she had put it, "peace
of heart." Something that had been done as an act
of sympathy had become for him a certain lifeline.

When he had written the first letter he had originally intended to explain, in his own *persona,* the situation of his sister's negligence. The task had proven
nearly impossible, however; Valerie could *not* be understood or forgiven for her rejection of her childhood friend along with all of those people of the *ton*
who had treated her so poorly. He had no words to
justify her actions, yet longed to both exonerate his
sister and suitably comfort Miss Tremain. The truth
from *Valerie's* pen might have somehow served. From
his own, every attempt sounded pompous, scolding,
and terribly impersonal.

In any case his conscience, grounded in the gentleman's code, shrank at allowing him to address a
letter to an unmarried girl. Somehow that code had
not seemed so important when he had begun to carefully write out a brief explanation *in Valerie's words* as
to why she had not written for so long; the bottle of
brandy had perhaps served to shroud it in good intentions. As the ink covered the page of that first let-

ter the long dormant image he had recalled of the sweet-faced young orphan-child saying good-bye to her dearest friend drove the scratchings of his pen. The words had practically written themselves. Valentine had concentrated on keeping his tone like Valerie's; she had written to him often while he was away, her letters always warm but very brief. His sister was not, he knew, an eager correspondent, and particular eloquence was not necessary. He would spell out the necessary information and leave it to Miss Tremain to accept gracefully, but likely with distance.

He had not counted on her generous heart, although in hindsight he supposed he should have. Sitting in his library that morning in late March, he had berated himself again and again for altering his sister's history to hide her scandal from her friend. He had had to come up with something, though, and an accident seemed serious yet eminently *fix*able. The event of his father's and brother's death could not be changed, however, and he imagined that this was at the root of Miss Tremain's desire to do something to help soften Valerie's mourning.

A riding accident had claimed the lives of Miss Tremain's parents when she was still of a tender age, Valentine recalled. One autumn, Anna's father was thrown from a lightning-spooked horse while riding with his wife. Anna's mother, determined to stay with him until the end she knew was near, disregarded the storm that came upon her and the dying man. Drenched by rain before help arrived, she took a fever and three days later followed her husband to her reward. Their nine-year-old daughter, left alone in the world, had learned the despair of loss at an early age. Valerie had met and befriended her when, after the funeral, the girl went to live with her aunt and uncle far from the home in which she had been raised. The two had become fast friends. Anna Tremain's sympa-

thy for her friend's new grief, Valentine understood,
would know few bounds.

Then too, Miss Tremain of all people understood
Valerie's tempestuous and largely one-sided relation-
ship with her parent. In her letter, with a few words,
a turn of her pen, Anna Tremain had suggested that
she well understood whence came her friend's greatest hurt. She knew nothing, of course, of the scandal,
the night at Vauxhall, and the elopement.

Valentine had been quite sure when he had devised
the fabrication that in her tiny corner of the countryside, at home with her recluse uncle and gentle
aunt, Miss Tremain would have little news of Valerie's
real situation. Why, when he had been at Hedgecliff
on that one occasion, he had learned that the family
did not even read the *Times*—ever! In his youthful
arrogance he had wondered aloud at it, and had been
told firmly by Mr. Masterson that the only news he
needed from London was that it had disappeared entirely in a cloud of smoke. The lady of the house had
laughed her quiet laugh and had then explained that
Masterson had been raised in London and at eighteen
had left it with the vow that he would under no circumstances ever return to it.

The young Valentine had been too self-absorbed to
consider at the time what that must have meant to
the young girl in the family. Valerie had once explained to him, however, that Anna, not a vain girl,
was little interested in Society. Their hamlet was small,
and she did wish to see some of the world—the things
her reading had shown her—but she was happy in
the absence of this experience to create a world of
color and even excitement out of the little bit of life
that she had been given. She immersed herself in the
stories of the people around her, and on her own she
spent her time reading, gardening, and riding. This
last she had taken up with a purpose remarkable in

one so young almost as soon as her grief from her parents' death would allow it. She had been determined not to fear that which had ended her parents' lives. She had become a bruising rider, according to her uncle, her courage and strength of character overcoming her grief and fear.

Valentine had learned most of this not from his sister, but from her friend's marvelous letters. He had thought to distract himself and innocently amuse Miss Tremain by requesting stories from her village. He had desperately needed some distraction, something to take his mind away from what it had learned to know best.

His dreams had been, throughout the winter and early spring, cruel in their repetitiveness, red with blood, and shadowed with fear and death. He had striven in the daylight hours to drive the images from his head, to fill his mind with estate business and tours of his newly acquired land. He had spent night after night reading his way through the darkness, sitting in his chair before the fire in the library, trying to find something in his vast collection of books that would paint over the memories he could not escape, that would ease the searing guilt that he felt. He had avoided the books that were his boyhood favorites; peopled by warriors, the ancient stories were dangerous ground for his imagination now. He counted as a fool that boy he had been, who had so longed to prove himself a hero in war. But nothing he read had served to lessen his bitterness or pain. For nights at a time, he drank his way into partial oblivion, just to be awakened out of his hazy stupor by images more violent than usual and gut-wrenching sickness in addition. It had been on one of these nights that he had finally opened and read the letters intended for

Valerie. Once it was done, he had no longer been an innocent party in the matter.

Anna Tremain's letters had given him something, a tangible something, to cling to in the light of day, and something to remember and imagine during the endless nighttimes. They were merely stories of her life and village, but told with an irrepressible humor and a vital compassion that made them sparkle with the simple joy of life. Valentine had not perceived this joy in his own world for quite some time, and had experienced something of a feeling—oddly, he thought—of *relief* when he had let himself first be led into her stories; and he had lost himself there for a short while.

After reading her first letter he had spent an entire afternoon without even trying to escape his own thoughts, simply enjoying his work as if it were the most natural thing in the world. He had even laughed so heartily while reading her stories that all that afternoon his mouth had had an unusual tendency to curl into something like a grin as he had ridden across his lands and seen to business that was, if not sad, certainly not amusing.

Now, regrettably, he could not deprive himself of this blessing. Daily he battled with his conscience, determining not to continue the charade any longer. He vowed to make some excuse that Valerie could no longer maintain the correspondence, to write his sister and tell her all, exhort her to draw a close to the friendship that only he was encouraging.

But with every letter that arrived for him he was further and further from any honorable resolution. He had come to *depend* on their exchanges, but especially on Anna Tremain's dreamlike presence in his life. Her words had found within him the joy for life that he thought had died that horror-filled day in

Spain over a year ago. Sometime during the summer he had reached a place from which he could not back out of his secret part in this game—or at least one at which he had given up the will to try.

Valentine put his pen to paper again.

The harvest begins tomorrow, and there is much to prepare for the week's work. I must make this letter short, therefore, but know that I am, as always,

Affectionately yours,
Val

FIVE

Dearest Valerie,

We have a new addition to our little community, just in time to liven up our cozy society as the winter weather descends. I shall endeavor to maintain maidenly restraint in describing this newcomer, but I fear I shall not be able to disguise my *particular interest*, or the interest of every young lady within miles.

The Honorable Jason Pendleton has come to complete some studies with his former tutor Mr. Thimbly, and, my friend, he appears to be a veritable paragon of manly virtue! I have met him twice now, once at a party given to welcome him by Squire and Mrs. Freekirk, and once accidentally when Aunt Louisa and I were leaving Mr. Thimbly's home and Mr. Pendleton was arriving to meet with his former teacher. Both occasions afforded me the opportunity to have speech with him, although upon neither occasion did we converse for long, I regret to say. For I will admit, Valerie, he has the most melodious voice and weaves the most charming and yet intelligent and respectful conversation with it! Aunt Louisa and I both struggle to maintain our feminine equilibrium when he has deigned to *speak with us, for his manner is so entirely* engaging *that we both find ourselves completely wrapped up in watching* him *and barely thinking to speak ourselves, as if his conversation were some sort of* entertainment. *Is it not wonderful?*

The news of him that is generally known is this: he is a younger son of a baron; he has come down from Town after only two years there to reacquaint himself with his old teacher, since he has just recently learned of Mr. Thimbly's retirement from Oxford; and he is a man of means but no particular wealth.

By his own admission, Mr. Pendleton finds country life relaxing, but prefers the bustle and busyness of London. He has assured us, however, that he plans to remain within our little fold until the Season begins in Town next spring. I wonder if you met him last year, Valerie? I would guess that he flies in less fashionable circles than yours in the haut ton, *and as he never mentions any persons other than those he is with, and his family, I cannot know through gossip who are his particular cronies among the Fashionable World. For now he seems content with us, I happily report.*

He ought to be! Every family of respectable status in our little hamlet is planning some sort of entertainment in honor of his presence among us. Aunt Louisa will have a musical evening, the music provided by myself, of course; Elizabeth Linsom, who is not quite of age yet, but who plays divinely; and the Misses Eversham, whose skills in harp and voice are unrivaled, I would merit, even in London. Mrs. Brown, the vicar's wife, will have an afternoon tea for him (our pleasures here, as you may recall, are humble). Mrs. and Miss Stottmeyer intend to gather a party for Christmas shopping in Crowsford (Do you remember that day we stole off to Crowsford unattended and bought those horrible *plush bonnets with the false cherries all over them?), at which Mr. Pendleton will naturally be the guest of honor. Dr. Beesle, a fine doctor, as you know from your experience with a sprained ankle that year, but a man who will not admit to his advancing years, is polishing his curricle in preparation for an intended race against our visitor to Pivey someday when the weather is expected to hold. All in all, it does seem as if I will have many opportunities to come into Mr. Pendleton's company, and I will freely admit to only you, my dear Valerie, that I do look forward to them. It has been an age or more since a suitable, personable, and intelligent young man has entered our company, and at the expense of appearing fast, I admit to being very pleased by the prospect of the coming months.*

I am certain you are unsatisfied with what I have as yet told you about him. I have been reluctant to say it, but for your sake I will. Please be assured, my friend, that Mr. Pendleton is extremely pleasing to look at; in fact, he is quite, quite handsome! For all I am worth, I am unable to deny that this has affected me a little bit. I shall only write details because I know you wish them. His eyes are blue, his hair like Adonis's, gold and wavy, and his person is slender but not too tall. I have been told by the Misses Eversham that when he is in proximity they lose their voices altogether in their admiration of his face and figure. They are a bit vulgar, I know, but I sympathize with them; however, I do not succumb to the same fits as the other young ladies of ____shire. I am far too sensible for that!

My dearest Valerie, I will tell you more when there is more to tell. In the meantime, I shall write soon with news of other things. Mr. Pendleton is not, after all, the only subject worth discussing these days, although to live in this little society you would not know it by how everyone cannot speak of anything but him.

Please give my warmest greetings to your brother. I am, as always,

Affectionately yours,
Anna

* * *

December
Hedgecliff

Dearest Valerie,

Mr. Pendleton has invited Uncle, Aunt, and me to join him at Mr. Thimbly's for dinner tomorrow. It will be an intimate group dining on bachelor fare, he warns us; but we are happy to have been asked. I am excited for the party and the possibility of stimulating conversation. As of yet, Mr. Pendleton has been reluctant to share with me any of the things he has been discussing with Mr. Thimbly. I do not think he trusts my capacity to keep up my side of the conversation, should we venture into waters deeper than the more common subjects. I shall take this opportunity to encourage him in this manner further, and see what I am met with. I believe I shall wear my jonquil muslin. . . .

* * *

December
Alverston Hall

Dearest Anna,

After reading your latest letter relating the events of the infamous shopping trip to Crowsford, I cannot but be concerned for your welfare. From all you have said, Mr. Pendleton seems like the veriest model of a gentleman; but I am ill at ease, nonetheless, and tend to agree with your uncle's grumblings, as you call them, that this young man seems to be too good to be true.

You will be openmouthed at my pronouncement. You will not believe how I can have formed such an opinion of this gentleman, not knowing him myself and you knowing me as well as you do. But perhaps I have a bit more experience than you with matters of gentlemen of the world, and I am worried about your very particular interest in him, not because I would deny you the pleasure of such an alliance, but because you still know so very little *about him. He could be* anybody; *and he could take advantage of you easily, since your aunt seems to have accepted him and allows him a greater freedom with you than I think is wise. (Forgive me for judging her discretion wanting in this one matter!) The isolated situation in which you found yourself with him that day in Crowsford should not be repeated, Anna. Do take care to protect yourself, and remain somewhat on your guard when necessary.*

In saying these things, I have only your welfare in mind. How I wish I could meet this young man and make an assessment of him myself. I shall have to trust to your good sense, however, that he is all you believe him to be. . . .

* * *

December
Alverston Hall

Dearest Anna,

The Hall is decked and the snow is lying thick on the ground; we are entirely prepared for Christmas. We cannot move far on account of the early weather, but the post arrives as usual and I have just read this afternoon your letter detailing your aunt's musicale, which I wish I could have attended. Mr. Pendleton seems to have acquitted himself with extraordinary grace and aplomb during the impromptu charade; I would have liked to see you miming Isolde to his Tristan! I am gratified that he is such an excellent singer, for I know how you enjoy your music. I cannot help but think that it is serendipitously coincidental that your favorite songs seem to be his as well. The two of you seem to have so very many things in common; the list grows with every letter that you write. . . .

Anna placed the letter she was reading on her lap, her brow furrowed in puzzlement. She could not understand why her friend had taken Mr. Pendleton into such dislike. Could she herself have possibly written something about him that would have caused Valerie to regard him with such suspicion and distrust? She was certain her letters contained nothing but praise for her new acquaintance.

In fact, Anna fully understood that this in itself could be the root of Valerie's concerns. In their girlhood years, Anna had been the less ingenuous one of the pair. Valerie had been almost too open, guileless herself and always expecting others to be the same. Anna had been trained to the healthy attitude "all that glitters is not gold," but she could not see how Mr. Pendleton's behavior merited such regular warnings from her formerly innocently trusting friend.

He was indeed quite without blemish. She still had not been able to engage his more intellectual side in conversation, but she supposed he was shy of embarrassing her, or calling too much attention to her own bluestocking qualities in company where others might observe. She expected that with more familiarity, in time, he would answer her invitations for such conversation. She knew he had an intelligent mind, and although dismayed at his reluctance to share his knowledge and thoughts with her, she had every confidence that soon the situation would change and she would find satisfaction.

In the meantime, his conversation was charming and always entertaining, and his attentions to her marked in comparison with those paid the other young ladies within their small community. While not vain, Anna was more than content to take the opportunities of mild flirtation that were offered her. She had thought Valerie would have entered into her adventure with the masculine sex with enthusiasm and encouragement. She had not anticipated the kind of reception her friend had given her news of a new admirer. She vowed that she would not censor her letters to Valerie in order to avoid feeling the discomfort of reading the evidence of her concern. She would write as usual, giving the appropriate amount of attention to news of Mr. Pendleton that his part in her life and her village merited, but not more. She was certain that with time something would happen that would acquit him of suspicion in Valerie's opinion.

Valentine stared down at the cold Christmas breakfast in front of him and realized that he had been daydreaming again. It would not do. His cook already thought his erratic eating habits reflected a dislike of her cuisine, when in fact it was the excellence of her preparations that had kept him eating at all this past year and more.

He looked again at the letter lying open on the stack of mail that had arrived in the post. The snow lining the breakfast room's broad windowpanes was days old, and the mail that had been forestalled for a short while due to the weather was piled neatly by the side of his plate of eggs and kidney.

He supposed he should be glad for the information he had learned this morning; he had expended enough effort to unearth it. The letter was from his solicitor in London, and told him all that should have calmed his mind concerning Miss Tremain's recent admirer. After making his own discreet inquiries by letter to various friends and some relatives in Town into the background of the Pendletons, and learning little of substance, though nothing negative, through this indirect method, Valentine had instructed his solicitor to find out all he could of the baron, his family, and especially his second son.

It seemed that Mr. Jason Pendleton was everything Anna believed him to be. He was well bred, well educated, and not without income, although by no means deep in the pockets. His family was sufficiently old, the baronetcy a gift from the king to the present baron's great-grandsire. There were three sons and two daughters, the girls still in the schoolroom, but generally understood to be as pretty as their brothers. Young Pendleton was just above legal age, but had not during his two years in London made much of a dash. In fact, he had barely registered within the more fashionable social circles in Town, despite what Miss Tremain had described as his engaging, almost magnetic manners and his love for London life.

Valentine ground his teeth. Then he took a sip of tepid coffee and stood up. He refused to be intimidated by Pendleton's tendency toward perfection. What did it matter that Miss Tremain found his conversation irresistible—if a little insubstantial? Why should he, the Earl of Alverston, worry if she found herself alone with the young scamp, unchaperoned in some snow-covered dell apart from a party of sledders, and in danger of being kissed, as had happened not a week ago according to her last letter? How on earth should it affect *him* if she danced until almost dawn, scandalously late for country hours, at Squire Freekirk's Christmas ball this very evening, blushing at the blond Adonis's every smile and whispered word of holiday intoxication?

This *petite affaire de coeur* was nothing to him, Valentine scowled. It affected him not at all except to provide him with an hour or two of pleasant diversion whenever he received one of her letters—letters that brimmed with life and excitement and the joy of finding herself admired, as she ought to be.

That night as snow once again fell outside in thick white flakes, the earl sat in silent contemplation, his hand around a warm glass of fine French brandy, his smoke-gray eyes gazing into the library's merrily crackling fire. Finally, smiling mockingly at himself, he lifted his drink in a silent toast to the young man who, at that very moment probably, was waltzing about the floor of a country squire's drawing room holding in his arms the woman to whom, ridiculously, and contrary to all imaginable events, Valentine had lost his heart.

SIX

March

Anna sat in the window box of her uncle's comfortable library and stared out at the rain falling steadily on the meadow behind their house. Since the sudden change in the weather that had heralded the end of winter, it had been raining for almost a week, and the roads were knee-deep in mud from Pivey to Ablesley. Her feet were tucked up under her, and since she expected no callers in this dreary weather, her dress was an old comfortable one and her hair was twisted, as befitted the country girl she was, into a simple plait that hung golden-brown down her back, tied with a red ribbon. Between her teeth, she worried the end of a quill pen, the ink on its tip long dried from disuse. Spread before her on the window cushion were the leaves of several letters, written in a neat, flowing hand, the dark wax seals on them maintained almost whole from careful opening.

She breathed in deeply and then let out her breath on a long whispery sigh. Why had Valerie drawn back from their correspondence as she had these past months? Why had Anna's entreaties to her friend to understand and accept Mr. Pendleton on his many merits met with such taciturn resistance? Then, when Anna had stopped writing as frequently of her grow-

ing friendship with the young man and had returned
to writing letters devoted to more general topics, as
she had in her last letter when she first told an anecdote about the Misses Eversham and then, with a
drastic turn of subject, poured out her heart concerning the issue of unjust taxes that were destroying the
country, taxes she had just learned of, why had Valerie
responded with diffidence and disinterest? Normally
her friend would have *something*, if not profuse com-
mentary, to say in response to Anna's radical, bluestocking notions. At the least she would usually have
commented on the way Emily and Katherine had simultaneously practically *hurled* themselves at Mr.
Pendleton that day on the skating pond.

Thinking of the day brought a slight blush to
Anna's winter-paled cheeks. She and Mr. Pendleton
had been skating together, arm in arm, enjoying each
other's company and what was probably the last of
the wonderfully cold days of frozen ice. They had
taken a turn around the bend in the pond, and he
had stopped them suddenly, using a tree branch
thrusting out of the ice as an excuse. She was not
sure if she had needed one, really; but when he had
moved to wrap his arm around her shoulders in
preparation to kiss her, she had still felt unsure, not
completely certain that she wanted what was about to
happen. The Eversham sisters had neatly deprived her
of the chance to discover her mind one way or the
other.

Perhaps it was Valerie's attitude toward her flirtation that served to dull the pleasure Anna felt when
she was in Mr. Pendleton's company. Anna had not
told her friend all of the details of the skating epi-
sode, but she had hinted at them, hoping that the
cooling trend in Valerie's letters would reverse when
she was presented with a romantic puzzle to solve.
The tactic had produced the opposite effect, it

seemed. Valerie's most recent letter had been so distant that Anna could only be amazed at the fact that her old friend had written at all. Valerie's letters had grown noticeably cooler shortly after Christmas, and they had not even improved when, sometime in January, Anna had tried to assure her friend that she would keep a modest distance, both physically and emotionally, from her admirer until she could know him much better.

In fact, this had not proven too arduous a task. Anna was still charmed by her suitor, flattered by his attentions, and always amused by his entertaining and openly warm conversation; but her heart was not in any serious way engaged. Try as she might to discover what he *or* she lacked to cause her to fall in love with him, and here the romantic turn of her character had caused her to mull over the absence of this necessity regularly during the past three months, she could not come to a conclusive answer. She had not shared these doubts openly in her letters to Valerie, but she thought they knew each other well enough that her friend could have understood this without explicit notification of it.

Given Valerie's last few letters, those that were lying before her only just reread in sequence, which were as regular as usual in arriving but so terribly im*personal*, Anna could only imagine one thing: that her friend had finally tired of her country acquaintance, and that this was her way of breaking with Anna without causing undue insult. The thought was lowering to Anna, not because she felt shame for feeling affection where there was none returned, but because she had grown to love Valerie even more during the past year they had spent writing to each other.

They had both grown during the years they were separated, after the death of Valerie's grandmother, Lady Greenwich. The person that Anna's childhood

friend had become was a subdued and more thoughtful one, however much she still maintained the humor with which she viewed herself and all of life.
Anna had discovered this through Valerie's letters,
and had come to depend on their friendship anew,
indeed in a way that she had never depended upon
it before. The companion with whom she had this
last year shared her stories, her thoughts, and her
dreams had become for Anna an intimate part of her
heart, a friend of the soul. She had thought, through
the brief but meaning-filled letters that she had received during the year, the experience had been
shared. Anna had indeed regretted that she could
only share the fraction of Valerie's thoughts that she
was able to put on paper. Her friend had never been
a particularly enthusiastic writer, but Anna knew the
spirit that guided the writing of the short missives was
profoundly more fluent than the pen composing
them.

She had hoped to be able to invite her old friend
someday soon, when the weather improved, to come
visit her and her aunt and uncle in ____shire, to take
her away from the dullness of Alverston Hall and
bring her into Society once again in a modest way. It
was time, she thought; Valerie's mourning period was
well over, and she was yet a young woman who could
easily find a suitable husband, with her dark curls,
sparkling eyes, and smiling way. Anna had devised a
plan by which she would slowly reintroduce Valerie
to the Society she had lately shunned by having her
go about with her in the little neighborhood for the
summer as they had done all through their girlhoods.
Thinking that a change of scenery would undoubtedly
have done her friend good, she had been on the
verge of proposing the scheme when Valerie's letters
had turned tepid.

Now, looking over her most recent letters, Anna

read again and again of the hard work being done
to restore some of the estate's more troublesome
areas of interest. Valerie seemed as much caught up
in the activity as her brother was, which was not unusual in normal circumstances, but was not quite in
character with what Anna had always thought of her
friend. It seemed odd to her that the earl was indulging Valerie so much as to allow her continued absence
from Society and her near seclusion at Alverston Hall
with him. She supposed he simply did not know what
it was Valerie most needed—the activity and friendship she would find with her friends back in Society,
that very thing upon which Valerie had always thrived.

Perhaps, Anna thought, the earl was so thoroughly
engaged with the tasks that beset him as owner of a
vast amount of land and a member of Parliament that
he was unaware his sister was moldering away in solitude in his country home. Anna could not judge a
man she knew only through his sister's words, and
she admitted that she knew little of the responsibilities of a Peer of the Realm, in any case. Perhaps he
had something in mind for her; perhaps there was a
prospective husband waiting in the wings, someone
who would, once they were married, take her back
into the Society that she had enjoyed so much before
the terrible events of almost two years ago.

Anna could speculate about this, but she could not
know. She had, however, given up her idea of inviting
her friend to spend the summer at Hedgecliff. Deeply
saddened by the loss of their new closeness, Anna
could nonetheless only concede that she had been
defeated. If Valerie wished to end their friendship this
way, or if she were simply tired of a correspondence
she had only reluctantly entered into in the first
place, then Anna could only respect her wishes and
bow out gracefully. Her heart rebelled at the prospect,

but given the evidence, she felt she had little choice in the matter.

As she moved her hand to lay her pen aside and fold up the last letter from Valerie, which would go unanswered for a while, at least, Anna heard a sound at the door and looked up to see her aunt entering the small, dimly lit library.

"Anna, it is terribly dark in here. Why don't you light some candles so that you can see to write." Louisa Masterson walked smoothly over to the small writing table that served as a desk for both ladies and pulled out of a drawer a match to light at the flaming hearth. She took it into her still-smooth hands and crossed to the fireplace, the soft folds of her gray morning gown brushing smoothly against her legs as she moved. Anna had inherited these long, slender legs from her mother's side of the family, but Louisa Masterson's dark coloring was uniquely hers. Anna thought that her aunt, at almost fifty, was still a lovely woman.

"I am fine like this, Aunt Louisa. The light here in the window is quite bright enough for my needs. In any event, I shall not be writing anything today, after all." Anna's voice was light, but there was a wistful tone to it that her aunt could hardly ignore. The older woman walked over to her niece and, picking up the letters strewn on the cushion, sat down beside Anna.

"You have been reading Valerie's letters," she noticed, glancing at the pages and weighing them in her hands. "Have you determined it is not in your imagination that she has grown distant these past months?" Mrs. Masterson's voice was full of compassion.

"I'm afraid this last is no warmer than the others," Anna said as she picked up the most recent letter she had received from Alverston Hall and scanned it.

"What I don't understand is why she still writes at all, and with such regularity. She seems so uninterested in our correspondence that it confounds me."

"I suppose you should be glad, my sweet," said Mrs. Masterson gently. "It is likely her good memories that keep her writing, which is a fine legacy of your friendship. Do not discount it, however odd it may appear."

"Mmm. Yes, perhaps." Anna could not express her strong feelings on the matter. It would sound strange, she thought, to another—especially to her aunt. She had always had ample love and affection from her foster parents, but sometimes Anna felt she must have inherited her father's tempestuous emotions. Although she felt disloyal even to think it on occasion, her mother's sister was tranquil almost to a fault sometimes. In any case, Anna told herself, Aunt Louisa likely guessed at something near enough to the truth of the matter.

"I have news for you that may rouse you out of your melancholy, Anna dear." Anna looked up as her aunt grasped her hands within her own. "Your uncle has had an invitation for us to make a visit to see some old, good friends of ours, friends we have not seen these fifteen years or more."

The words were spoken expectantly, but Anna could not understand her aunt's enthusiasm. Uncle Robert never traveled on account of his infirmity. Early after his removal to the countryside from London, a fever had deprived him of much of his ability to walk; while here at the farm he had a system of wheeled chairs and railings which made mobility possible, anywhere else he was confined to a sitting chair all day long. This was abhorrent to him. In response, Robert Masterson had defied nature by becoming a master horseman despite his handicap and had made a home for himself where his activities need not be curtailed in many ways. Anna admired him, but she sometimes chafed at her own lack of experience in the world as a consequence of her uncle's lifestyle. Her uncle possessed the means to be a man of Style, and however much Anna did not inherently value this, she did think it gave one an opportunity to see some of the world. However, although their little family was often invited to friends' and clients' homes for extended visits, they never accepted.

She raised her gaze again to her aunt's face in inquiry. Louisa narrowed her eyes for a moment and then smiled slowly.

"The invitation," she said, "is to Mr. and Mrs. Greeley's town house"—she paused—"in London."

Anna's heart skipped a beat, and then she guarded her senses again. "What does it signify to where it is, Aunt?" Her tone was even, not displaying any of the disappointment she could not help from feeling every time such an invitation was tendered and then refused.

"It signifies a great deal, my sweet, since this time your uncle has consented to have us go."

The words hung in the air as if too brilliant to dissipate quickly in the still, warm room.

"Aunt Louisa? He cannot have!" Anna's voice was breathless, unbelieving.

Her aunt smiled broadly. "Indeed he has! He greatly esteems these friends—he has known Mr. Greeley since their days at Eton, and Mrs. Greeley is a kind and intelligent woman. You will perhaps remember when they visited Hedgecliff with their daughter, Lucinda, many years ago? You were, I think, not yet seven at the time. They go up to Town every few years or so for the Season, and it seems that this year Lucinda, who just last week turned eighteen, will be having her come-out. Samantha—Mrs. Greeley, that is—knowing your circumstance here in your uncle's home, had the idea that you might want to join her daughter in being introduced to the *ton* this year as well."

"Aunt! But what of you and Uncle Robert? I cannot leave you *alone* here for that many *months!*" Anna exclaimed hurriedly, and her aunt smiled. Anna was ever one to think of the difficulties to others rather than the benefits to herself in any circumstance.

Louisa Masterson patted her niece's hands, which were clenched in her lap in bridled excitement. "My dear, *I* shall accompany you to Town"—Anna gasped in happiness—"and your uncle has insisted that a few months of solitary activity here at Hedgecliff will do him good, as he has much work to do to prepare for the racing season, many contracts to see completed, etcetera." Louisa's eyes danced with pleasure at her niece's barely contained excitement; Anna was nearly rising off of her seat in anticipatory glee. "He has assured me that he will miss us dreadfully, but he feels that it is time for you to have some excitement in your life." She leaned forward and lowered her voice. "I think he recognizes the fact that you are too good for any of our country gentlemen, and he hopes to see you wed to a respectable man of quality."

Anna's cheeks flushed lightly; then a thought came to her. "He thinks I have been too much in the company of Mr. Pendleton," she said a bit conspiratorially, as if understanding. "And that this has not been proper."

Mrs. Masterson nodded sagely, but the smile did not leave her lips. "Perhaps he believes that Mr. Pendleton's suit could use a little healthy competition."

Anna grinned and grasped her aunt's hands more tightly yet. Her voice was warm when she spoke. "Aunt, you and Uncle have made me so very, very happy." In her mind she was thinking how, despite her previous decision, she could not wait to share the wonderful news with her friend at Alverston Hall.

March
Alverston Hall

Dearest Anna,

I am delighted to hear of your proposed journey to Town. I hope your Season will be everything that I had anticipated for mine.

I will not be able to join you there, as your letter hopefully suggested. In fact, very shortly I will travel quite a distance farther away from London to care for an elderly relative who is rapidly declining in health. I have been asked to act as companion to her while needed, and have accepted the responsibility. As yet I lack the desire to return to Society, and expect to be occupied thus for many months.

My brother plans to spend the Season in London, and he has instructed me to offer you his services as escort whenever you should need them. He will shortly be traveling to Town, and tells me he shall call upon you when he learns that you and the Greeleys have arrived. I have already given him your direction. He encourages me to stress that you should consider him at your service for the duration of your sojourn in London.

I shall not have the opportunity to write to you during the next months, as I shall be quite busy with caring for my relative and seeing that her home is kept in order. Excuse me for this little while, and know that I am, as always,

Affectionately yours,
Val

SEVEN

April

The Earl of Alverston strode purposefully down St. James's Place, having just left his club after a rather harrowing two hours of further reestablishing himself among his London acquaintances. Bramfield had not been there, but would meet him later at Tattersalls to give him his opinion on an exceptionally fine pair of grays that Valentine wished to purchase for his use now that he was back in Town.

He was looking forward to seeing Timothy. He had seen his old friend only briefly when he had passed through Town to see the family solicitor after his father's and James's deaths. Timothy had visited Alverston once since that time, and had been a welcome companion for the weeks that he had stayed, but still it had been almost a year since they had seen each other. Valentine was, as it turned out, particularly glad he had at least one ally in Town this Season.

He had been gone for too long. Most of his friends were changed; either they had become serious and stuffy, respectable fellows or they had become bored and overly arrogant. A few had drifted toward dandyism or too much gaming, squandering their honor and wealth as they went. Some, of course, had died in the war. None were quite as he remembered them, and he was not what they had expected, either.

His self-alienation from Society had been remarked in Town since his return from the Peninsula and his elevation to the status of Peer. Many at Brooks's this morning had regarded him with either morbid curiosity or barely concealed disdain; he had, remarkably enough, acquired the character of both an eccentric recluse *and* a too-proud coward who shirked his social duties. The former was understandable, given the bare contact he had maintained with most of his acquaintance. The latter was mainly on account of his sister's scandal, banishment, and subsequent disappearance from Polite Society. It seemed that while Lady Monroe had largely been forgiven her transgressions of two years ago, he, *Valentine,* was being criticized as an ineffective and inappropriate guardian for the willful young beauty. The general agreement, it seemed, was that a girl so beautiful and spirited would only be controlled by marriage and should not, under any circumstances, be left to become a spinster. Somehow it was known—or assumed, given the lack of information about her—that Valerie had not married yet, and this deficiency was attributed to her brother's unskilled management of her.

Valentine had taken the sustained ribbing as well as the disdainful silences and pinched noses in stride, with a casual aplomb that would have left that master of manners Brummel himself satisfied. While not correcting any of the assumptions made about him, he had behaved as the perfect gentleman, greeting the men he met that afternoon and discussing matters both social and political with them, as well as answering any questions put to him with direct honesty. He did not, however, disclose Valerie's exact location or speak much about her. She desired anonymity, and he would respect her wishes. Otherwise, he was acting as a man of his upbringing and status dictated; he appreciated the wise and suffered the fools lightly. His situation might have changed, but Society would always remain the same.

By the time his thoughts had run through the morning's experience at his club, the earl found himself near the residence on Field Street which he sought. He had passed through some of the more fashionable neighborhoods in Town, and had turned onto a less brilliantly arrayed street, but one on which the houses were still of respectable size and appearance. The families of country squires and well-to-do untitled gentlemen tended to inhabit this square of Town, and Valentine, who had once or twice found himself here before, felt satisfied that Miss Tremain's friends were people of sufficient wealth and taste to choose such a neighborhood. He had caught himself worrying that the Greeleys were not what he would wish for Anna's sponsors—perhaps of the vulgar or social-climbing sort—and had quickly berated himself for the thought. They carried Louisa Masterson's blessing, and that was enough for his satisfaction.

It did not signify to him, anyway, with whom Anna would stay while she was in Town; he would brave the worst Society graspers in order to finally meet her face to face.

The thought stopped him in his tracks as his stomach did an unexpected somersault, and a flush of chagrin suffused his face. He could not remember the last time he had either blushed *or* felt butterflies. His association with Miss Tremain was driving him to behavior that he would not have been able to imagine in himself two years ago. How, he wondered, could a woman, however extraordinary in both character and mind, cause such havoc in a man's life? And as of yet he had not even *seen* her, a thought which this time caused his stomach to clench.

What did he remember of the little girl, anyway? She had been a stick of a child then, all legs and laughing mouth. Her hair, he thought, was of a medium color, a little gold perhaps from its exposure to the summer's sunshine; even his own sister had returned each year from her summers at Hedgecliff with sun highlights in her dark curls. Mostly, though, he remembered the girl's doelike eyes, wide and dark and serious in a pleasing little-girl's face. She had been, he supposed, a typical country girl.

How she must have changed in the intervening *seven years!* Whatever the case, it was not her appearance that had caused him to tumble into love with her. It was her quick mind; her warm and often absurd sense of humor; her genuine, unrestrained caring for everyone she knew, including those whose own behavior more usually attracted censure or disdain among Society; and her unfailing hope in a world that offered to so many so little in recompense for making the hard journey through life. She had touched him with her caring and courage in the face of indifference and loss; her righteous anger over the injustices she had herself witnessed and had learned of under Mr. Thimbly's guidance; and her burning desire to make some difference in the world, a desire as yet bottled up inside her, unable through her naïveté, ignorance, and situation to find a way to employ itself. Perhaps, Valentine thought with frustration, if she married a man like Pendleton, whose intelligence went only so far as to provide him diversion in the company of other men, it never would.

He took a heavy breath and looked up the street toward the town house the Greeleys inhabited during the London Season; then he steeled himself. His breath caught in his throat: The knocker was up on the door.

The earl had made this walk every day for the past

week since he had been in Town, guessing that none of his particular cronies of the *haut ton* would know if the less fashionable Greeley family had arrived, and not particularly anxious to spread their names about just yet. He had designed his strategy carefully; the war had provided him with a few useful skills in acquisition tactics, and he was determined to put them to work on his own personal behalf for the first time.

He winced at the direction his thoughts had taken and felt a familiar ache in the pit of his being. Those same skills had not helped anyone that searingly hot summer day in the foothills of Spain. This, however, was another time and place, a new age for him. Anna had shown him that with her courage.

He looked carefully to confirm the information signifying that the Greeleys and their guests had arrived in Town. He could see evidence of their moving in: a traveling carriage parked in front of the house, a footman hurrying forth from the opened front door to gather more baggage from the vehicle. Valentine stared. A woman, apparently young, had come through the door, hastening after the footman and reaching her hand out to him in a gesture to get his attention without actually touching his liveried shoulder. The distance was too great for Valentine to make out her features, but he could see the glimmer of gold-brown hair beneath a simply ribboned straw bonnet and the lithe figure of the girl revealed by her rose-colored traveling dress. She exchanged words with the footman and turned, retracing her steps up to the house and disappearing once again through the door.

Thursday he would call, he decided as he turned and made his way back the way he had come, toward Mayfair. He would give them a day to settle in; then he would present himself at Number Ten Field Street and humbly offer his services as escort and guide for the duration of the young ladies' stay in town. In the meantime, he would close himself in his study and write a long-overdue letter to his little sister far away in Boston, Massachusetts.

EIGHT

Anna gaped at the number and quality of gowns arrayed before her in the dressmaker's shop.

"Aunt, I cannot imagine how one can possibly choose the styles let alone the fabrics!" She turned her soft brown eyes to her aunt, away from the bolts of both brightly colored and subtler hued cloth and the fashion journals laid out around her. Mrs. Masterson grinned in understanding.

"My dear Anna"—the strong but cultivated female voice came from across the room—"you will learn to understand what is needed for a young lady's Town wardrobe in no time at all." Samantha Greeley, arrayed in a modest matron's dress of emerald green that neatly matched her bright eyes, moved toward Anna, a bolt of sapphire blue silk balanced across her outstretched forearms. Her daughter, whose eyes were quite as bright as her mother's, like Anna stared wide-eyed at the wealth of material around them with a mixture of excitement and dismay in her expression. "You will wear a great deal of white this Season," continued Lucinda's mother, "despite your slightly advanced age for a girl making her come-out." She looked down at the fabric in her arms and *tsk-tsked* as if in response to what she had just said.

Anna sighed as she watched her sponsor lay the

richly colored fabric on the table behind her and pick up instead a pale yellow muslin to consider.

"Now, Samantha," Louisa Masterson spoke up, "Anna has been going about in our little Society of ____shire for two years already. Surely she could perhaps have a *few* gowns of more mature cut and color." She glanced at her niece fondly. "She is no longer a girl."

Anna's dark eyes strayed to the bolt of sapphire silk and then rose to see Lucinda looking merrily at her, green eyes sparkling with a mixture of delight and playful envy. Miss Greeley would not be able to escape the barrage of white garments this Season, and perhaps for longer, unless that is, she found herself a husband to provide her with instant maturity. The two exchanged conspiratorial smiles.

Anna turned her attention back to the conversation continuing between her aunt and Mrs. Greeley. The younger matron agreed that Anna might have gowns made in a style more befitting her nineteen years than the simple white muslins that would be ordered for Lucinda. Although white for a woman of any age was *de rigeur,* pale colors and pastels were all the rage this Season, which suited Anna well enough, although she herself preferred slightly darker colors. Her aunt, who knew her tastes, proceeded to guide the choice of fabrics and dress styles throughout the course of the next few hours.

When the women emerged from the shop at luncheon time, Anna was to expect delivery at her home the next morning of at least two new gowns: one of a muted peach-red hue and another, a walking dress, of azure blue and white striped jaconet. The other gowns she and Lucinda had ordered would be delivered within the week. By then the girls would hopefully have become comfortable in their new surroundings, and would be ready to make their combined social debut at a small gathering held by Lady Jasmine Ethridge, one of Mrs. Greeley's oldest and dearest friends, and the wife of Baron Ethridge of Hughbottom Sill. Mrs. Greeley and Louisa Masterson felt certain that this respectable but unformidable matron's party would be the ideal venue for introducing their charges into London Society.

Anna was anxious to wet her feet as soon as possible. She was more interested, if truth be told, in visiting the Tower and having a look at the famous Elgin marbles, and getting a peek inside Astley's Amphitheatre than meeting the *ton* quite yet. She was a bit nervous about the latter, and only wished for the first difficult and anxious social occasions to be over with, so that she could feel if not at home then at least comfortable in London. Its immense size had not subdued her adventurous spirit, but learning the kind of constant social activity that was expected of a young lady upon her first Season in Town had startled her quite a bit. Anna was glad to have Lucinda Greeley as a sympathetic companion in this new experience. The younger girl, though, was extremely shy, if unfailingly sweet. She would prove a charming companion, but not one to help Anna through the more difficult and worrisome social situations that could arise.

She was delighted therefore when the next morning, sitting in the drawing room with her aunt and Lucinda and arrayed in her beautiful new sunset-colored dress, a visitor arrived who, with his entrance, removed these worries from her mind. She rose and smiled as she watched her aunt stretch out both her hands in greeting to the young gentleman attired in a dun brown coat and rust pantaloons. His smile was genuine as he turned to Anna and offered her his hand to shake.

"Mr. Pendleton," Louisa Masterson said, "it is a pleasure to tell you that you are our first visitor since we have arrived in Town. I suspect you cannot have been here long yourself."

The Honorable Jason Pendleton reluctantly withdrew his hand from Anna's and turned to her aunt with a smile. "Indeed not, madam. I arrived yesterday night, but made visiting my most cherished friends from ____shire my first order of business today." He glanced at Anna for a moment. "I thought I might steal a march on all of the other gentlemen who will be flocking to your drawing room as soon as the two loveliest ladies in town make their debut." With this charming comment he turned to a blushing Lucinda and was properly introduced before they all sat down and Mrs. Masterson rang for tea.

Anna immediately asked Mr. Pendleton for information of Hedgecliff and her uncle. She and her aunt had left home over two weeks ago, first traveling to Cotswold and the home of the Greeleys, where they had resided for a few days during which preparations for the Season were completed and the young ladies acquaintance reestablished. The entire party had then made the three-day journey to London. Anna felt that she had been away from her uncle for much longer than a scant two weeks, and she begged Mr. Pendleton, who had traveled to London on horseback, and therefore much more quickly than the Greeleys' train of three carriages, to tell her what he knew of Uncle Robert's goings-on during their absence. He was indulgently fulfilling her request when the butler entered and announced the arrival of yet another visitor.

"His lordship the Earl of Alverston," intoned the young but pompous retainer, and he stepped aside to admit perhaps the handsomest man Anna had ever seen.

He bore a fleeting resemblance to Valerie in his coloring and the confident yet somehow gently amused expression in his eyes, but there the similarity ended. The earl was tall, his frame dwarfing the diminutive butler who was just then making his backward retreat and closing the drawing room door behind him. Lord Alverston's broad shoulders were encased in a coat of blue superfine that fit his athletic frame superbly, allowing for no suggestion of padding or corsets. His tasseled hessians shone from across the room, and his hands rested at his sides with confident grace. His rich sable hair was cut into a fashionable style that had likely been tousled—*To the bearer's advantage*, Anna thought—by the removal of his hat before he had entered the room. But despite his admirable form and dress, his face was the most stunning thing about him. Noble cheekbones flattered a well-cut jaw and a fine, expressive mouth. The crowning glory were his warm eyes, charcoal gray and long lashed, which had been unwaveringly trained on Anna's own since the instant he had walked through the door.

When he turned his gaze to her aunt, after what seemed an eternity but was likely only a fraction of a moment, Anna realized that she had stopped breathing, and she slowly allowed herself a few bits of air as she watched the earl remake her aunt's acquaintance.

"Lord Alverston." Louisa Masterson extended her hand and the earl bowed over it. "How kind you are to call on us this morning, before anyone else even knows we are in London. You make us feel quite at home in this land of strangers."

"It is my delight, Mrs. Masterton, to be able once again to make your acquaintance. I have very fond memories of the evening I once spent at Hedgecliff with you and your husband." The earl's voice was smooth and resonant, and Anna could not help but instantly like the way his mouth curved ever so slightly upward when at rest, instead of bearing the perpetual

downturn that graced so many masculine faces among
London's fashionably attired. "I hope Mr. Masterson
is well?" he politely asked, his tone bearing a sincerity
unusual for the banal question.

"He is, thank you. He is having to get along without his womenfolk for a few months, however." Louisa
smiled warmly and turned to draw his attention to
the young ladies present. "My lord, may I present to
you my niece, Miss Tremain, and our good friend,
Miss Greeley?"

Anna barely knew what she did when the earl once
again turned the power of his shadow-dark eyes upon
her, but she supposed she executed something of a
reasonable curtsy, as his expression did not alter when
he bowed to her. His gaze lingered upon her only a
fraction of a moment longer than was necessary before he turned to Lucinda, whose emerald eyes were
at the moment as wide as Anna had ever seen them;
but the younger girl did not embarrass herself in
greeting their exalted guest.

"And this is Mr. Pendleton," her aunt continued,
"a friend of ours from ____shire, who has also just
recently arrived in Town for the Season."

Valentine's heart froze. Later he was sure that he
had nodded the proper greeting or made the requisite remark, but at the moment when he discovered
the identity of the man standing next to Anna Tremain in the Greeleys' London drawing room, he was
temporarily bereft of the capacity to think.

He had prepared himself for many possibilities, and
had told himself that whatever her appearance, if he
was not particularly attracted to her right away, it
would not matter. He had learned to love her mind
and her spirit, and he would undoubtedly love her
person as well in time. Valentine had never been
much of a romantic, despite his obvious attractiveness
to the opposite sex. He had borne the flattering at-

tentions of many women in his twenty-seven years with as much grace and humility as possible, as well as a great deal of honest indifference. He had once or twice fancied himself in love with a pretty face, but had grown out of these infatuations naturally, if with the usual amount of puppy-love pain and discomfort such things caused. He had never, though, felt that his heart was truly engaged; not at least until this past Christmas when he had realized that his interest in Anna had shifted over the course of a year of letter-writing from appreciative amusement to friendly caring to, finally, what he thought was love.

He had not been prepared for her simple yet radiant beauty, and now that he had seen her, all other images of what she may have looked like scattered in the truth of such unanticipated exquisiteness. Long honey brown hair, gathered softly in a knot at the nape of her neck, framed a delicately flushed face graced by high cheekbones, a full, sensuous mouth, and the most beautiful soft brown eyes that he had ever had the good fortune to gaze into. She was over medium height for a woman and bore herself regally, her shoulders straight and her hands lightly resting on the fine fabric of a gown whose perfect late-summer shade set off her creamy complexion. She was a lovely country blossom, down to the few freckles that dappled her slightly up-turned nose like drops of morning dew on a velvety petal. Valentine Monroe, the earl of Alverston, was smitten all over again.

That he had arrived just in time to witness the re-union of Miss Tremain and her greatly esteemed admirer served to rouse his ire quite violently, he was chagrined to note. Accepting Mrs. Masterson's invitation to sit and partake of the tea that had just been delivered into the room on a broad silver tray, Valentine found that his jaw was clenched, and he loosened it. He took the opportunity of the pouring and passing of teacups to make a covert assessment of his scholarly rival, and was impressed by the neat, understated quality of the man's dress and demeanor. Pendleton was an attractive fellow, blast it all; but Anna had been most intrigued by his address. Valentine determined to attend carefully to the fellow's speech so that he could judge for himself what Anna had described as his magnetic conversation. Louisa Masterson made the job simple.

"Lord Alverston, Mr. Pendleton was just now telling us news of Hedgecliff and our little village. I hope it will not bore you if we implore him to finish his story."

Valentine smiled. "No, indeed. In fact I would very much like to hear news of your good husband." Mrs. Masterson smiled and the group turned its attention to the light-haired gentleman.

"Mr. Masterson has been particularly involved this past week, I take it, with the sale of his two very best mounts," Mr. Pendleton began, his attention equally divided among the people seated around the tea table.

"Those would be Sheldrake and Felicity, if I am not mistaken?" Anna interrupted, looking to her aunt for confirmation. Louisa Masterson nodded, and they both returned their attention to the gentleman speaking.

Valentine was happy to be witness to Miss Tremain's honest enthusiasm for her uncle's business. As Pendleton continued, her cheeks flushed to a warm rose glow and her eyes sparkled with interest in what he was telling them. The earl was somewhat pained to think that her heightened beauty was perhaps solely on account of her interest in Pendleton's speech, which admittedly proved pretty, even in discussing the practical matters of the opening of the racing season and how that would affect sellers and buyers this year. He was gratified that when Anna began a brief exchange about the farm with her aunt, her eyes maintained the same brilliancy as before; perhaps it was the topic of her uncle and his business that enthralled her more than the young man sitting by her side. Valentine noted, with rising irritation, that Pendleton had somehow moved himself a fraction of an inch closer to the fall of Miss Tremain's dress on the settee, a fraction which put him in easy touching range of her arm if she but moved an inch. She did not. She did, however, take the opportunity of a lull in the conversation to turn her questioning chocolate gaze upon Valentine himself.

"Lord Alverston," she began, her lips parting to reveal white, even teeth. "I am anxious to ask you about your sister, if I may. How does my good friend go on this spring? I have not heard from her in quite some time, and I would like very much to learn how she is finding her life so far from London this Season."

Having her attention trained entirely on him almost robbed Valentine of speech, but by lingering over a sip of tea, he was able to gather his wits together and make a reasonably vague yet honest reply. "My sister is well, thank you," he said. "She is finding her present employment rather oppressive to her spirit, I am sorry to relate, and wishes to be free of it as soon as is reasonably possible." This much, at least, was true. Denbridge had written to him months ago of how Valerie was almost more miserable in Boston Society than she could possibly be in the London Society that had so ostracized her after her unfortunately unacceptable behavior. Valentine did not know, however, where she hoped to go next to comfort her still wounded heart, although a trip to visit friends in Italy had at one time been mentioned and then discarded quickly.

"Oh, I am terribly sorry to hear that!" Anna said with fervent concern, her eyes clouded as she gazed as if unseeing into his. Valentine wondered if she was seeing in her mind's eye his sister instead of him, her gaze was so strangely distant. But then, in an instant she was back from where she had gone, and he was again struck almost physically by the remarkable expressiveness of her doelike eyes. Unexpectedly, she smiled, and Valentine felt his insides melt within him. "Do you think her unhappiness with her situation now will possibly convince her to leave her post and come down to Town for the spring?"

He returned her smile. "I hope for your sake that it will, Miss Tremain." And for mine, that it won't, he prayed silently to himself, but he continued smoothly. "I am certain she would like very much to see you, although she may not be able to at the present moment."

The gratitude that these words evoked in Miss Tremain's eyes reached out and enveloped him, and Valentine, struck speechless yet again, was tremendously glad that the conversation just then took another turn. But for at least a moment while she had gazed at him with such hope and what seemed to him almost longing, he had felt as if she and he were the only two people in the room—or in the world, for that matter—and that everything in her eyes was meant especially for him.

NINE

Both gentlemen lingered in the Greeley home not long beyond the appropriate half-hour of a proper morning call. As the party stood up for their departure, Valentine once again turned toward the older lady in the room.

"Mrs. Masterson, I will be honored if you would allow me to serve as escort for you, your niece, and Miss Greeley while you remain in London."

Anna could tell that Lucinda was looking at her meaningfully behind the earl's back, but her gaze remained fixed on his heart-stopping profile, and a warmth invaded her as she realized that he was doing this on account of his sister's wishes.

"Lord Alverston, we are most happy to accept your offer, especially as our kind host, Mr. Greeley, has so many responsibilities that require his absence from Town during these months," Louisa Masterson said, inclining her head gracefully.

Valentine smiled. "I was hoping you would join me tomorrow afternoon for a drive in the Park?"

"I thank you for the invitation, my lord," Anna's aunt said with a thoughtful look, "but that might prove a bit too sudden an experience of Society for the young women." Valentine nodded in understanding, hiding his disappointment. "Perhaps were we to require your escort for a stroll tomorrow, sometime before the more fashionable hour, I could gratefully accept on behalf of us all. Although we do not wish to upset your schedule, of course."

"On the contrary; I am at your disposal and should be very pleased to take a turn about the Park at an earlier hour," Valentine replied lightly.

"A fellow can barely move his cattle, in any case, when he tries to ride too late in the day, for all of the carriages lined up to display their occupants," Pendleton said good-naturedly, and Valentine had the grace to agree with him. The earl looked again at Louisa Masterson, who quickly said that she hoped Mr. Pendleton would join their little group on the morrow. Pendleton gratefully accepted, and Valentine supposed that he would rather be present than not when the blond Adonis was near Miss Tremain; at least that way he could keep an eye on them.

The moment the earl and Mr. Pendleton departed, Lucinda breathed an airy sigh and said in a wondrous voice, "My but he *is* terribly handsome!"

Returning to her seat and embroidery, an image of smoky eyes and a mouth-curling smile came to Anna, and she thought that she could not agree more.

"Why," Lucinda went on in breathy accents, "I wish I could get *my* hair to shine as gold as his. Perhaps he uses some kind of lemon wash. What do you think, Mrs. Masterson?"

Louisa Masterson looked slyly at her niece's surprised reaction to Lucinda's words. "I think it unlikely that young Mr. Pendleton uses any sort of hair color or color enhancer on himself, Lucinda," she responded to the blond girl, her eyes straying back to Anna, who suddenly found it necessary to bend down to rummage in her embroidery bag for an item.

Mr. Pendleton, indeed! Anna thought. How could a woman even *glance* at another man when Lord Alverston was in the same room? Lucinda Greeley must be collecting cobwebs in her attic!

Anna instantly berated herself for her unfairness. Perhaps the innocent and less worldly Lucinda was attracted more to the younger man's golden air of youthfulness and boyishness. Anna did not recognize that her own tender age and country-bred status could have easily merited her the same consideration. There was nothing whatsoever boyish about Lord Alverston. Anna could barely remember now the vague image she had of Valerie's brother from the time he had come down from Oxford to Hedgecliff almost eight years ago; it was entirely eclipsed by the very masculine and mature vision she had now of the earl. He had certainly grown up since she had seen him last—or perhaps *she* herself had, Anna mused. Whatever the case, he was extraordinarily beautiful.

The earl had not seemed to her in character a vain or arrogant man, though. His conversation had been unassuming and pleasant, and his address polite, though perhaps just a bit warmer than might have been usual for a first or second meeting while not overly familiar in the least, something which Anna attributed to her close association with his sister, his sole companion during the past two years of grieving and healing. He had been the perfect gentleman, from his sparkling boots to his quiet air of confidence. Anna wondered if *all* London gentlemen would be so breathtakingly wonderful. She secretly doubted it.

Anna's gaze was trained on the broad span of shoulder covered by dark gray superfine that, she had noticed earlier, perfectly matched the shade of its wearer's eyes. Lord Alverston was walking in front of her, her aunt's hand resting on his arm as they strolled slowly along the Hyde Park footpath in the midmorning sun. Louisa was saying something about how unfashionable they were to be out and about so early in the day and that Lord Alverston had been terribly kind to begin his day so early on their account.

His reply was lost in the spring breeze, and Anna reluctantly turned her attention back to her walking companion. Mrs. Greeley was admiring the unusually clear sky and the bright yellow and pink flowers along the pathway for the third time since they had set forth from the house. She turned her head around partially to ask the opinion of her daughter and Mr. Pendleton, who made up the last of the morning's walking party, and the two agreed that indeed the weather could not be finer. Anna remained silent, content to be strolling through the Park, breathing in the day's fragrance and sharing the quiet of the prefashionable hour with her new friends.

Oddly, though, she *was* experiencing something that was not *particularly* enjoyable. It amounted to a sort of uncomfortable nervousness, but different from the one she had been feeling on account of her debut into Society; now that she and Lucinda had the escort of not one but two fashionable young gentlemen, this no longer preoccupied her as it had.

It was an odd feeling, like the feeling she got when she was watching a young thoroughbred race for the first time: a kind of *singing* in her blood; she could find no other way to describe it. She had felt it this morning when she rose, and had been able to consume little of the chocolate and toast she had been served in her room on a silver tray. (Mrs. Greeley was indulging her charges for their first week in Town, saying it was essential that they live the lives of true ladies of the *ton,* at least for a little while.) The sensation had remained with her after the arrivals of Mr.

Pendleton and the earl, and stayed with her still as they walked leisurely along the winding paths.

Perhaps, she pondered, it was just the excitement of finally entering Society as a young woman and not as a green girl, as she had been when gradually introduced into their little ____shire community. It was a heady thing, living in a fashionable town house, being served breakfast in bed every morning, sharing the gracious company of attractive gentlemen of the *ton*, and being treated as if she were particularly unique, due to her status as a girl making her debut.

Anna was resolved not to let it go to her head, however it had seemed to affect the rest of her extrasensitized limbs and her fluttering midsection. She would seek out Mr. Greeley's library when this walk was over and lose herself in something intelligent and challenging, she vowed; and then she did immediately lose herself once again in the beauty of the sunshine falling through the tall trees and onto the lush spring grass of the Park.

Suddenly the party came to a halt as a horseman cantered toward them on the pathway. He reined in his spirited roan and smiled down at the little group, his eyes lingering for an appreciative moment on both Anna and Lucinda before moving to Lord Alverston.

"Well met, Val," said the gentleman in cheerful tones, his hair glimmering like copper in the bright sunshine.

Valentine grinned up at his friend. "Good day to you, Tim. May I present to you my companions?" As the earl named the persons in his group, Timothy Ramsay, Viscount Bramfield touched his high-crown beaver to each in turn, raising his brows a fraction in greeting the two young ladies in the party.

"I am very pleased to meet you all," he said, holding his feisty mount at bay with his strong legs as if it cost him no effort at all. Anna glanced aside and noticed that Lucinda was already gathering that by-now-familiar amazed expression in her eyes, and she looked back to the viscount. "Taking in a bit of the fair weather this morning?" His voice was friendly and entirely without a trace of Town boredom that, even in the few short days she'd been in London, Anna had learned to recognize among its more fashionable inhabitants.

Mrs. Greeley, as the hostess of the party, answered for them all. "Indeed we are, my lord. If you did not have your horse to consider we would urge you to join us."

"Thank you, madam. As it is, I must be on my way. But I hope our paths will cross again soon." And with a wink toward the wide-eyed Lucinda, he cantered off along the path on the way they had come. Mrs. Greeley *cluck-clucked* the viscount's teasing of her daughter, but seeing Lucinda look to the earl blushingly, she took up Mr. Pendleton's proffered arm and continued along the path.

"Lord Bramfield is a particular friend of yours, Lord Alverston?" Anna asked as they resumed their stroll, finding herself walking alongside the earl this time. She had to concentrate to keep from staring at the place on his neck where soft sable locks curled ever so slightly around the back of his ear.

"Yes, he is," Valentine replied easily. "We have been friends since we were boys at school together. He is a very good fellow, my closest friend," he added. "I am happy to have been able to introduce him to you." He glanced to the side to see her looking at him, and returned his gaze to the view ahead. He was surprised at how her nearness served to unnerve him. Valentine spoke to cover his confusion, not thinking what he was saying until the military metaphor had already escaped his lips. "Bramfield is a staunch ally against the forces of the absurd in this town." Em-

barrassed, he stole another glance at Miss Tremain
and met a frankly amazed stare, amusement lifting
the corners of her shapely mouth. There was a question in her eyes that she dared not speak.

"What I had meant to say—" he began quickly, but
Anna's gentle laughter cut him off and he looked at
her in chagrin.

"What you said, Lord Alverston, was not at all what
one would expect to hear from one of your status, I
am quite certain," she said, a ripple still in her voice.
"One does not have to spend very much time in Society to understand that personal opinions of that sort
are left unsaid." Anna touched her hand to his sleeve,
and was instantly shocked by her own forwardness.
She clasped her hands together in front of her.

"I do beg your forgiveness, Miss Tremain, for my
rudeness. I cannot think what devil caused me to say
that." Valentine was thoroughly embarrassed. Never
before that could he remember having made such a
social gaffe. Miss Tremain would think him a churl,
too arrogant and too sure of himself by far.

"Come now, my lord. I may not have been in London for long, but human nature is much the same
wherever life takes one. Pay me the courtesy of allowing me to take your words for truth, devoid of pride."

Valentine's eyes widened. She had known what he
was thinking and had gone right to the heart of the
matter, without dwelling on his poor behavior. As his
embarrassment dissipated, the earl felt a rush of admiration for the young woman by his side. She was,
as he had known already, honest and forthright yet
utterly graceful.

"I shall, Miss Tremain," he said, and smiled at her.
"But only because you request it of me." Her eyes
were sparkling in the bright morning light as they
looked up at him for a moment and then away again.
His gaze traveled over her shining hair and high poke

bonnet, across her soft-skinned face, and took in the fashionable and very flattering cut of her blue and white striped gown. Valentine took a deep breath to still his tingling nerves.

"And speaking of requests that you must make of me," he went on, lightly tapping his silver-handled cane on the path beside him in a staccato rhythm, "I wish you to tell me what London sights you would like to see before the whirl of social engagements begins to eat up all of your time. Are there any places you have in mind to visit for which I may serve as your happy escort?"

Anna's heart leaped in excitement. "Oh, yes, Lord Alverston, indeed!" The animated enthusiasm in her voice brought a smile to Valentine's lips. "I should *very* much like to see Lord Elgin's infamous marbles. I have heard so much about them that I am anxious to see them for myself." Suddenly she lowered her tone. "I understand that they are not quite proper viewing material for young ladies, however."

He nearly chuckled at her swift change of moods, from enthusiasm to imminent disappointment, but held himself in check. The earl was amazed at how quickly the mature young lady could, from a wise observer of life, become an innocent country girl and then again resume her Town role with easy grace. He wondered if she was at all aware of the change in her manner and decided that she could not be. She was not self-conscious enough for that. Valentine thought her any number of remarkable women all wrapped up into one.

"Shall we apply to your aunt for a judgment on the matter?" he asked solicitously. "I trust her to be the best arbiter of etiquette for such issues of maidenly modesty."

They slowed their pace and turned, still walking, to hear Mrs. Masterson's opinion on the subject of the ancient Greek marbles. Anna's aunt was walking just behind them, arm in arm with Miss Greeley. When the issue was put to her, she looked thoughtful for a moment only, and then pronounced her opinion that Anna was quite mature enough to see some silly old rocks, and that as long as she was in the company of a highly respectable earl Society would not blink one eyelash at it.

The earl for his part expressed gratification at her trust in him, while he privately pondered whether he was not the best person, in Society's eyes, to be acting as escort to Miss Tremain in this endeavor. He had only this morning fielded yet more oblique questions concerning his sister, this time from some of the old biddies he had encountered in Leicester Square where he had gone to purchase an item at the milliner's for his old housekeeper's birthday. Not everyone saw him as a man who knew what was right and proper for a young lady of Quality. He would despise himself if Anna acquired negative publicity due to anything he did or failed to do on her behalf. When he put this last concern to her, in a slightly less personal way, she laughed her rippling laughter and smiled all the more brilliantly in her anticipation.

"I have no fear, Lord Alverston, nor should you," Anna said as they resumed their walk side by side. "Society does not frighten me, although I do respect the power it has over a young lady's future." Her brow furrowed slightly at this last remark, but quickly cleared. "Perhaps," she said, looking up again at his face, "we could go very early in the day and thereby avoid any prying eyes that might be looking for innocents such as myself swimming in waters too deep for them."

The earl could not resist her enthusiasm. "That sounds like just the perfect strategy," he paused, and then added meaningfully, "given, that is, the *absurdity* of the situation." Valentine watched her eyes flash to his and the edges of them crinkle delicately as her lips curved into a broad, uninhibited smile.

TEN

Anna accepted the glass of lemonade from her former dance partner, a slender young man with an extraordinary excess of pomaded hair and, she had discovered, two left feet. Unfortunately, the lemonade, like her companion, was rather flat. She thanked him for his kindness in acquiring it for her, sipped at it, and wished for her aunt to turn her attention away from the old fellow in uniform with whom she was speaking and back to her. Nothing could be more exhausting, she had found, than the inane conversation and painfully obvious posturing and jostling for recognition that she had witnessed this night at what had been advertised to her as the most important social venue in London. In Anna's opinion, Almack's was nothing more than a hot, crowded, and mediocre version of what amounted to a prettified barnyard—with cackling chickens, strutting roosters, and the rest. She flexed her toes in her satin slippers and wondered when she would be able to go home.

Beside her Mr. Bimly was stammering something about her heavenly glow when Anna spied the Earl of Alverston and his friend Viscount Bramfield moving in her direction from across the room. She felt a welling of warmth within her, and she sighed in pleasure at the potential for interesting conversation and amusement the evening suddenly offered. Knowing it would not do for her to be seen anticipating the approach of the noblemen with too much relief, however, she turned to her companion and smiled with compassion at the expression in his watery eyes. He had apparently asked her a question, but she was entirely ignorant as to what it was.

"I say, Miss Tremain, it *is* a bit loud in here. Perhaps you did not hear what I have asked you?" Mr. Bimly's face wore the look of a wounded dog as he gazed at her with thinly veiled melancholy. Anna shook her head ever so slightly and raised her brows.

"You have it, sir. If you ask me again, however, I shall endeavor to listen especially hard this time." She had suffered her modest share of doting young men in the countryside, the difference being that those she had known all of her life, since the years when they were all playing jackstraws on their parents' drawing room floors. Here the faces and names were new, but, she was sorry to admit, many of the approaches were very much the same. For Anna a gentleman's behavior toward her mattered little, however; she treated them all as she treated everyone.

To some, however, she had not been able to help revealing a few more aspects of her character.

She had spent much of the past week being fitted for yet more gowns and acquiring all of the necessary items that a young lady in London would need: a China paper fan, a pair of gold sateen ballroom slippers to match the ball gown which she would wear at the come-out ball she shared with Lucinda in several weeks, a new bottle of lavender water for her toilette, and any number of new bonnets, gloves, ribbons, and delicate underclothes that, Mrs. Greeley insisted, she could not live without in the coming months.

The rest of the time she and Lucinda had been gradually making their way into Society. After attend-

ing the Baron and Lady Ethridge's fête, the girls were
shepherded to a musical evening at the Carmichaels',
a ladies' tea at the home of the widow of Sir Edward
Leeds, and an intimate dinner party for thirty given
by Mr. and Mrs. Stilver in honor of the debut of their
only daughter, Felicity. Miss Stilver had proved an entertaining companion, and although in Anna's humble opinion the girl was more likely to be concerned
about the color of another woman's dress than the
speech coming from that person's mouth, she was
pleasant enough.

Since the morning of Anna's first walk in Hyde
Park in the company of Valentine Monroe, she had
seen the earl a number of times, but not once yet in
Society. She supposed, and was largely correct, that
the parties and entertainments the earl and his friend
Bramfield frequented were a bit above her acquaintance's humble touch. Few of the people she had met
in Town were of the nobility, and those that were,
were largely younger sons and a very few ladies married to untitled gentlemen. Anna was not surprised
that she and her friends had not crossed paths with
Lord Alverston and his friend at social functions over
the busy course of the past week.

She had met him on several occasions away from
Society's interested gaze, however. He had, as
planned, taken her to visit Lord Elgin's marbles, and
their party that day had been a very merry one. If
indeed any other people had been in the exhibition
rooms at the same time they were, they could not
have missed the giggles and exclamations of the small
but enthusiastic group of antiquarians. Aunt Louisa
had acted as Anna's chaperone, Lord Alverston had
invited his friend the viscount, and together with Mrs.
Greeley, who, although she would not allow her young
daughter to be exposed to the most intimate sculp-
tures, had a healthy curiosity about them herself, the

five passed through the rooms in a mood vacillating somewhere between sincere artistic appreciation and sheer playful irreverence. At only one moment during that morning's gay adventure had the glow of pleasure been dampened for Anna. It had been when Lord Alverston surprised her studying a particularly magnificent frieze of a Lapith soldier fighting a centaur.

Fascinated by this representation in stone of the myth she had read of in her Latin studies, Anna had fallen behind the rest of her group in contemplation of the marbles, musing over the story they depicted. She recalled that the myth told how the Lapiths had invited the centaurs to a wedding celebration, but when the centaurs descended into their cups and began making brazen advances toward the Lapith women, including the bride herself, the hosts turned on their guests and a battle erupted.

With the myth running through her mind, and engrossed in the lifelike quality of the marble figures, the elegance and expression of the lines of sculpture, Anna had forgotten to maintain a modest distance from the piece. Unconsciously, she moved closer to study the forms more carefully and marvel at the sheer force of energy radiating from the white stone. The controlled power of the masculine figures was extraordinary and, Anna agreed fleetingly as her palms grew warm, decidedly *not* fitting for the eyes of an unwed girl. She was in fact so intensely engaged in her appreciation that she did not hear Lord Alverston approach from behind her, and she almost jumped in surprise and sudden shame at her own demeanor when he spoke at her shoulder, commenting benignly on the sculpture that had enraptured her.

Anna recovered her composure quickly, but not before she spied a light of deviltry in the earl's eyes that were trained on the marble before them, and she wondered in irritation why he could find amusement in discomfiting her so. She was, perhaps, even more vexed with her own shortness of breath and the flush that she could feel staining her cheeks under the earl's acute gaze. Consequently, her reply to his question was curt, and she had moved away from him and the betraying sculpture with rather less courtesy than comportment. Although it took her some time to regain her feeling of contentment after this brief but embarrassing incident, the rest of the visit passed without further upset, to Anna's great relief.

Two days later the earl had taken Anna and Lucinda for their first drive in the Park, still at an early hour so as to avoid the heavy traffic, chaperoned again by Anna's aunt. The ladies had complimented the earl on his team, his carriage, and his driving; he had been immensely gratified; conversation had been amusing and general; and after it was over and she was sitting quietly in the parlor writing a letter to her uncle, Anna could not remember when last she had had such an agreeable morning. Lucinda had finally learned to speak in the earl's company, due to his frequent appearance in their lives, and her still-shy yet uniquely observant part in every conversation, balanced what Anna suspected must seem to the earl like her own unending string of questions regarding London Society and national politics, made for few dull moments when they were in company together.

The earl had again taken up Mrs. Masterson and Anna in his carriage two days ago, in order to show them some of the countryside closely surrounding London, the Viscount Bramfield riding alongside on his spirited roan; and yesterday he had made an appearance at the Greeley house in the morning, when the ladies were receiving the many visitors whose acquaintance they had made during the past week through their many engagements. Anna had not had an opportunity to speak with Lord Alverston then, as he was engaged for most of his call in conversation with the fair-haired Felicity Stilver. Her aunt, it seemed, was something of a distant relation of the earl's.

Sitting beside Mr. Pendleton, who had arrived some time before the earl that morning and had quickly made his way to her side, where he stayed for the remainder of his visit, not far from the earl and Miss Stilver, Anna had inadvertently overheard some of their amicable conversation. She did not know why when, during a lull in her conversation with Mr. Pendleton, she heard the earl and Miss Stilver discussing something which seemed to be far removed from the subject of family trees, and she had felt a peculiar sense of unease suddenly descend upon her. She had shaken it off and forgotten it, but for some reason the anticipation of meeting the earl again had grown since then.

Anna was amazed at how quickly she had come to feel easy with her childhood friend's brother. Well, not exactly comfortable, for she was still feeling an uncharacteristic nervousness in his presence, which she attributed to both his influence among the *beau monde* and his truly breathtaking handsomeness. While there was still that odd singing in her blood most of the time, she did recognize a familiarity between herself and the earl. Valerie had, in all likelihood, told her brother here and there of her friend in ____shire, and Lord Alverston probably felt that she was an extension, as it were, of his adored little sister.

Anna was glad of it. She was enjoying his company, his interesting conversation and his guidance in matters of *ton* etiquette, though the latter he gave only reluctantly and with enough amusement apparent that Anna could not be sure if at times he was not roasting her. Still, she trusted him, as she would have trusted her own brother had she had one, and she was very grateful to have his friendship, especially during these nervous first few weeks of her and Lucinda's debut.

Now, seeing his approach out of the corner of her eye, she gave all the rest of her attention to the young man standing beside her struggling to speak.

"Miss Tremain," stammered Mr. Bimly, "I would be honored if I could have the pleasure of calling upon you tomorrow morning at your residence."

Anna smiled graciously, if a little distractedly. She could see that the earl and viscount had nearly reached her location in the stuffy assembly rooms. "Why Mr. Bimly, certainly you may. We are often at home accepting callers in the morning, although tomorrow I think my aunt may have some letters she wishes us to write," she added, in thought.

"I am most grate—"

"Bimly old chap, how is it that you are monopolizing the company of the most attractive lady in this old shack this evening?" Viscount Bramfield's voice was jovial, his tone one that no one could take offense at, although often his words were not quite in the appropriate style. He beamed a broad, white-toothed smile down on Anna, and she nodded her head in polite recognition of his flattery. She liked the viscount and thought his loud, merry manner both honest and entertaining. Looking into *his* eyes did not produce in one the strangest sensation of sinking— not in the least. She looked into them now.

"Mr. Bimly has just kindly brought me a glass of lemonade," she said smoothly, without a trace of the laughter that bubbled up in her in response to the ever-present absurdity of their situations, an absurdity which had once been pointed out to her. "It is, I am sorry to say," she said in a conspiratorial tone, "not the very *best* refreshment I have taken since I have been in London."

Bimly's lips thinned and he nodded, dismally looking down into his own glass of pale liquid. The viscount chuckled.

"And where have you partaken of a *good* refreshment during your weeklong sojourn among the *crème de la crème* of society, my dear Miss Tremain?"

Anna's cheeks dimpled unintentionally, but the earl stepped in to save her from having to rate her week's entertainments in such a manner.

"You must stop roasting Miss Tremain, Tim, or she will imagine that you do not have a serious cell in your brain cavity," Lord Alverston said, and rested his dark gaze upon Anna's slightly flushed face. "Miss Tremain, you look very lovely this evening. I would be unreasonably proud if you would honor me with a dance."

Anna responded that she would be pleased amidst the viscount's protestations that he did not indeed have any cells at all in his skull, and he would thank the earl and everyone else to remember that. She was glad of the distraction. She had been dancing all evening it seemed, and her feet were aching with the need to sit, but somehow the thought of being partnered by Lord Alverston in a dance infused her with a new energy. She was certain that he would not step on her toes, at least she hoped he would not.

She was justified in her assumption. Lord Alverston was an excellent dancer, guiding her in the patterns of the dance and around the other couples in their set as if he had been born to do just that. She had witnessed him drive his cattle with much the same grace and expertise, and wondered if there was anything at all that this man did not do superbly.

When they had opportunity for speech, his conversation was light and friendly. He asked her if her evening at Almack's was pleasurable, and she responded appropriately. Although she was in danger of finding herself responding to the twinkle in his eyes by sharing some of her more irreverent observations of her night's entertainment, Anna restrained herself. She did not know the earl well at all, regardless of how comfortable and familiar she felt with him, and she did not want to appear a vulgar or disrespectful country clod to him—or to anyone else for that matter, she added with a mental pinch to herself. She would first have to learn what lay beneath the sparkle in Lord Alverston's eyes, the smile in his expression, before she ventured to reveal more of her irreverent self than was seemly. She was curious, however, to know more about him.

The music brought them together for a few minutes, and when his hand gently grasped her gloved fingers, Anna suddenly felt the strength in him that she had only imagined. She spoke to cover her confusion.

"Do you take your Seat in Lords, my lord?"

The earl's brows rose a fraction, but his response was even. "I have not had the opportunity to leave my estate during the past year and a half, I am afraid, Miss Tremain. I should like to join Parliament as soon as possible, however." His dark gaze rested on her thoughtfully as he turned her underneath his arm through the pattern of the dance.

Anna caught his expression. "I hope you will not think me forward for asking, my lord," she paused, "or rude for adding that I think it a peer's duty to fulfill the obligation and responsibility given him." Her voice was genteelly modulated, but her soft eyes shone a bit brighter than Valentine had seen before, as if with some spark of restrained militancy. She was holding her chin perhaps a fraction of an inch higher than usual, and he felt unaccountably warmer under the strength of her gaze. He nodded, his expression neutral.

"I am glad I can agree with such a beautiful woman on such an important issue," he said, and had the pleasure of seeing her cheeks flush slightly pink, with a mixture of embarrassment and indignation, he imagined. Her lips parted to speak, but he continued. "And a woman of intelligence, of course." He watched her eyes flash toward his in barely veiled surprise.

Valentine spoke next as if changing the subject entirely. "Your uncle and aunt have not traveled often during your lifetime, I understand?"

Anna replied as they walked down between opposite lines of dancers to the bottom of the queue. "No. Because of Uncle Robert's infirmity we do not often go about in Society." Her voice held a note of compassion but none of self-pity.

"And yet your conversation is unusually—and refreshingly, I must emphatically add—learned for a woman your age." The dance separated them for a moment, and Anna peered at her partner to detect any hint of displeasure or disapproval in his expression. Finding none, she felt pleased beyond all reasonable accounts at his words.

"Due to my uncle's business, Uncle Robert and Aunt Louisa saw much of the world before my father died and I went to live with them. They have shared with me stories of their lives since I was a little girl," she said when the dance reunited them. "Too, I have read a great deal, my lord." She looked somewhat shyly at him. *"You* have been to the places I have only imagined, though." Her voice held a whisper of a sigh. "How I envy you that." She smiled up at the dark-haired earl, surprising an almost grim look on his face, his eyes suddenly shuttered and his fine lips with no hint of smile at their edges. Anna resisted the urge to reach up and touch his cheek, a response that seemed to come naturally, to her surprised dismay. Then the earl's gaze softened, and one side of his mouth raised in an almost imperceptible grin, as if the moment before had never happened.

"Sometimes the imagination does a better job of it than the real thing, Miss Tremain," he said. "But I do not deny that the world has many wonderful adventures to offer, too." His smile was genuine now, almost tender. Anna wondered what memories the earl was recalling at that particular moment to make his eyes glow so warmly.

"Will you tell me of some of your adventures, my lord?" The words were out of her mouth before she could even think to stop them. Anna felt like the veriest fool, and knew she must sound like a schoolroom child asking for a bedtime story. But the earl's slight smile only broadened.

"I shall," he said, "but only if you will tell me some of yours in return." His expression was again open, his tone even, and Anna could tell that he was sincere. She smiled, and the brilliance of her expression nearly deprived Valentine of breath. He marveled at the expressiveness of his partner's face, at how her lovely visage could hint at so many different meanings with a mere narrowing of the eyes or a curve of the mouth.

"Then I shall, too, my lord." Her lips twisted into a half-grin, and she added, on a dangerous whim, "And after that perhaps I will tell you exactly what I think of the coal taxes, the plight of underworked weavers in Leeds, orphans, Napoleon Bonaparte, and the war in general. What should you think of that?"

Anna's eyes sparkled with mischief and a hint of wariness. She had decided upon the spur of the moment to test his mettle all at once, to discover in one go what kind of a man he was—if such a test were possible. His regard mattered little to her unless he was a man who could respect her in return; yet she felt a tension in awaiting his response to her blue-stocking challenge. Nonetheless, she thought she knew what his answer would be. He did not disappoint her.

"I think that I shall be learning a great deal about many things in the near future, I should say." His smiling eyes laughed down at her. "And as I plan to take my Seat sometime soon, I do hope you won't mind my taking notes."

Anna felt the satisfaction ripple through her as if it were a physical thing.

"Indeed not, my lord. I will expect it!"

ELEVEN

Valentine stood with his back to the front window of the Greeleys' front parlor, his hands clasped behind him. The sun, valiantly attempting to push its way out from behind a curtain of spring clouds, shed its bright afternoon light into the room and glimmered off the yellow satin-upholstered furniture. Two riderless horses stood outside on the paving stones before the house, saddled and bridled, tended by a groom mounted on a third horse. They had been standing thus for almost a quarter of an hour, and Valentine was about to walk out into the hall to summon a footman to take his groom a message to have them walked when the door of the parlor opened and Lucinda Greeley stepped into the room followed by a maid.

The young woman was wearing a riding habit of spring green which admirably complemented the emerald of her eyes and set off her light curls. The dress itself hugged her ample, and still charmingly young, round curves with attentive care. Miss Greeley was not an undesirable partner with whom to share his afternoon's ride, thought Valentine, even if she had not been the companion he had originally intended for himself.

"I am sorry to have kept you waiting, my lord." She smiled from beneath her gold lashes as he took her hand and bowed over it. She was not as shy with him as she had been two weeks earlier, when they had first met, but she was still not the outspoken, confident girl that her friend was. Valentine thought her sweet and perfectly pleasant, if not particularly stimulating, company.

"It is my pleasure, ma'am. Perhaps, though, we should not keep the horses waiting any longer." She put her hand on his outstretched arm, and they made their way out of the house and to their mounts.

"I do apologize for my tardiness this afternoon, Lord Alverston," Lucinda said when they were a short distance away from the house. She was riding one of her father's horses. It had been brought to town by Mr. Greeley, who had correctly guessed that his young house guest, Miss Tremain, would miss her country pleasures and so had kindly seen to providing her with a mount in London. Anna had already ridden out in the morning several times since she had arrived in town, sometimes with a groom and sometimes with her host himself, and had been very happy for Mr. Greeley's kindness. Not much of a horsewoman herself, Lucinda had not ridden the dappled mare before this morning. Valentine saw that she held the reins with unnecessary tightness and that the gray consequently played the bit in her mouth more than was desirable, especially in such a confined area as the Park they were approaching.

"I was engaged in a project and had not noticed the time until just before you arrived," she continued. "I am so happy to be out this afternoon, though, and I do thank you for your invitation."

Valentine noted the slight puffiness around Miss Greeley's usually wide eyes and the powder, so unusual on a girl of Lucinda's age, hiding a flushed face. The project must not have been a happy one, he imagined as he directed his bay through the Park gates. His voice was gentle when he spoke.

"I am delighted to have your company, Miss Greeley. Please do not give it another thought."

Lucinda looked at him quickly from beneath lowered eyes. "I know I should not say as much, but I *am* sorry that you became obliged to escort *me* this afternoon when I am perfectly certain you wanted to ride with Anna instead." She said the words on a rush, as if afraid her courage would desert her partway through her speech.

Valentine's brows drew together slightly, but he looked at her without expression. "Miss Greeley, permit me to say that you do both me and yourself an injustice."

Lucinda looked, if possible, even more than before like a frightened rabbit trying to cross a busy thoroughfare. "I am terribly sorry, my lord. I did not mean to suggest that you had been less than gracious. I only wished you to know that I was embarrassed at the way my mother . . . ah . . . *encouraged* you to make an invitation to me after Mrs. Masterson told you that Anna was already engaged for this afternoon."

Valentine was on the verge of responding with polite benignity when he noted the clear glimmer in the girl's eyes, and he peered at her more carefully. Her mouth was set firmly, and her hands were not so unsure on the reins as he had thought before, but clenched tightly in agitation. Lucinda Greeley, it seemed, was not afraid and embarrassed at her lateness, which if truth be told was irritatingly common for women of Valentine's circle, as much as she was angry at something. He could not imagine what.

Her mother had been, admittedly, somewhat forward in staking her daughter's claim to his afternoon when the night before at a musical *soirée* he had asked

Louisa Masterson if *her* niece would be able to join him to ride in the Park the next day. But many match-making mothers had been using the same tactics on him for years, whether in London, Spain, or the English countryside. In any case, her comment had been more of a suggestion than a forced invitation for her daughter; Valentine had not felt obligated to take her up on it, and could have easily turned the conversation in another direction without having had to ask Miss Greeley to ride with him in Miss Tremain's stead. He did not understand what could be causing the flush on the blond girl's already pink cheeks, cheeks which, if he wasn't mistaken, had been tearstained not so many minutes ago. He chose his words carefully.

"I am honored by your company this afternoon, Miss Greeley, and can only be pleased that the situation turned out as it did. I would have extended my invitation to both you and Miss Tremain from the outset if I had been able to provide the other of you with a mount from my own stable," he added. "My sister has not been in Town for several years, however, and I do not have a mount suitable for a young lady, I regret to say."

Lucinda Greeley was not mollified—he could tell by the glint in her unsmiling eyes—but she gallantly attempted a gracious smile and a nod of her silver-gold head before something caught her attention across the Park.

"And there are Anna and Mr. Pendleton now," she said, as if continuing a thought she had been having.

Valentine's heart did a little leap and his horse, feeling the change in his rider's grip on the reins, sidestepped a bit. He berated himself for his foolish schoolboy behavior as his eyes sought out the place where Lucinda gestured with her crop across the green. A modest curricle, one among many more elaborate conveyances, traveled slowly along one of the Park's crowded pathways. The earl recognized Miss Tremain and her companion even in the distance. The couples were on the same path, moving toward each other, and would meet in a very short time.

Lucinda turned to him, shifting gracefully in her saddle. "Would you like to meet them, my lord? I should like to say good afternoon, if you don't mind." Her words were unexceptional, but Valentine felt something was not quite right in her tone. The girl's eyes were bright again, greener than he had seen them before.

"As you wish, ma'am." The pair in the curricle recognized their friends and reined in when they came abreast of them. Valentine noted that Miss Tremain's lips were curled in laughter, as were her companion's, as they came to a halt. He raised his hat to her and nodded to Pendleton in greeting.

"Lucinda, how lovely to come across you here. How do you do, my lord?"

Anna had spent most of the previous evening in the company of several of her aunt's old acquaintances and their daughters, and although Valentine had been present for the musical evening at Lady Granville's home, hoping for an opportunity to speak with her, they had exchanged only the briefest of words by the end of the night. He had been in the company of his friend and Bramfield's mother, the viscountess, who had professed a dislike for one of Louisa Masterson's circle, although she had been delighted to remake Mrs. Masterson's acquaintance from many years since; the parties had not mingled. In any case, it had been a large gathering. Valentine was sorry that the one social occasion that had been likely to throw them together had proven too large, after all, for convenience's sake.

Not for the first time during the past fortnight the

earl found himself wishing that his sister was in Town, that things had somehow happened differently. He knew by now that even had Anna not revealed her character to him through her letters over the past year, he would still have come to know her and to admire her. Of course, if he had not read those same letters, he may never have found the strength and peace of heart to heal the wounds he had received before his return to England. He may never have had the desire to leave his estate again ever.

He bowed from atop his horse. "I do very well, Miss Tremain. I see you are taking advantage of the afternoon's reluctant sunshine."

"Which certainly is threatening to be outdone by the clouds," Pendleton said with an appreciative smile at Lucinda, who, atop her dappled mare, was doing her best not to look at any of them while still appearing polite. In fact, the girl appeared to great advantage upon the elegant gray, her lush young figure appealingly erect despite the downward tilt of her golden head. But Valentine could not help wonder at the tears that he thought perhaps only he could see standing on the rims of her wide eyes. Whatever their cause, he must try to wrest her from the predicament she was in.

"Indeed," the earl said heartily, and he gently tugged on his mount's reins and discreetly pressed his heels into the bay's lean sides, trying to distract the two in the carriage with a bit of staged restlessness on the part of his horse. Pendleton seemed to take the bait; Valentine saw him looking critically over the particularly fine horseflesh dancing about on the pathway. When he looked to Anna, however, her full lips were still smiling, but her eyes held a question in them, and she looked swiftly to Lucinda. Valentine cursed himself silently for trying such a ploy on a woman who knew horses so well; he had not thought quickly enough. "Perhaps we should be on our way before it disappears altogether and we are forced to cut short our promenades due to rain." He almost heard the sigh of relief from his companion.

"Will we see you tomorrow evening at Lady Bramfield's, Lord Alverston? The viscountess has kindly included us in her dinner party. My aunt is so happy to be renewing their acquaintance." Valentine could tell that Miss Tremain had decided to play her part in not drawing attention to Lucinda's distress. He smiled at her, still unsure of the role she played in Miss Greeley's troubles. She was wearing a walking dress of figured golden brown muslin that elegantly set off both her tawny hair and her dark eyes. He found himself imagining her thick hair unbound and tangled about her shoulders, and swallowed hard.

"I regret that a previous engagement will not enable me to accompany you to the party, but it will be my greatest pleasure to meet you there." He bowed again from his seat.

"Thank you, my lord. You are very kind."

"Not kind," Valentine said, "only honest." He smiled, once again tipped his hat to the carriage occupants, and looked to Lucinda to depart. She smiled gamely, looking both her friend and Mr. Pendleton in the eyes, and then spurred her horse along the path. Valentine followed.

When they had ridden in silence for a short time, followed by Mr. Greeley's groom at a discreet distance, Valentine heard a muffled sniffling sound and he drew his handkerchief from his waistcoat and handed it across to his companion. Lucinda met his eyes with a wide tear-filled stare, and took the cloth with no ceremony. She carefully wiped her eyes with its corner. They had ridden off along a little-used path, and no one but the groom was within close proximity to them.

"I cannot imagine what has come over me, my lord," she said with admirable calm. "I am not usually such a watering pot. Perhaps it is the coming of summer in the air."

"Or alternatively the possibility of rain."

The girl looked with confusion at him, and Valentine saw that his comment had gone wide of the mark. He had gotten too used to thinking of all young women as necessarily quick-witted. Lucinda was not a fool, by any means, but her wit was not quite what he was used to in his sister and her childhood friend. It was clear, however, that Miss Greeley was suffering from some upset, and it did not serve in any case to make light of it.

"Perhaps if you would care to share your trouble with me, Miss Greeley," he began again, "I might be able to help you." His tone was gracious and gentle. She looked over at him with large, watery green eyes, and Valentine felt the oddest urge to smooth back her silver-gold hair from her delicately furrowed brow. This must be what it is like to have a daughter, he thought, and surprised himself that he had even imagined such a thing.

Lucinda's words were hesitant at first. "I would not want to burden you with my silly problems, my lord, really." When he looked at her, however, with genuine concern in his expression, she sniffled again and straightened her shoulders.

"Really, it is the most foolish thing, after all." She glanced at him quickly, then looked ahead of her. "You will think me the veriest ninnyhammer, and you would be perfectly correct in your estimation."

"Allow me to be the judge of that, please, Miss Greeley."

"I would speak to Anna, or I should, but given the circumstances, I cannot," she went on, as if talking to herself. "I cannot tell my mother, for she would make too much of a fuss, and might look unkindly upon Anna afterward." She turned to him with pleading eyes as if he could indeed help her in this matter. "I would never wish that. It would make me above all things unhappy."

Valentine nodded, thinking he understood at least that the girl's problem stemmed as much from suffering it alone as that it existed. "Your concern for your friend's comfort does you credit, Miss Greeley. But what of Mrs. Masterson?" he suggested. "Could you take her into your confidence?"

Lucinda's eyes grew round again. "No! I am afraid she would not understand at all, or sympathize." She looked down at her hands, which were twisting the reins into circles in her lap. "She thinks so highly of *him*, and I know she wishes great things for Anna."

Valentine felt a frision of fear stir his midsection. "Of whom are you speaking, Miss Greeley? Do you mean that Mrs. Masterson thinks highly of Mr. Pendleton?"

Her gaze shot to him, and her mouth opened in a little O of dismay.

"Have I been so obvious then, my lord? Is it so clear that it is *he* who has in such a short time become so important to me?" Her words were almost anguished, and thoroughly distressed.

"Certainly not, Miss Greeley. Your conduct is always ladylike and discreet." Tactfully ignoring her odd behavior in the park just a quarter of an hour earlier, Valentine hastened to reassure her. "You will recall that I have been privy of late to more of your company than others of your acquaintance in Town. I am aware that you and Miss Tremain have been often in Mr. Pendleton's company," he explained, "and I drew a conclusion that others would not have been able to deduce. You may rest assured that your feelings for the gentleman are not in any way apparent to the common observer."

Her calmed expression convinced Valentine that she believed him, and he waited for her next speech. She waited a few minutes before speaking again. When she did, the threat of tears had cleared from her voice, as if simply sharing her secret with him had relieved her of some of the pressure of the pent-up emotion she had been feeling.

"I should feel very grateful to have such a wide and distinguished acquaintance so early in my Season in Town," she said. "And I should be happy that my friend Anna has won the regard of someone so gentlemanly and kind."

"I do not wish to pry into Miss Tremain's affairs, Miss Greeley, but is it a settled thing, then?" Valentine held his breath.

Lucinda shook her head. "Oh, no, indeed, my lord. Not yet, at least." She sighed. "They have had so much time to know each other in the countryside, however, and it is very clear that *his* affections are engaged. My mother and Mrs. Masterson seem to think it a foregone conclusion that the two will become betrothed before the Season is out." Her voice was thinly wistful, as if the future were already secured to her own disadvantage. Although feeling his heart drop somewhere into the region of his boots, Valentine refused to be so easily beaten.

"But by all evidence they are not yet, Miss Greeley. This should give you hope." His tone was firm, taking her by surprise.

"Do you think so, Lord Alverston? I am not so certain." She was looking mournfully at his handkerchief in her hands, as if planning to put it to use again before too long.

"I do not see, Miss Greeley, why you should give up the battle before it is even lost," he said, "if you will excuse a military man his metaphor." This won a watery smile from his companion, and he reached out his hand to take hers in a firm grasp. "A person must sometimes work to get what she wants. If you want it badly enough, I believe there is nothing that should stand in your way."

Emerald eyes looked into his with newly found hope, and Valentine felt the pressure on his fingers demurely returned. "I do believe that you are right, my lord," Lucinda said with some strength to her voice. "But how am I to reconcile this with the desire to see my friend Anna have all that will make her happy?"

"Does Miss Tremain return Mr. Pendleton's regard?" Valentine was more afraid of the answer than he could even admit to himself. He believed what he had said to Miss Greeley about fighting for what one wanted, but he admitted to himself he lacked the courage to hear that her heart was already given to another. He felt a stab of despair at just imagining the possibility.

"I do not believe so, but I am not certain," Lucinda answered. Her eyes turned soft. "Anna is so kind to everyone, so unfailingly polite and friendly. I wish I had her poise and ease of speech among company. It is hard to know exactly how she feels about *him*, and I have been afraid to ask her directly."

Valentine considered this information a minor blessing, for the time being at least.

"Then you have nothing to keep you from the field," he said, resuming the metaphor. "If you do not risk betraying your friend in winning Mr. Pendleton's affections, then you have every right—and a duty!—to turn his affections toward yourself. Neither you nor Miss Tremain lack for suitors, Miss Greeley," he added, and watched a blush steal onto her pale cheeks. "If you choose, both you and she can have your pick of suitable beaux."

"Oh, Lord Alverston—"

"I am saying that you will not deprive your friend of her only opportunity at happiness if you succeed in turning Mr. Pendleton's eye your way in the end."

And I will, if given the chance, do my best to be the opportunity for that precious happiness that she finally accepts, Valentine vowed to himself as Miss Greeley smiled at him with renewed hope. And after a bit more conversation and planning, as they spurred their horses down the path to resume their ride, the earl blessed the good fortune that had made Lucinda Greeley his riding partner this day after all.

TWELVE

"I understand she has been a recluse these two years past." The voice was reedy and thin, even as it rose out of its whisper.

"Indeed, she has not dared to set foot in Town, and well she should not, I say! Her brother cossets her, you know," responded another female voice in lowered tones, but just loud enough for Anna to hear from her position in a chair arranged back to back with the sofa on which the two women sat. They had been speaking in very low tones since they sat down, at about the time when the ancient matron to whom Anna had been talking dozed off. Now their voices had become audible to her, and she was trying to think of a way to take her leave of the sleeping Mrs. Barkley so as to avoid overhearing the ladies' conversation. Her intentions turned contrary to her breeding however when, as she gathered her skirt to stand, the next words came across the small space to her.

"The earl is unexceptionable, Marybeth. I should not go about blaming him if I were you." The woman's tone had turned cool with warning.

"Well," stammered the other, "I don't mean to say . . . And he *was* seen holding the hand of that Country Nobody in the Par—"

The first woman cut off her friend's dissembling. "He is a fine figure of a man, if a little too preoccupied with his estates. Of course that gossip about him and that girl means nothing. She is not of his consequence, after all. My Priscilla, however, is a perfect match for him. It is his sister who is wild and uncontrollable. She acted shamelessly and paid the price for her behavior."

"But her father's death was such a tragedy, don't you know, coming so soon afterward." The second woman was proceeding with care now. "And her eldest brother, too." Anna almost heard the woman's lips pursing.

"Certainly tragic, but it did not seem to do her any good," responded the first.

Without turning her head, Anna recalled the face of the speaker, Lady Chetham. They had been introduced to each other earlier in the evening, before the large party had sat down to dinner at Lady Bramfield's town house. The daughter she had mentioned, ivory pale and very becoming in a slim white gown, now sat across the room conversing with their hostess. Her mother continued, "The present earl will have his hands full trying to find a suitable match for her, if he ever makes the attempt."

Silence followed and Anna imagined Lady Chetham's companion nodding sagely at her heavily jeweled gossip partner.

"Ah, there are the gentlemen now from their port," Anna heard Priscilla Chetham's mother say a bit more loudly. "I will go and secure the earl's promise to attend Priscilla's come-out ball next week." With rustling silks, both ladies stood, and Anna turned her head a fraction to watch the women stroll purposefully across the room toward Lord Alverston and engage him in conversation. He was dressed in a wine-colored coat and dark pantaloons, his evening shoes sparkling almost as much as his eyes, and his hair was tousled just enough to make him look to

Anna impossibly handsome—as usual. Reluctantly she drew her gaze away from him and turned her thoughts to the words she had heard just spoken by the two ladies of the *ton.*

Certainly they had been discussing Valerie and her brother. Who else could match the description so well? Two years of secluded life, the death of both father and older brother, and—*Best, or perhaps worst, of all,* thought Anna—the description of the girl as wild and uncontrollable. That certainly described her old friend well, Anna mused, even if it did not reflect too well on Valerie's reputation.

But she was not surprised. She had long held the suspicion that Valerie had been injured two years ago in London in an accident resulting from her typically overspirited behavior. Anna had warned her friend that she must try as best she possibly could to behave as an earl's daughter was supposed to behave during her come-out Season, but Valerie had laughed away her best friend's cautions. Although the late earl's daughter had never written to her of the details, Anna imagined that her friend had perhaps engaged in a carriage race of some sort—she had always been challenging the local boys in ____shire to some such thing during their summers—and had taken as a consequence both a fall from her curricle seat as well as from the grace of the sticklers in the *ton.* It was the simplest and most likely reason for Valerie's defection to the countryside and for her sustained pain over the loss of her father and brother from such an accident. The words of these town biddies that Anna had just overheard merely confirmed it.

Her suspicions—well, more like certainties—on other matters were bolstered too. The earl, it seemed, was the Society catch that Anna had imagined he was. He was young, wealthy, titled, very personable, and devastatingly attractive. Neither a doting mother, a concerned father, nor a hopeful unwed daughter could find anything to complain about in a suit brought by such a man, but much to praise. His eligibility was such that even sour talk about his sister was laced with sweet words for his own person; and gossip concerning his apparent interest in one woman could not serve to dampen the hopes of certain scheming mothers of other debutantes.

Anna glanced across the room again at the earl and found herself simultaneously pleased for him and irritated with him. She did not truly understand why Valerie was still cooped up in the countryside while her brother was enjoying himself on the Town these weeks. How she would be enjoying her old friend's company if they were together in this often ridiculous, sometimes exhausting, and always entertaining whirl of London Society! Granted, she still felt concern over the cool tone of Valerie's last few letters to her; but she had decided to attribute that to her friend's overlong seclusion, which must be serving her badly in spirit and mind. Anna strongly felt that the time for healing had passed and that Lady Valerie needed to take her place among her kind again in Society.

She vowed to tell the earl these very thoughts the next time she had the opportunity. She was certain Lord Alverston would listen to her with his usual open kindness if, that is, she could manage to get over the lump that rose in her throat when she tried to speak to him of late. It was most annoying, really, and quite unaccountable. Whyever, when she felt as if she were getting to know him better, almost as a friend, did she feel less and less at ease in his presence? Anna vowed that she would not succumb to these silly fidgets the next time they spoke.

She had hoped to have some chance to converse with him tonight, in fact. Since yesterday when they met in the Park, she had wanted to question him about Lucinda's odd behavior, to ask him if he was privy to the distress exhibited by her young friend. It had been so clear to Anna from her place in Mr. Pendleton's curricle. The earl had acted a bit strangely too; Anna had noted that despite her *own* quite unexpected and very unwelcome discomfiture.

It had been the oddest thing, really. For some strange reason, when Lord Alverston and Lucinda had approached the curricle on horseback, an image had popped into Anna's head of the marble sculpture she had been looking at when the earl startled her at the museum the week before. She had looked at the earl atop his tall bay thoroughbred and had pictured suddenly the raw strength and naked muscles of the battling soldier and centaur in the ancient Greek masterpiece. As Lord Alverston reined his horse to a halt, Anna once again felt the memory of his presence behind her at the museum as she gazed intensely at the muscular figures, and her face flushed with heat as it had then. Sitting beside Pendleton, she had spoken to cover her confusion, and was then quickly distracted from her own embarrassment by Lucinda's odd humor.

Before bed the night before she had tried to speak with Lucinda, to ask her if she was troubled, but had not been able to find an opportunity to be alone with the girl before the candles in the house were extinguished. Today, amidst the bustle of visitors in the morning and shopping later in the day, Anna and Lucinda had barely spoken at all. The carriage ride over to the Bramfields' town house this evening had been less than comfortable, with Anna's aunt doing most of the talking in the absence of conversation from her niece or Lucinda. Anna had repeatedly looked to her friend with concern and questions in her eyes, but the girl had kept her face averted and immobile. Anna had wished that this night particu-

larly they had the distraction of the earl's company
as escort.

Then, almost as soon as they had arrived at Bramfield House, Lord Alverston had drawn Lucinda away
in conversation, and the two had spoken together—
only very briefly joined by the viscount—until the bell
announcing dinner rang. The earl walked Lucinda
into the dining room, and the two were seated next
to each other at the table, far down the room from
Anna herself. While she conversed perfectly content-
edly with the gentlemen on either side of her during
dinner, Anna stole glances at them across the room,
and was rewarded with repeated views of smiling profiles and animated expressions. She noted that the
earl and Lucinda were sharing their witty conversation—only thus could she imagine it to be, considering the general tone of the entertainment at the
other end of the table—equally with their other dinner companions, but felt irritated all the same. Didn't
either of them know that she had particular matters
to discuss with both of them? Clearly their enjoyment
of each other rendered all others invisible to them
these days.

Suddenly, with this thought, the gossip Lady
Chetham referred to concerning the earl consorting
with a "country chit" came back to her. Lord Alverston was seen holding . . . *Lucinda's* hand? It must
have been when she and Pendleton had met them,
Anna thought with sudden clarity. No wonder Lucinda had been behaving so oddly; she had been hiding something of great import from her friend.
Anna's heart grew heavy. Apparently a romance had
been blossoming under her very nose and she had
not been made privy to it by her young friend. Certainly the gaiety of the pair at dinner this evening
proved something of note was afoot. *Why, perhaps they
already shared a secret agreement!* she thought as her eyes

opened wide in dismay, and overwhelmed with con-
sternation, she felt her body tense.

Coming back to herself in an instant, and looking
quickly about her to see if anyone had noticed her be-
musement, Anna grinned at her own thoughts. Really,
when she started imagining things that weren't there
she had to take herself in hand and begin thinking
rationally again. Why shouldn't the earl and Lucinda
Greeley enjoy each other's company? It made sense; *she*
certainly enjoyed the company of both of them. And
what should it matter in any case to her if they had
been behaving during the past thirty-six hours like two
peas in a pod, with their cozy ride in the Park, their
private conversations, and their smilingly satisfied expressions? And their hand-holding. Anna was pleased
that her friend was making such a notable conquest;
Lucinda was a lovely, kind girl and deserved all of the
attention she received from the admirers that had gathered around her in the past few weeks since they had
been in London.

In distraction Anna raised her bewildered gaze
again to the party, and met the dark, smiling look of
the earl himself. He was standing in a group of people across the room from her, but he had turned his
head from the conversation, and his warm, intense
gaze invited her to smile in response.

Anna felt her lips curve and—amazingly—her heart
flutter. She tilted her head in recognition and willed
herself not to drop her gaze first. His eyes seemed to
glow even more warmly, and then he turned his attention back to the others in his small group. Anna
took a breath of much-needed air, not even bothering
to scold herself this time for her foolishness. She was
certain it would pass soon enough, after all.

In the carriage on the way home, Lucinda nearly
bubbled with animation. The party had been perfect,
the guests sparkling, the conversation diverting, the

food delectable. Louisa Masterson gracefully agreed with the young woman, occasionally directing concerned glances at her niece who sat quietly on her corner of the plush seat, neither agreeing nor disagreeing with her friend's enthusiastic comments, but pleating with her fingers countless folds in the skirt of her new primrose silk gown.

She had been extraordinarily beautiful tonight in her pink evening gown, her thick and blessedly unfashionably long hair swept up in a loose knot tied with silver ribbons. When she had smiled at him across the room after dinner, Valentine had had to muster all of the strength that was in him not to run across the room and sweep her up into an embrace that would have scandalized London Society for a month.

He didn't quite know how he could go on much longer acting the polite and courtly gentleman, he realized as he sipped a glass of brandy and then swirled the dark contents around absently. All he really wished to do was spirit her away to Alverston Hall where he could be with only her, have her conversation, bask in her marvelous wit and intelligence all day long, and where he could kiss her delectable rose pink lips during the darker hours. Indeed, he would kiss her and hear her and see her all day *and* all night, if he had his wish. The images accompanying these thoughts caused the earl to tug uncomfortably at his snug cravat.

Fantasy, of course, was just that: fantasy. Anna Tremain barely knew him, and there was nothing guaranteeing that if she knew him better she would come to love him. He had hopes, though, and his hopes drove his actions. He had vowed to himself to act the courteous escort to Anna and her friends, but not to press his company on her too much. He wanted her to have a clear idea of the world of London Society in which he did not quite fit any longer, vainly he supposed, counting on her good sense, to bias her in his favor.

Valentine had taken up the project of gently disengaging Mr. Pendleton from her side both to assist the shy Miss Greeley in her quest for happiness, but also to distract himself from wanting to spend every moment he could with the girl's friend. So far the plan was not working. It had only seen one day, though, and Valentine had tried so very hard to enjoy himself at Timothy's house, chatting and scheming a bit with Miss Greeley and keeping his distance from the most lovely woman in the room.

It had been torturous. He was convinced after the trial of this evening that neither he nor she needed any breathing space. Walking away from Bramfield House—he had dismissed his carriage, feeling restless and out of sorts after dinner and needing the walk—he vowed he would take the next opportunity to speak his heart to her, or better, to take her into his arms and make mad passionate love to her until she was forced to accept him.

His silver-tipped walking cane snapped against the cobblestones beneath him in agitation. What a rot to be honorable! What a rot to respect women! It made falling in love with one of them damned inconvenient.

Lost in his thoughts, he finally found himself at Brooks's, but politely declined any company from the various acquaintances he met there. Sometimes a man wanted to be amongst others, yet alone. Fellows understood that; most fellows, at least. Sir William Wimster, an old and near forgotten acquaintance from school, decided to ignore the earl's quite obvious desire for privacy and, upon seeing Valentine, planted his rounded figure in a chair next to him.

"What ho, old chap? See you're drinking some of Boney's finest. Don't mind if I take a sip of that myself, do you?"

Valentine nodded to the nearest footman who produced a clean glass for Sir Wimster and poured out some of the earl's brandy for the man. His expression was benign, but Valentine hoped that with no encouragement in conversation Wimster would soon take himself off in pursuit of more interesting company. He continued to contemplate the toes of his evening shoes.

"Don't suppose we ought to congratulate those wily Frenchmen on the quality of their brandy," Sir Wimster said, gazing into the amber-brown liquid, "but we certainly can enjoy it." He looked suddenly over to Valentine. "Say, you was fighting the dastards there for a while, wasn't you, old chap? Wondered why I hadn't seen you in some time."

Valentine's eyebrows rose slightly, but he guessed correctly that the more than half-foxed baronet needed no response to continue.

"Quite something, the war, I say. Just talking to another chap earlier today at a posting house on my way into Town, don't you know? Camfield. Why, Alverston, you know Camfield, I'm sure of it. Went up from Oxford some years before us, of course, but I remember the two of you had some wager going or some such thing. Had something to do with— Hmmm . . . Now what was that wager of yours all about? Must've been six or seven years ago if it was a day, now that I think of it."

Lost in the intoxicated haze of his memories, Sir Wimster failed to notice the earl's mouth thin to a line, the expression on his face harden to stone. If the drunken man had been watching more carefully,

he would have seen the Earl of Alverston's eyes bank down to dull gray embers and his hand curl tightly around the delicate stem of his brandy glass. When Sir Wimster did look up from his reveries it was because the voice he heard was so quiet as to seem disembodied.

"We wagered on which one of us could kill the most Frenchmen." Valentine's eyes stared sightlessly at the man next to him in the pause that followed his words.

Sir Wimster finally coughed uncomfortably. "Well, yes, and I should expect that between the two of you, you cleaned up Boney's men right 'nd tight." He spoke hastily to cover his discomfort. "In any case, seems Camfield's back in Town; talked with him at the Swan, don't you know. Might want to look him up now that he's back, swap war stories 'nd the like. Never quite understood you fellows wanting to get yourselves all banged up over there," he said with an uneasy glance at Valentine's walking stick leaning against the wall behind the earl. "Glad you did it, nonetheless," Wimster muttered. "Grateful for it 'nd all of that." He stood up with another cough.

"Well, old chap, must be on my way." He set his glass down on the table after one last deep swallow. "M' thanks to you for the drink. Evening, Alverston."

Valentine nodded and stared after the man who turned and wove his way unceremoniously to the room's exit. When the doorway was empty, he set his own glass down almost too carefully on the table beside him, and all at once felt overcome with a breathtakingly powerful weariness.

Camfield had returned.

Two years, and the man had finally chosen to come back to the place he had left with so little so many years ago. Two years since they had last seen each other. Two years since Valentine had learned of his

friend's betrayal, two years since he had *experienced* it, in those two days of his life that now seemed like a horrible glimpse of hell. And finally Drew Camfield was back.

Valentine knew something of man's nature. He had been an avid studier of humanity from the time he was a small boy, and had had ample opportunity to understand better the people of his aristocratic world while on the Town in his university days and afterward. His experience in the war had only knocked the final scales of naïveté from his eyes. He knew it was no accident that his old friend had returned just now, after these many years away. The earl knew, as surely as he knew he loved a woman with all of his heart and soul, that Drew had come back, after all of this time, because he knew that Valentine had too.

THIRTEEN

Anna was having the time of her life.

Seated in a box high above the raucous cluster of rowdies on the floor below, alongside her aunt, the Greeleys, and Lord Alverston, she was enjoying her first taste of London opera. Around her throughout the theater women's jewels sparkled on their heads and fingers, at their wrists and nearly bared bosoms. Hundreds of candles flickered, reflecting light throughout the house and bouncing off shining hair, glittering satins, and dozens upon dozens of quizzing glasses and opera-glass lenses. Everyone was watching everyone; from the highest stickler to the most tawdry bird of paradise. Anna had been told that this kind of behavior continued even when the opera was in progress. She was entirely delighted.

The Earl of Alverston had invited the Greeley party to join him in his box for the opera this evening. After almost a week of seemingly endless morning visits with Mrs. Greeley's and Aunt Louisa's ever-expanding acquaintances among the women of the *ton*, drawn-out sessions with the seamstress, and constant housebound activities having to do with the planning of the girls' come-out ball in a week's time, Anna was practically bursting with pleasure at being out and about and enjoying the sights of London again. Too, in their anticipation for the evening's activity, she a-

Lucinda had found themselves more comfortable with each other than they had been for a week's time at least.

Anna had been relieved when Lucinda came to her room while they were getting ready this evening and offered to dress her hair for her. The girl had braided it into two long plaits and curled them around the back of Anna's neck, leaving golden brown tendrils trailing down the sides of her face and her creamy brow clear. The effect had startled Anna with its elegance, an elegance she was unaccustomed to seeing on herself. She had looked up from her own reflection in the glass to the gleaming gaze of the emerald-eyed girl, and then Lucinda had looked away.

Anna was puzzled still by her friend's distant behavior this week, since the day they had met in the park with Mr. Pendleton and Lord Alverston. She had not found an appropriate moment over the course of the busy sennight to speak to either Lucinda or the earl, but had become more sure as to the reason Lucinda was appearing so distracted lately, not why this should have translated into her acting particularly cool to Anna herself, however. Anna found that she wanted to consider the possible explanations and in fact the whole situation less and less as the week wore on.

She was happy, though, at this little change in the pattern that had been developing, and savored its sweetness. Looking beyond Aunt Louisa to her friend, dressed this evening in a pale yellow gown with butterflies embroidered in white silk on the fabric, and looking very young and lovely, Anna was not surprised to see her head bent to Lord Alverston's. The earl and Lucinda had been much in each other's company although Anna thought he had not made any ar appointments with her friend that had not uded herself, and sometimes Mrs. Greeley

We'd Like to Invite You to Subscribe to Zebra's Regency Romance Book Club and Give You a Gift of 4 Free Books as Your Introduction! (Worth $19.96!)

If you're a Regency lover, imagine the joy of getting **4 FREE Zebra Regency Romances** and then the chance to have thes lovely stories delivered to your home each month at the lowest prices available! Well, that's our offer to you and here's how you benefit by becoming a Zebra Home Subscription Service subscriber:

- **4 FREE Introductory Regency Romances are delivered to your doorste**

- **4 BRAND NEW Regencies are then delivered each month (usually before they're available in bookstores)**

- **Subscribers save almost $4.00 every month**

- **Home delivery is always FREE**

- **You also receive a FREE monthly newsletter, *Zebra/ Pinnacle Romanc News* which features author profiles, contests, subscriber benefits, boo previews and more**

- **No risks or obligations...in other words you can cancel whenever you wish with no questions asked**

Join the thousands of readers who enjoy the savings and convenience offered to Regency Romance subscribers. After your initial introductory shipment, you receive 4 brand-new Zebra Regency Romances each month to examine for 10 days. Then, if you decide to keep the books, you'll pay the preferred subscriber's price of just $4.00 per title. That's only $16.00 for all 4 books and there's never an extra charge for shipping and handling.

It's a no-lose proposition, so return the FREE BOOK CERTIFICATE today!

Check out our website at www.kensingtonbooks.com.

Say Yes to 4 Free Books!
Complete and return the order card to receive this
$19.96 value, ABSOLUTELY FREE!

FREE BOOK CERTIFICATE

YES! Please rush me 4 Zebra Regency Romances without cost or obligation. I understand that each month thereafter I will be able to preview 4 brand-new Regency Romances FREE for 10 days. Then, if I should decide to keep them, I will pay the money-saving preferred subscriber's price of just $16.00 for all 4...that's a savings of almost $4 off the publisher's price with no additional charge for shipping and handling. I may return any shipment within 10 days and owe nothing, and I may cancel this subscription at any time. My 4 FREE books will be mine to keep in any case.

Name _____

Address _____ Apt. _____

City _____ State _____ Zip _____

Telephone ( ) _____

Signature _____ RN020A
(If under 18, parent or guardian must sign.)

and Aunt Louisa as well. But the few times that they had gone into Society this past week, Lord Alverston had been there, offering Lucinda his arm and maintaining his gentlemanly courtesy with her in the sight of many. At Almack's on Wednesday he had danced with Lucinda; of course he had partnered Anna as well, but it had *looked* as if he had enjoyed himself so very much more with Lucinda.

Anna was, as always, very pleased with his company; he was interesting to talk with, did not hide his views on issues not concerning the *ton*—or issues concerning the *ton*, for that matter—from her because she was a woman, but spoke to her as if she were an equal and as if he valued what she had to say. She supposed he thought her something of an oddity, but he appreciated her nonetheless for her knowledge and opinions. He was accustomed to the company of his sister, Anna reasoned, and although he spoke little of Valerie, his affection for and admiration of her were apparent in the few things he did say. Anna imagined that she herself could thank Valerie's place in her brother's heart for the attention the earl paid to her, and the occasional entertainment she could provide for a man who seemed to be at odds with the high Society in which he lived.

She wondered often what kept him in Town when it was obvious, to her at least, that he was not quite at home in his social surroundings. Certainly he had friends, such as Viscount Bramfield, whose company he appreciated. But although he treated those of his wide acquaintance with polite attentiveness and amiability, Anna suspected he was not quite himself among most of the *beau monde*. She knew this from the few hints Valerie had given her in writing over the past year or so, and from her own observation of his behavior since she had known him in London. His smile was broader when he conversed with Aunt

Louisa, for instance, and his laughter was freer when she heard him with the viscount; she had noticed that his manner, while never stiff, was particularly comfortable when he was in the company of Lucinda, and even perhaps herself. A week ago she had even imagined that his eyes sparkled just a bit more brightly when he looked at her.

Glancing again at where he sat, in conversation with Lucinda, just below her in the box, Anna knew that that particular notion had been born of her own fertile and lately unchecked imagination.

She looked about the theater, noting the many opera glasses trained on their box, focused especially on the earl and his lovely young companion. Watching Lord Alverston speaking cozily with Lucinda as the curtain rose, Anna wondered what Priscilla Chetham's mother was thinking now, and how Felicity Stilver and various other contenders for the earl's attention imagined their own prospects were dwindling away to nothing.

Anna turned her gaze toward the play beginning below, and as she did so, it crossed that of Mr. Pendleton, whose box, not far from the earl's, contained a matron and two well-dressed young ladies. His expression was clouded, however, and his brow drawn. He was staring at her own box, Anna realized, directly at Lucinda and Lord Alverston. As she watched, the earl grinned and patted Lucinda on her delicately gloved hand, and they turned their attention to the stage. In doing so, Lucinda looked straight at Mr. Pendleton. Meeting his gaze, she smiled almost too brightly, her eyes widening characteristically, and her chin dropped just a tiny fraction as she turned fully away from both Pendleton and the earl and focused her attention on the stage. Pendleton wore a mask of angry agitation. Anna looked to Lord Alverston. He was smiling, his attention apparently on the opera in its opening moments. His hands rested lightly on his knees—his long-fingered, strong, beautiful hands.

Anna felt a pain in her midriff, so at odds with her happy mood and general feeling of good health that it startled her. She blinked and turned her attention fully to the front of the theater.

She would watch the play, concentrate on the opera and the music, and lose herself in the story—a tragedy. She would *not* try to think what that three-way incident had been about: the strange behaviors of all of her friends, the meaningful looks whose meanings *she* could only guess at, her own body's shocking response. She would simply throw her imagination into the spectacle on stage, and perhaps when it was over everything would be back to normal again.

Her self-discipline did her credit, for when the curtain came down on the first act and she felt a touch on her shoulder and a voice at her ear, she nearly jumped out of her seat in surprise.

"Miss Tremain, would you care to take a turn with me about the corridor, and perhaps enjoy a bit of refreshment, while we await the next act?" Lord Alverston was bending over her, offering his arm. Glancing around to see Lucinda engaged in earnest conversation with her parents, Anna stood and put her hand on the sleeve of his coat, willing her heart to still its sudden frantic beating.

"Thank you, my lord, I would like that."

He led her out of the box and into the hall, gesturing to an attendant to bring them champagne. The beverages arrived in short order, and Anna raised the glass to her lips and took a much-needed sip.

"What do you think of the opera, Miss Tremain? Are you impressed with our London thespians?" The earl gazed down at Anna as she looked about her at all of the finely dressed theater patrons, recognizing a few acquaintances in the large crowd. She sipped her champagne and glanced up at the earl.

"I am, my lord. The performance is quite excellent, according to my humble country tastes." She grinned unselfconsciously, and he responded in kind. "Miss Dimmelford has the most heavenly voice, don't you think?" Anna continued, trying to sound calmer than she felt, standing so close to the earl. "I was really quite enthralled by the aria she sang just now at the end of the act, when she finally realized she was in love with the painter's son and cast to the wind her father's plans for her to marry that wretched count. She was—" She glanced up to find the earl looking at her with an intense warmth in his smoky eyes, and both her voice and gaze faltered.

Then she forgot entirely what she was saying.

"She was quite passionate, indeed," the earl finished for her after a pause during which neither spoke, and to Anna it sounded as if his voice was perfectly normal. She looked at him over the rim of her glass and saw that his expression reflected that normalcy. She wondered with amazement if she had imagined the other look.

"Do you think," he asked, his mouth curving upward at the edges, "that she sets quite the right example for our young English ladies?" There was a laughing tone to his otherwise very proper voice.

"My lord," Anna said, brandishing her fan both as a prop and to cool the blush she had felt staining her cheeks when she'd spoken her last, unpremeditated words. "A respectable young English lady would never leave a count for a painter! Even were the count as poor as a church mouse, which of course *this* count is decidedly not, he would still be able to gain entrance into the *most* fashionable homes and establishments in both the country and city. What would a beautiful young English woman *do,* for heaven's sake, without her endlessly diverting activities among the *crème de la crème* of Society? Even were her clothes threadbare and the bill collectors knocking at her door day and night, she would still have her afternoon tea gossips, her embroidery circles, and her musical *soirées* to attend."

Anna was speaking to calm her nervousness, but the earl was smiling and the sparkle was back in his eyes—or at least the sparkle Anna imagined she could see.

"No, an English maiden had better stick with her count, after all. Love or no, she would be miserable with the painter." She added, "She might have to *cook* for him, or something dreadful like that, after all." She peered up over her champagne glass with mischief in her eyes.

Lord Alverston laughed. "But what about the possibility of having her likeness made by her true love? What of potentially becoming the next Mona Lisa, a face adored by so many for being painted with such intense feeling and mastery? Would that not be enough temptation to entice even the most innocent yet dedicated socialite miss from her lordly suitor?"

"You have offered an excellent argument, my lord," she responded, pursing her lips a bit and raising her curved eyebrows. "But I am afraid I shall have to maintain my original idea." Anna was feeling the effects of the champagne she had nearly finished now. She was having the most difficult time schooling her lips out of a silly grin into a more seemly expression.

"And you, Miss Tremain?" the earl asked, taking the empty glass from her hand and giving it and his to a nearby footman. As his fingers brushed hers, Anna felt a tingling sensation where they touched. "I do not count you among England's typical milk-and-water misses. If given the chance to choose between a lowly undiscovered painter whom you adored and a wealthy, titled man who adored you for your great beauty, whom would you pick?"

Anna laughed and then made the mistake of looking directly into the earl's eyes, which were dark as coal in the dimly lit corridor. She opened her mouth, but found that the words of her clever retort would not come. She stared into his eyes, speechless, willing something amusing or at least sensible to come to her lips.

The earl spoke first, his voice low and earnest in the noise of the crowd returning to their seats for the next act of the performance. His words were a complete, heart-deadening surprise.

"Miss Tremain, I must speak to you regarding Miss Greeley—"

"Lord Alverston, I am simply thrilled to see you here tonight!"

Anna turned her head to see Lady Chetham and her daughter Priscilla coming to a halt beside her. Priscilla's tapered hand was on the arm of a young man whom Anna suspected by his looks was her brother. His dull locks did not rival, however, his sister's attractively short and shining chestnut coiffure. "We *do* look forward to seeing you at our ball tomorrow night in honor of my dear Priscilla," the heavily jeweled woman said, extending her gloved hand to the earl while beaming at her tall, elegantly clad daughter. Lord Alverston took the matron's hand in his and bowed over it, beginning to speak, but the woman cut him off with her thin, high voice.

"How do you do, Miss Tremain? And how do you like the opera? Is it your first? I understand that there is not much in the way of sophisticated entertainment in your part of the country, isn't that true? You must be quite overwhelmed with our little London, mustn't you?" Anna simply stared as the woman went on speaking, not even pausing for breath. "Oh, it seems they are ringing the bell for the next act already. Alverston, I twisted my ankle coming out of the box just a few minutes ago. My son Philip will give me his arm for the return. Would you mind very much escorting dear Prissy to our seats?" She was moving down the corridor toward the entrances to the boxes before the earl could even open his mouth to respond.

Anna watched Priscilla Chetham slide her narrow hand through Lord Alverston's arm and lift her calculating gaze to his face. Of course, Anna thought grimly as she walked beside the earl and they made their way down the corridor, the fair Priscilla's expression would not appear calculating to a man entranced by the girl's bronze-and-ivory beauty; it would just seem adoring. And what man would not want a beautiful young woman to look adoringly at him, to grasp his elbow just *so* in that helpless manner, and to speak to him in that feathery feminine voice?

By the time they passed the Alverston box, Anna was feeling almost dizzy with the wash of contrasting emotions she was experiencing. She did not look around to see the silent apology in the earl's eyes as he was led away from his own box and further down the corridor by his beautiful companion. Anna smiled to her aunt, to the Greeleys; and was introduced to the two young ladies who stood in the small space on either side of Mr. Pendleton, who met her with a cheerful greeting. The girls with Mr. Pendleton were his cousins, and they had wanted to make the acquaintance of both Mrs. Masterson and Miss Tremain, he explained. They had heard so much of ____shire and wanted to know the people who had kept their dear Jason so happy while he had been in the country. Would Mrs. Masterson, Miss Greeley, and Miss Tremain join them on the morrow for a picnic in Richmond if the weather held? The invitation was accepted, plans were made, details were quickly discussed, and the three Pendletons made their exit just as the curtain rose for the second act.

Grateful for the opportunity to be alone with her whirling thoughts, Anna turned her face again to the diva on the stage and unknowingly breathed a heartfelt sigh.

"Pray, do not despair just yet, Miss Tremain. She will win her man in the end," came the softly spoken words at her shoulder. Anna swiveled her head to see Lord Alverston sitting down quietly beside her, his eyes on the stage but his attention apparently on her. She looked at him quizzingly, and he glanced at her out of the corner of his eye.

"Your sigh," he explained in a smiling whisper as the music swelled below them. When she could think of nothing to say to that, he spoke again, his expression serious now. "I apologize that I had to leave you like that, it was unspeakably rude; but I am especially sorry for the interruption of our conversation."

Anna nodded slightly in acceptance; then the actors came on the stage and the singing began, and conversation was temporarily at an end. But her heart felt like a sodden weight inside her. She could not erase from her mind the possessive look she had spied in Priscilla Chetham's eyes, nor could she ignore the words the earl had spoken to her just before they were interrupted in the corridor. He had been about to tell her of his feelings for Lucinda, Anna had no doubt. And even were that not the case, it would not be long before Priscilla Chetham or some other cunning-eyed debutante of the *ton* conquered him with her rosebud smiles and fluttering lashes.

Anna suddenly felt tremendously sad. And overwhelmingly foolish. Unbeknownst to her own heart, she had pinned her hopes on the earl—on the wealthy, titled and entirely inappropriate brother of her best friend. She had ignored her racing heartbeat in his presence, her anticipation of seeing him each day, her unqualified enjoyment of his company. In the few short weeks that she had known him, she had come to think of him as a friend and had turned a blind eye to the more unfamiliar emotions that had begun to stir within her.

But as she sat there beside him in the cushioned seat at the opera, hearing again in her mind Priscilla's laughter and the earl's last words in the corridor, feeling his nearness now, and hearing the soprano's voice rising in gloriously tragic tremolo, Anna recognized her self-deception. She would have laughed could she have summoned the energy. It had all been used up, however, on imagining that she—humble, bluestocking, unsophisticated Anna Tremain of ____shire— could have something of value or interest to offer the charming, intelligent, handsome, and much-sought-after Earl of Alverston.

Anna steeled herself to take one last glance at the earl before making the futile attempt of nobly vowing to forget him and lose herself anew in the tragedy unfolding before her on the stage. Her own little drama unraveling right now was minor in comparison, of course. She almost did summon up a chuckle then, and the corners of her mouth curved up a bit as she turned her head ever so slightly to the side. Anna raised her eyes finally and met the earl's dark gray gaze, staring directly into hers.

Unwillingly, she smiled, her heart thudding desperately inside her, and then she gasped silently as his smoldering gaze traveled to her lips, lingered there for a moment, and then returned to her eyes. Instead of dropping her gaze instantly, Anna found herself looking back at him, willing the moment to last, willing it not to end and thus become forever a piece of her imagination/memory.

She knew from the flashing of opera-glass reflections in the corner of her vision that they were probably being watched. But though she supposed their actions could be seen, she could only hope that the dimness of the theater hid from both the spectators and the earl the love for him that she was sure was clear as day in her eyes.

FOURTEEN

She had the headache.

She was unwell, resting, taking a day to recoup her energy from all of the new and busy goings-on she was experiencing in London.

Whatever the reason Louisa Masterson had given him as he stood in the Greeleys' parlor, hoping for the miracle that would send Anna walking past the door so that at least he could get a glimpse of her to fill his near overwrought senses, she would not see him.

Her aunt had actually said that Miss Tremain did not wish to see anyone. She had given specific instructions that she wished to spend a quiet day alone, and her aunt was respecting that wish. Mrs. Masterson understood it herself, missing the country as she did after this near month spent in the noisy city. She would not be averse to a little peace and quiet with only her family for company.

Certainly the earl was nearly family, of course, being the fond brother of Anna's beloved friend Valerie. Still, the girl really did need her rest if she were going to be able to attend Priscilla Chetham's come-out ball this evening, and she was so sorry to have to turn him away since Anna was always delighted to see him under normal circumstances. Mrs. Masterson was so glad he had called and was looking forward to seeing him tonight at the ball.

Anna would not have been delighted to see him that day, for certain.

Sitting through the remainder of the opera the night before had been torture for her, or worse than torture, if there were such a thing. She had felt every quizzing glass, every pair of opera glasses in the theater trained on herself and Lord Alverston for the duration of the performance. By the time they entered the blessed darkness of the earl's carriage, which was to convey them home, Anna felt as if she never wanted to enter another opera house for as long as she lived. It was like sitting in a fishbowl! Even then her head had been aching from a combination of confusion, shame, and too much champagne taken on an empty stomach. She vowed never to drink another glass of the dreadful stuff for as long as she lived. It had been a nightmare. A nightmare in a fishbowl.

Granted, her behavior had not been all that was perfectly acceptable and ladylike; but she could stand the social censure for that. What Anna was silently agonizing over was the way the earl himself had reacted to what had happened—or had not happened, as she now supposed was the case. When she had finally dropped her gaze from his, she had almost immediately *felt* his body stiffen beside her, and when she peeked up at him she had seen with shock that his face, now turned toward the stage below, wore a stern and almost angry expression. Anna had gotten the distinct feeling that he had turned to ice in the seat beside her, and with that, she had wanted to leap off her own chair and flee through the labyrinthine corridors of the building and out onto the streets below, into the night.

It had been terrible sitting there next to him knowing of his displeasure and disgust. She had gone from feeling surprised to bereft to furious to despondent all in the course of the measly hour it took for the performance to come to its tear- and bloodstained conclusion. By the time her party moved out onto the cobblestones and into the carriage Anna was mostly feeling numb with the exhaustion of having experienced more emotions in one night than she had in her whole lifetime. To make matters worse, somehow during the ride home she had been seated facing the earl, and when the carriage went over a rut in the road and her knees brushed his, she had felt the acute humiliation of a woman who has displayed her heart on her sleeve and been summarily rejected.

When they had arrived at the Greeleys' town house, the earl had handed her out first, and Anna had avoided meeting his eyes so as not to see the disdain in them. Maintaining her equilibrium long enough to say good night to her aunt and the Greeleys, she had burst into tears the moment her door was locked behind her. Lucinda's scratching at the same door a quarter of an hour later earned the girl a less than coherent denial that anything at all was wrong and a soggy but firm good night. Anna had supposed that Lucinda was probably insulted or at the least confused by her behavior; but for the first time since she had started feeling the more green-eyed of the two, she did not give a fig for what Lucinda was thinking.

This pitiful pettiness did not last long, and she had cried herself to sleep in a few minutes, exhausted by the revelations and emotions of the evening. If only her troubles could be solved with a few dramatic sword or dagger thrusts, as they were for the lovely Donabella in the play that evening, she had been thinking when she had finally drifted into an at first fitful and then too deep sleep. Anna awoke in the morning with a head splitting from side to side and a heart heavy in its newfound happiness.

She was in love. She was rejected. Worse yet, she was in love with and rejected by her best friend's brother, her best friend's only living family member. It was the worst possible scenario Anna could have dreamed up for anyone, and she herself had fallen into it headfirst, with her eyes shut.

She did not want to see anyone ever again. She wanted to sleep, to dream, and not to think about any of this anymore. She wanted it all to go away.

But then, when she thought that, she imagined his beautiful stormy eyes, his hands, his expressive mouth, the dark tousled locks of hair curling around the edge of his shirt collar; and she wanted to breathe in her images of him until she was filled to the bursting point. Having discovered her own heart was very satisfying in that sense, Anna found.

She desperately wished, though, that she was a strong enough woman to take her feelings and use their power to make her even stronger. She was not sure that she was capable of doing so, however. It would take a certain effort to distance herself from the object of her affections, and having only last night discovered that was the earl, Anna was not yet prepared to give him up so easily from her heart.

In any case, she did have a headache. She sent a note by a maid to her aunt to beg forgiveness of Lucinda and Mr. Pendleton and his cousins; she would not be joining them on their picnic today due to her indisposition. She felt it was only fitting, after all, since among Lucinda's conquests during the past week Mr. Pendleton was coming in only slightly behind the earl in the suitor race. Anna did not think she could fully enjoy her friends' company today when she was sure she would be gnashing her teeth at every kind word and wide-eyed soft look wasted on

Pendleton while Lord Alverston's back was turned, metaphorically, of course.

Anna surprised herself with her loyalty to the earl, considering it was not in her favor to wish him Lucinda's constancy; but she did think the girl might want to make up her mind as to which man she was going to claim before they started getting unpleasant with each other. The scowls directed toward the earl last night from the Pendleton box would have been enough to encourage a less honorable man than Valentine Monroe to challenge their bearer to a fight.

Anna could not imagine things coming to such a state, of course; she had probably been reading too many of Mrs. Greeley's Minerva Press novels lately. She did think her friend, Mr. Pendleton, a kind and amiable man who deserved kindness in return. Anna hoped that Lucinda Greeley was using the brain and heart God had given her under that halo of golden curls and that rounded figure. Anna did not wish to see Pendleton hurt, and she wanted even less to see the earl suffer any unhappiness.

The pain of imagining Lord Alverston the victor in this particular battle was almost blinding in its intensity. Nonetheless, she wanted for him what he most wanted for himself. Anna supposed, when she was able to stop crying, wipe her eyes, and blow her nose, that was what love was, after all.

Valentine scanned the crowded ballroom from the top of the steps leading down into it. There were hundreds of people present, all packed into the Chetham's spacious and elaborately decorated ballroom. An orchestra played at the edge of the dance floor, and a dozen or more couples moved around the small space to the patterns of a minuet. He heard the butler intone his name, saw the queue before and behind him move, and Valentine began his descent into the ballroom with an acute feeling of disappointment.

He had not been able to sight her from the steps. It might take him hours in this crush to seek her out, and by then her dance card might already be filled and she might not have a free set left for him to claim. That all depended, of course, upon whether she wished to even speak with him, let alone share a dance with him.

He must find an opportunity to talk with her. He had to make certain he knew what she felt, that she knew what he had been trying to say the night before. From the way things had happened last night, he could only imagine the worst, but he had to give himself one more try before giving up and skulking back to the countryside in defeat. He did not expect good news tonight, but Valentine knew he had to be more sure of it all before he made a decision that might not serve him well in the end.

It was torture imagining that she had been shamed by the expression of his feelings last night, those feelings he was sure she had been able to read on his face in the silence between them. They had surfaced unbidden, and he had been caught outright, staring at her like some schoolboy half-starved with calf-love. He had been thinking how beautiful she was, how free of spirit and full of both thoughtfulness and laughter. He had been reveling in her presence right next to him, after having been deprived of even the sight of her during the first act while he and Miss Greeley enacted their little charade on behalf of the blond Adonis in the nearby box. Valentine had been overwhelmingly satisfied when Pendleton reacted the way he had in response to their little playacting, breathing a sigh of relief that at least for this night, and perhaps forevermore, he could stop dancing attendance in public on Lucinda Greeley and start putting his attention where he truly wished it to be.

He had talked himself into believing that it would not hurt his suit to help little Lucinda win Pendleton away from Anna by paying the girl a bit of extra attention; in fact, it could only clear the field for his own campaign. It had worked so easily—the foolish, jealous boy!—that Valentine wondered if it had ever been necessary in the first place. He expected to hear a positive update from Lucinda this evening, or at the latest by the end of the week, when hopefully he would be blessedly free to leave off making up to the wide-eyed chit and to do some real lovemaking instead.

But somehow it had all gone horribly wrong last night. One moment he had been gazing at Anna's graceful profile, admiring her pert nose and creamy skin and the way her peach silk gown clung lovingly to her young, supple curves; then she had looked up at him and he had lost his mind. He remembered having an overwhelmingly powerful desire to kiss her and feeling as if her remarkable chocolate brown eyes were somehow devouring him in their heat. Then she had dropped her gaze and he had absently, as if in a dream, let his own trail away and across the theater and into the clear, piercing stare of Andrew Camfield, Marquess of Drysden.

After that, it had all proceeded like a bad dream. When Valentine had come back to himself after a few moments, he had become aware of Anna's hands clasped tightly together in her lap, trembling, and he had ached to take them in his and still their tremors. Then he had noticed the spectators, all of the most curious and catty of the *beau monde* watching and waiting to see what the Earl of Alverston would do next. He instantly realized the censure to which he had exposed Anna, the gossip and nasty rumors that the *ton*

would make up and circulate for lack of anything better or more worthy of them to do. An innocent glance
could head the week's gossip columns in the London
newspapers; a longing, desire-filled gaze could ruin a
young lady before dawn the next day.

Valentine had schooled his features to a fashionable
mask of nonchalant disinterest and boredom, and had
maintained that expression throughout the rest of the
evening until they were safely in the confines of his
carriage with the door shut behind them, on their
way home. But the damage had already been done.
She would not raise her eyes to his, and as he wished
not to embarrass her in front of Lucinda or her
aunt—the Greeleys had ridden with other friends to
the opera—he had been struck mute with the inability
to act. Making her good-bye on the steps to the
Greeley town house, she was all that was polite and
genteel, but it was the first time since they had met
that first day over three weeks ago right there in that
house that she had not looked straight and unblush-
ingly into his eyes and told him what a lovely time
she had had. It seemed silly, he mused miserably, but
that omission was what struck him as the most awful
aspect of the entire evening. Because of his actions,
her spirit had been bowed, the fire of her heart
banked, and he cursed himself as a wretched fool for
ever thinking he was good enough for her in the first
place.

Now tonight he knew he must see her, look into
her eyes and try to understand—if he could not yet
ask her outright—what she felt and if she returned
his affection at all. He was sure he would know from
her behavior, that her honesty would force her real
feelings to the surface where he could perhaps read
and understand and try to accept them. He did not
expect the best, but he had to give it one good try,
at least.

Valentine pushed politely through the crowd, greeting friends and acquaintances as he moved along. He
was just reaching one side of the ballroom when he
felt a slender hand wrap itself around his elbow and
saw a smiling, ruby-lipped girl move in front of him
and lift her porcelain-perfect face to his. Like Venus
in all her glory, and arrayed with all of her weapons
of cunning and spite, Priscilla Chetham was the an-
tithesis of what Valentine admired in women. He had
come to her ball only to find and to speak with Anna.
He suspected that the young Lady Priscilla imagined
he had something else in mind from the proprietary
way she was clutching his coatsleeve now.

"My lord, I am so happy to see you here," she purred
in her feathery accents, using the excuse of a number
of people passing them in the crowded room to move
closer to him and press her bosom against his arm for
a fraction of a moment. Impressed, he was; she was a
well-shaped and, in the filmy white dress she was wearing this night, well-exposed female. Intoxicated, he was
not. He stepped back a bit.

"May I congratulate you on your party, Lady
Chetham. It appears to be a successful crush." He
hoped the banal words and impersonal tone would
dampen her ardor. Apparently, they did not.

"My mother is likely to be floating on air." She
waved a white-gloved hand in an insouciant gesture.
"I am happy only to be dancing the entire night away,
without ceasing. . . ." Her eyes glittered green sparks
at him as her words trailed away; and as the opening
strains of a dance were at that moment drifting across
the crowded room, and no partner seemed to be coming to claim the party's guest of honor, Valentine felt
honor-bound to ask Lady Chetham for the dance and
lead her out onto the quickly filling floor.

He was chagrined to find that the music playing
heralded the supper dance. Valentine vowed to dance

very carefully, so that the conniving chit did not have
an excuse to trip against him or enact some other
such nonsense. Girls like Priscilla Chetham, he knew
from his own and his friends' experience, would stop
at nothing to get what they wanted. Happily, she
seemed content to be dancing, and he relaxed and
let himself enjoy the music at least, while keeping her
firmly at a maximum distance from himself when the
patterns of the dance allowed it. She chatted away at
him, apparently not expecting a response, and Valentine allowed his gaze to circle the room, still searching
for Anna in the crowd. Consequently, he missed the
smug little smile his partner threw toward the young
lady dancing with her own partner just behind him
at that moment.

Anna drew in her breath sharply and tried to attend to what Mr. Pendleton was saying to her as they
moved around the ballroom in elegant patterns. The
arrogant beauty's triumphant sneer, directed straight
at her, had taken Anna entirely by surprise, and she
realized belatedly that she had been following the
earl's progress across the floor with her eyes. Anna
berated herself. She would *not* be baited by Priscilla
Chetham or any other dreadful flirt who chose to dig
her claws into Lord Alverston. She did not care a fig
about whom the earl danced with, or at least she
would try to pretend that she didn't. While she was
at it she would pretend she did not feel the constant
ache in her midsection that seeing him so close to
another woman was producing in her.

She must be more careful not to lose herself in
admiration of him every time she saw him. *That* would
not do at all. What would the morning spent crying
her heart out and the afternoon spent recovering and
convincing herself she was perfectly satisfied with her
situation have been worth, after all, if she found her-

self tonight behaving in the same foolish and unguarded way she had at the opera?

Anna stole a fleeting glance at the earl again. The
dancing was turning him to face her. She willed a
smile to her lips and laughed up into Mr. Pendleton's
face. She hoped he had said something funny.

". . . a sister, do you not, my lord?"

Valentine caught the last few words spoken to him
as he swallowed down the altogether unpleasant physical sensation that had struck him when he had finally
located Anna among the dancers. She was dancing in
the circle of the arms of that young jackanapes: Valentine's nemesis. She was smiling, her eyes twinkling
at the handsome blond man guiding her about the
candle-brightened room. Her chin was tilted up, and
she was conversing gaily with her partner, her sensuously full lips expressing her delight as did her eyes.
Her entire being was animated. She was exquisite.

Valentine looked away and turned his partner in
the dance. The measured, regular rhythm of the qua-
drille played by the orchestra did nothing to help dis-
entangle his thoughts from Anna. Apparently she was
feeling quite well this evening, entirely recovered
from her tiredness by her day of rest. He must speak
to Lucinda and learn what if anything had happened
with Pendleton. If that bounder was playing one or
the both of them false, he would have to pay for it,
at the end of Valentine's shooting site, if necessary.

"I beg your pardon, Lady Priscilla." He managed
to draw his attention back to the cold beauty in his
arms. "I am afraid I did not hear your question."

Priscilla Chetham's lips began to form a pout, but
then she decided to change her tactic and smiled instead. "I wondered whether your sister would be returning to Town this Season, my lord? I have heard
she is quite as beautiful as her brother is handsome."

Valentine was unused to direct compliments from

unwed girls; those from older, married women were much more common. He repressed a moue of distaste, admitting to himself that if Anna Tremain had said the same words to him he would now be floating somewhere several feet above the dance floor.

"Thank you, Lady Priscilla. I am not certain of my sister's plans and cannot say what she will be doing in the near future."

Truth be told, he had not heard from his sister directly since her response to his letter of two years ago telling her that their father and James had died. She had not replied to any of his other letters. He certainly did not expect an answer to the latest one for some months yet, the one he had written to her on the day the Greeley party had arrived in London. In it, Valentine had told her everything, and he knew that when she received it—if she read it—she would be forced to respond. He still wondered if she would be furious with him for his deception. He expected her to be; he would be if their positions were reversed. His anger at her inconsiderate behavior had started the whole thing, but that was no excuse for what he had done to Miss Tremain. Perhaps, Valentine mused, it would be better if Pendleton were to put *him* at the end of a bullet's journey.

"She left London in some haste, I have been told. I would not for the world wish your dear sister any harm, but did she suffer some injury, my lord?"

Valentine was escorting Priscilla Chetham off the dance floor and into the supper room, and he glanced down at her, disguising his distaste for this girl who was the focus of the ball's attention. Many of his acquaintances had sidestepped around asking him about his sister during this past month in Town, but none had been so brazen.

"You are kind to be concerned, ma'am," he said in an icy voice. "I was not in the country at the time, so I am afraid I cannot give you an answer to your question." *At least not one that will keep those lobster patties on the table in front of us from being thrown at my head were I to say it,* Valentine thought humorlessly to himself as he chose food from the buffet for their supper while his companion clung to his arm, making his actions especially difficult. He led her to a table at which he recognized some acquaintances, and they sat down to partake of the typical ball supper of mediocre food.

Soon he was feeling more relaxed among the larger group of guests. After two glasses of surprisingly fine champagne, he even felt fine enough to chuckle a bit at one of the witticisms spoken by a member of the party seated around him, and did not even flinch when Priscilla Chetham laid her hand on his on the table for an instant. Instead he drew his hand away from under her cold fingers slowly and discreetly. Really, but she was a tiresome baggage. He could not wait for the supper to end so that he could deposit her with the unfortunate man whose name was written next on her dance card and seek out Miss Tremain. As they stood up to return to the ballroom, he was feeling so relieved at the prospect that he even smiled at the chestnut beauty.

Anna saw the smile from across the supper room where she had been sitting with Mr. Pendleton and a group of his friends. She had also seen the earl's hand clasping Priscilla Chetham's on the table as they were finishing supper, had watched him withdraw it after a moment, but slowly, as if reluctant to do so. She had cringed inside.

Now, leaving the room on the arm of Mr. Pendleton, she wondered what could have made her think that the earl might have had any romantic interest in her at all. His behavior with her had been all that was kind and polite and considerate, true. But he had never maneuvered to get her alone in a gathering, like Mr. Pendleton had when they were still back in ____shire, in order to kiss her—or at least to try to. He had not paid her compliments by the dozen every day, and unlike Mr. Pendleton and other young men who had admired her, he had never cast sheep's eyes at her. She might count the look the earl had given her the night before, Anna mused, but in reality that had felt more like a wolf's gaze than a sheep's; she had felt positively like *dinner* when he had looked at her.

Anna Tremain was no fool; she knew—at least she knew now, after last night—what desire looked like on a man's face. She also knew that desire was not love, and the love in her eyes must have disgusted him as much as it had driven from him any misguided stirrings of desire he might have been feeling. Shamefully, she knew not whether to count the latter a blessing or a curse.

She looked up at Jason Pendleton as he took her hand in his at the edge of the dance floor.

"My dear Miss Tremain," he said, grasping her hand in both of his like an old friend, "dancing and dining with you has been, as always, a delight. I thank you."

"Thank you, Mr. Pendleton. I am happy to have had your company, and your patience with me, especially after my defection from your party today." She smiled warmly at him.

"Do not give it another thought, my girl. We missed you, but we shall make up another party very soon. My cousins are great ones for outdoor entertainment, you know."

"They seem to be very congenial girls," Anna said noncommittally. She had been wondering today, in her spare moments from despairing over Lord Alverston and rallying from that despair, whether either of the Misses Pendleton had her sights trained on their fair-visaged cousin. Anna resented their intrusion into the Greeleys' cozy little society, but not for her own sake. This afternoon, when Lucinda had arrived home from the outing to Richmond, Anna thought she had never seen the girl happier or more brilliant in her soft, spring-fresh beauty. Lucinda had positively radiated happiness.

And it had not been hard to guess why. Anna had been sitting in the window seat of her room when the Pendleton carriage pulled up in front of the house after the day's entertainment. Lucinda and Jason Pendleton's leave-taking had been drawn out, and had consisted of a great number of words on his side and a great deal of blushing and dimpling on hers. This evening, while they were getting ready for the ball, Lucinda's eyes had glittered brightly as her maid put the finishing touches on her shining coiffure. The girl needed no powder or rouging to bring color to cheeks that were already rosy from high spirits.

Although she had not shared the news yet, Lucinda Greeley, it seemed, had chosen her man. Anna could not remember having ever seen her friend appear quite so besotted after an occasion spent with Lord Alverston. She was happy for her: Mr. Pendleton appeared to return her regard, and it was an excellent reason for Anna to think of something other than her own pitiful situation. At least, she thought glumly and not without a stab of pain while making her own final preparations for the Chetham ball, she would be seeing less of the earl as a consequence.

"They are indeed," Mr. Pendleton responded in agreement, drawing her thoughts back to the present moment. "But I must tell you, *dear* Miss Tremain," he went on, his voice trembling, "that I believe I have discovered the very *most* congenial girl in the whole world on my very doorstep." He paused and looked over across the room to where Lucinda stood conversing with her mother and a few other ladies. He brought his eyes back to Anna's face, and his expression was anxious.

Anna looked up at him expectantly, hoping she was showing the enthusiasm she felt.

"Dear Miss Tremain, we have been such *good* friends. . . ."

"Sir, I must admit to you that I think I know what you are going to say." Anna only spoke to relieve him of the agony of self-justification, but his eyes widened in alarm. "And I will save you the effort of saying it," she continued, "by asking you why you are here right now talking with me when you should be over there asking Miss Greeley to join you for a stroll on the balcony?"

Anna was gratified by the look of happy understanding that suffused her friend's face.

"Oh, Anna—may I call you that? We understand each other so very well, do we not? It seems foolish to remain so formal with each other." She smiled her real affection for him. "You are true gem among women." His hands grasped hers again, and he smiled at her warmly, his eyes glowing in gratitude and anticipation. "I thank you for calling me friend and for putting up with my whims."

"I hope this time it is not simply a whim, Jason?" she said, knowing the answer, but wanting to hear him say it to satisfy herself for Lucinda's sake.

He shook his head firmly. "Indeed not, my dear Anna. I have found the only woman I could ever want for my wife. I await an answer to my suit with eager anticipation."

Anna smiled again at him and squeezed his hands with hers. "You shall not have long to wait, I promise you." She released him and watched as he again took her hand and raised it to his lips this time.

"You are too kind, dear Anna. I thank you."
Pendleton saluted her hand again, and she just had
time to admire his golden curls bent over her hand
when she felt the presence of another with them in
the corner of the ballroom behind a broad Corin-
thian column. She raised her gaze and saw the Earl
of Alverston standing before her. Clad in formal black
ball attire, an unusual severity commanding his handsome features, he was both starkly imposing and devastatingly attractive.

"Good evening, Miss Tremain," he said and, turning his head to nod shortly at her companion, added,
"Pendleton." Anna's heart raced, but she made her
curtsy as Jason extended his hand and the earl—even
in her confusion, Anna noted he was standing very
straight and immobile—took it to shake. Turning
back to Anna, he set his dark gaze on her and spoke
almost without expression in his voice.

"I cannot presume to hope you have a dance yet
unclaimed at this late hour. But if you do, I should
be honored if you would share it with me."

Anna was so stunned that she barely thought to
answer. Mr. Pendleton looked at her, anxious to be
away and at Lucinda's side before she was claimed by
her next partner. She smiled at him, wishing he would
stay and willing her pulse to stop beating so violently
in her neck. She looked again at the earl.

"It so happens, my lord, that I am not engaged for
the next dance. Thank you."

There, that had sounded fine, hadn't it?

Anna nodded to Mr. Pendleton and reached for
the earl's arm, proffered to lead her out onto the
dance floor. To her dismay, she heard the opening
strains of a waltz as she moved into place, and she
held her breath as Lord Alverston's hand circled her
waist and he grasped her left hand with his right.
Anna willed herself to breathe as the heat from his

touch penetrated her glove and gown and infused her with a tingling warmth.

"It seems the waltz has become popular very quickly," the earl said as he began to guide her around the floor to the lilt of the music.

Anna was surprised at the banal comment, but immensely relieved. Maybe, despite the pounding of her heart and her dry mouth, being in the earl's presence would not be as torturous as she had been imagining. Still, she could actually feel her *lips* trembling, and so decided to make use of them as little as possible since she was unsure of how successful speech would be, given their instability. She smiled slightly, close-mouthed, and kept her gaze directed just over his right shoulder. That seemed safe enough; maybe she would get through the dance that way, by simply not looking at him, not allowing her heart to get swept into the depths of his storm-cloud eyes. God knew she could *feel* him well enough.

She knew he was looking at her and imagined that his expression was as stiff and strained as his body seemed to be at this moment. He waltzed divinely, nonetheless, guiding her about the floor as if they were one, regardless of the fact that she was about as far away from him as was possible when still in his arms.

Valentine felt his heart sinking with every graceful step she made in perfect synchronicity with his. She would not even look at him. He made another attempt at conversation, this time more personal.

"You are looking very well this evening, Miss Tremain. I hope your day of rest was satisfying."

Another bare smile and a slight nod. "Thank you, yes, my lord," she said without looking at him. He wished he could see what she was looking at over his shoulder. He guessed it wasn't anything in particular; it just wasn't *him*. He wished he had the courage to draw her close in his arms and force her to look at him. Mostly, though, he wished they were in private so that he could at least have enough of her attention to speak with her in earnest.

He let his own gaze drift over her clear face, her shining hair and graceful neck, her smooth shoulders, and he could not wish that he had forsaken this one dance with her. It was heaven holding her, even if only in this impersonal, formal way. The music swelled around them, as if accompanying a grand drama, but one in which it seemed he and she could not partici- pate. At least not together.

Clearly she did not care to be with him. She was distracted, most likely looking for Pendleton, wher- ever he was in the crowd. Approaching them earlier, after finally having found her in the young fellow's company, Valentine had heard the last words the two exchanged, and he had turned cold, his blood as frigid as any Pyrenees winter. He had heard her sweet promise of an answer to Pendleton's suit, and he had seen a door closing, had seen himself alone and out- side of the happiness of their dreams. He had gotten it wrong, all wrong somehow, and now he saw his own future suddenly in stark, solitary relief, deeper and more shadowed than the ancient marbles he had mar- veled at in her company. His voice had sounded strange and distant even to his own ears when he had asked her for the dance. Now, with his heart con- stricted in his chest, and feeling as if his spirit had flown and left an empty shell, he could not summon up the hope or fortitude to challenge what he knew must be the truth.

His hand tightened around her waist, and he whirled her around swiftly as the music finally came to an end, bringing them to a smooth halt directly in front of Pendleton and Lucinda Greeley. Valentine released Anna and she stepped back a bit, startled by the suddenness of the dance's end. Her foot came against an obstacle, and she discovered it was Jason Pendleton's shoe; she had been unaware of their surroundings since the beginning of the dance, her attention fully concentrated on trying unsuccessfully not to feel anything while she was in Lord Alverston's arms. She heard a light feminine chuckle—Lucinda's—and felt Mr. Pendleton's hand at her elbow to steady her as she finally looked at the earl.

He was looking at her arm, where Jason held it. Anna disengaged herself and squared her shoulders.

"Thank you for the dance, my lord," she said in as steady a voice as she could muster.

"The pleasure, ma'am," he said as he bowed, "was all mine." His head came up and his eyes met hers, and for an instant, Anna thought it seemed they were filled with sorrow. Then, as if she had blinked away the image, they were hard steel gray again, and he turned about and walked away through the thickening crowd.

Anna took a step forward, lifting her hand involuntarily, as if in a dream inspired by his shadowed gaze. Then someone laughed very close to her, and the world came back to her in a rush: the candlelit ballroom, the heat, and the finely dressed people all around her, the humming of voices and the tuning of the orchestra for the next set. She turned and saw Lucinda and Jason standing close to each other and talking, wrapped up in their own world of interwoven dreams and reality.

Anna turned again, scanning the crowd for Lord Alverston's sable locks and broad shoulders, but she did not see him. He had departed, it seemed, before she had recognized her own mistake. He was gone, and she was again left with only herself and her regret—this time not for her love, but for her deception that had denied it and that had produced in her a wound that somehow she knew would never heal.

FIFTEEN

The week leading up to the Greeleys' ball passed swiftly for most of the members of the household amidst final preparations, last-minute matters that needed attending to, and countless calls on every friend in London who could savor and share the excitement of a come-out ball with the young ladies for whom it was being thrown.

Lucinda happily threw herself into the preparations. The day after the Chetham's ball, Mr. Pendleton had an interview with Mr. Greeley, and then, after a satisfying session with Lucinda, took himself off to his father's home in the countryside to discuss particulars and arrange to have his family in Town for the wedding in a month's time. The public announcement would be made the evening of the ball, but until then the engagement was to be kept a secret. If people commented on Lucinda's high color and gay spirits, they naturally attributed it to her excitement about the approaching ball, and her mother and Mrs. Masterson did not dissuade them from the notion.

To Anna, each day of the week passed with agonizing slowness. She offered help when she could be useful—writing invitation cards, consulting on floral arrangements and decorations, and doing small tasks that could be accomplished far away from the bustle of ball preparations. Claiming either too much work to be done at home still, letters to write, or tiredness from all of the activity, she managed to avoid most of the social visits that her aunt, Lucinda, and Mrs. Greeley made. She could not absent herself from the parlor, however, when callers came to see them at their home. Thus it was that she had to endure an almost unbearable half-hour three days before the ball when Lord Alverston made an appearance in the Greeley house for a morning visit.

Keeping her eyes on Mrs. Stilwell, with whom she was speaking, she managed to avoid looking at him directly when he entered; there were quite a few people in the room at that hour, it being the day of the week when the women of the house were known to be at home to visitors. When she finally did steal a glance at him, she saw that Lord Alverston was crossing the room, and Anna noted every inch of his very masculine elegance as he moved. Her heart constricted, and though she was instantly sorry she had looked, she could not draw her gaze away from him. Lucinda held court with some of her regular admirers at the fireplace, and Anna watched the earl approach her, speak with her for a moment, and then move to stand with her aunt who was engaged in discussion with Lady Bramfield on the other side of the room. Out of the corner of her eye, Anna watched him conversing with the two older women and noted his lack of animation and stiff demeanor.

My, but he certainly has become stuffy since Lucinda's defection to Pendleton! she thought critically, lowering her gaze to her embroidery as she listened with half an ear to what Mrs. Stilver was saying to her. But Anna found herself justifying his behavior; he was, after all, doubtless suffering from a wounded heart from Lucinda's defection. Or at the very least, a bruised ego.

Furrowing her brow over her work, she conceded that it wasn't fair to accuse the earl of acting strangely

when she herself had contributed to bringing on his
diffidence in the first place, with her embarrassing
show of unwanted affection at the opera. She wished
it could all be undone. She wished she had never let
herself imagine that he felt something for her. As she
watched him talking with her aunt and Lady Bramfield, Anna wished mostly that there was some way
they could go back to the way they had been before,
before that unguarded moment at the opera.

She missed his company. She missed his wit and
his irreverence and his thoughtful conversation. Why,
she hadn't had an intelligent conversation in almost
a week! It seemed the most important and interesting
topics available for discussion lately were what Prinny
had worn to his last scandalous dinner party and how
the price of an ice at Gunter's had gone up a penny.
Anna hadn't realized how necessary to her weekly
nourishment of good conversation was the earl . . .
until he was no longer available to share her thoughts
with.

She supposed she had been spoiled while growing
up in having two such wonderful companions to raise
her. She had always had an insatiable curiosity about
the world, and they had encouraged her. She had en-
vied Valerie for having social standing—not to mention
distant relations across all of Britain who would be willing to host the earl's daughter—and freedom to do all
the exploring she wanted if she had so desired. Anna
had sometimes felt frustrated when Valerie had not
shown more interest in traveling, even in England itself. If given the chance as Valerie had been while growing up, Anna would have surely taken it.

But Valerie had been more interested in parties and
adventures and in thwarting her father's wishes. Her
adventures had centered around doing outrageous
things to shock or anger her parent, thus the carriage
races and cockfights. Valerie, however, understood Po-

lite Society very well, and although she had a quick mind, she was not one to spend her time in extended conversation; like many of Anna's female friends, she found herself in need of almost constant diversion.

Most of the women of Anna's acquaintance in Town, in fact, did not seem to want to exhibit their intelligence very often, and when they did talk about something other than bonnets and beaux, they did so only in private, certainly with no gentlemen within hearing distance. The war was, admittedly, a topic of much speculation among both men and women. But Anna found that most people's opinions reflected less their own thought on the matter than popular trends. Concerning this and other issues, many women of her acquaintance seemed to regard Anna as something of an acceptable bluestocking: too cerebral by far for a woman, but charming and feminine enough to be admitted into their circles.

As for the men she had met in London, Anna had early tired of being patted on the head by older men and being gaped at by younger ones when she spoke of something more profound than the weather and more complex than the color of flowers. Thinking back on the winter months in ____shire that she had spent flirting with Jason Pendleton, Anna was amazed at her own lack of perception. How could she ever have overlooked his disinclination to talk of anything of substance with her? She had truly deceived herself in making excuses for him by seeing only his charm and good looks. Jason Pendleton was a kind man and a very pleasing companion, but he was certainly a better husband for Lucinda than he would ever have been for Anna herself.

Lord Alverston was the only person of her London acquaintance who did not shy away from engaging her in conversation, and he did so in public, in front of her family and friends and anyone at all who happened to be near. Too, he did not withhold his appreciation of her opinions nor his disagreement with them. She never felt as if he were patronizing her or merely amusing himself with her peculiar penchant for discussion. Until the night of the opera, she had felt as if he thought of her as a friend, an equal of sorts, regardless of her sex. That had all changed with one look, to her great unhappiness.

Now, hearing him make his good-byes and knowing that he was leaving, Anna felt more alone and bereft than ever in this noisy, crowded, posturing city. She wished her Season over, the ball and all of the meaningless social calls far behind her, and herself back sitting under the peach tree behind her uncle's house. She wanted peace, an end to her aching heart, and distance from the man who, unbeknownst to both of them, had raised hopes and dreams in her that could never be satisfied.

Valentine wished he had never come to London. At least in the countryside he had Tilly Brubanks to provide intelligent conversation, even if the topics tended out of necessity to center around issues of livestock and harvests. It had been almost a week since he had had a normal conversation with Anna, unless one counted their brief speech at the opera before the incident that had ruined their friendship, it seemed, and left him an interloper in her world of happiness.

He missed her more than he had anticipated he would. The weeks over the past year during which he had gone without news from her as their letters had traveled across almost all of England seemed to him now unimaginable, after the desert of this past week without her company. He knew not whether seeing her at the ball this evening would provide him with sustenance for his empty head and heart, or more frustration and insatiable longing.

He looked up from his meal to attend to what his dinner companion was saying. Timothy was still discussing his cattle, trying to urge Valentine to make a visit with him to Tattersals yet again in order to find just the right mount for his youngest sister who would be coming to Town with her children in a few weeks' time. Elizabeth was a widow, her husband having perished in the Peninsula just before Valentine had made his own lucky escape with a wounded spirit and leg, but with his life intact. Timothy was usually excellent company, but he had been particularly busy with the affairs of his womenfolk this month, squiring them around Town in the absence of his other brother-in-law who usually did the job; Matthew had remained at home this Season as Timothy's other sister, Clara, was approaching her confinement. Valentine had seen precious little of his best friend, and now he was more than slightly irritated that the viscount's present course of conversation was leaving him wishing he was seeing less of him still.

"I think you ought to buy Patterson's mare and have done with it, Tim," he said sharply, taking a full swallow from his wineglass. He put the glass down with unaccustomed force, and the clink of breaking crystal on the mahogany table rang throughout the dining room. The well-trained footman attending the gentlemen did not even flinch, but the viscount sat back in his chair slowly, placing his napkin on the table beside his now empty plate. He crossed his arms over his broad chest and looked with an even expression in his blue eyes at his friend as Valentine handed the ruined glass to the footman.

"Forgive me for saying so, Val, but I think you ought to consider taking out your anger on the one who is fueling it." His voice held no hint of caution, only consideration.

Valentine looked up, suddenly alert, and searched his friend's expression. "What can you know of that?" he said finally, after a pause in which he scanned his friend's face for a hint of knowing.

"I mean," said the viscount, "that you ought to face the fellow down and get some satisfaction. People are beginning to wonder if you care or not whether your good name is slandered. I think," he added quietly, "that they are beginning to believe the knave."

Valentine was confounded. "What are you talking about, Timothy?"

The Viscount Bramfield furrowed his brow and shook his head. "I am talking about Drysden, my friend. What else could be making you such a complete ogre lately?"

The earl drew himself back in his chair again, immensely relieved that his private business concerning Miss Tremain was not public knowledge after all. Then he took in what his friend had said, and his expression hardened.

"A business problem, Tim—something I am trying to resolve at the Hall," he fabricated smoothly. "But what of Drysden? I know he has returned to Town, but I've heard nothing else of him as of yet." He was sitting in strained anticipation in the high-backed dining chair. The evening light coming through the windows of the room glinted off his dark hair and the single black opal in his cravat.

"Then you don't know," said the viscount, "that Drysden has been spreading the rumor that Callanera was your fault?"

Valentine's hands came into fists and he sat forward in his seat. His heart was racing suddenly, as if he had been running, and his palms were coated in sweat. "He is saying this? Who has he told, do you know? What has he said?"

Timothy shook his head again. "He hasn't said anything in my presence, but I've not seen him above twice in the past two weeks since his return, and he steers clear of me, knowing our association," he explained cautiously. "But Berswick told me just this morning at Jackson's that the knave has been making not-so-subtle suggestions as to who actually ordered the defense of Callanera, and dropping hints as to what, according to his story, actually happened there."

"The villain!" Valentine spat out, wishing he could strike out also, but at what, he could not decide. His own guilt was so deep, still so painful even after two years that hearing of Camfield's treachery brought back every single detail of the hellish two days as if it had all happened just yesterday. He understood why Drew Camfield felt he had to do what he was doing, slandering his old friend's good name. Perhaps it was the only way in his eyes. But understanding the man did not make Valentine feel less anger—less fury—or less helpless impotency at the outcome of events that had happened too quickly and too long ago to reverse. Perhaps had he felt at peace with himself as he had before Christmas this past year, perhaps if he had allowed the healing and the forgetting to continue, as he had been learning to do with the help of Anna's loving and open letters, and gathered courage to go on in this way, he would be reacting now with less rage and more compassion, more confidence.

He could not convince the whole *ton* of his innocence, after all, especially since he could not truly convince himself. Valentine believed that however far away those days became, he would never be able to rid himself of at least a remnant of the guilt and pain he felt. He could learn to live with it, though, and

could continue to ignore those in Society who wished
to believe the worst of him, to listen to only half of
the story.

Now, though, he was not afraid of his honor; he
could live with the ignominy, however Drysden tried
to paint him. He had been absolved by the foreign
office, after a long and arduous process through
which he had relived every moment of the two days
over and over again for the benefit of the military
tribunal. The members of the tribunal had come to
understand early in the hearing's proceedings why
Valentine had made the decisions he did. He had
walked away from the tragedy forgiven, if not com-
mended; his actions had been unorthodox, but necessary under the circumstances.

Valentine could not, however, live with the idea that
Anna might hear the gossip and come to think him
a coward, the villain that Andrew Camfield was painting him to be. This he would not bear, and because
of it, he turned his thoughts to the viscount's earlier
advice.

"Yes," he said quietly, as if there had not been a
lengthy pause between himself and Lord Bramfield,
during which the footman had cleared the table of
covers and placed a bottle of port in front of them
and Timothy had lit a long, savory-smelling cigar.

"Yes, you have heard about the gossip he is spreading?" the viscount asked him, breathing a thin cloud
of smoke into the air.

Valentine turned to face him. "No, my friend, I
mean 'yes,' I will face him." Viscount Bramfield pursed
his lips and made a soft whistling sound through them.
"I am not sure exactly how yet," Valentine continued,
"but I shall have to do something before his poison
spreads beyond the ears of those whose opinion I care
not about." He fell once again into thought, his hand

around a glass of ruby port, his eyes on the candles burning on the table before them.

As he tapped his cigar against a silver tray on the table and brought his own glass to his lips, Timothy Ramsay wondered in amazement that there was finally someone in Town whose opinion his friend *did* care about.

"Louisa, Mr. Greeley bumped into an old acquaintance of his at his club today and invited him to join our party this evening."

Samantha Greeley was sipping a cup of tea and looking over the final guest lists for the ball. They lay on the tea table before her, several sheets of paper covered with rows upon rows of neatly scripted names. Louisa Masterson turned from where she stood at the mantel, arranging a bouquet of flowers—white, yellow, and gold, the colors of the ball decorations. Guests were not expected to enter the private rooms of the family, but all of the public rooms were being turned out in case those escaping the crowded ballroom for a breath of air or to rest their feet wandered into them.

"Samantha dear, there are so many names on those lists whose faces are entirely alien to me that one more is not going to make the slightest difference. We have food for many hundreds," Mrs. Masterson said, finishing the arrangement and joining Mrs. Greeley on the settee to take some tea.

"Yes, even if we don't have room for them," Lucinda's mother said on a sigh. "But this is a titled gentleman, and it seems he is also an old friend of your Anna's Lord Alverston."

Louisa Masterson looked sharply at her friend, but Samantha's expression was entirely innocent as her eyes scanned the pages of names. Certainly their hostess could not have noticed what Louisa herself had come to suspect over the course of the past several weeks, but especially the last. The earl and Anna had not spent any more time in each other's company than was usual; it was how they had been looking on those occasions when they were together that had set Louisa Masterson to speculating and, since the night of the opera, to worrying too.

"It seems that Lord Drysden and the earl spent some time together in Spain," Mrs. Greeley said, standing and covering an incipient yawn with a lace-edged palm. "Oh, my, I must have a little rest before it gets too late. She moved toward the parlor door. "I shall see you in a few hours, Louisa dear. Do get some rest yourself."

Left in the room alone, Louisa Masterson took the pages of the guest list in her hands, running her eyes over the names as she turned from one sheet to another. It had been decades since she had hosted a party of such magnitude, but she was not concerned about the music or the catering or any other minor aspect of the party. Her real anxiety was for her niece, who, as the evening of the ball had drawn nearer, had shown less and less interest in the celebration; Anna's aunt thought she had an explanation for the reason why.

Anna lay in her bed, staring sightlessly up at the canopy above her. The image she saw in its stead was the face of the man she had seen only once in the past week, but who had been in her mind almost constantly.

She knew he would come to the ball; she knew he would look as handsome as ever; and she knew that it would be the longest night of her life and that she would spend it waiting for it to end, hoping to get

through it without either screaming, crying, or faint-
ing dead away at his feet. Of course she had never
done any of those before. Well, except for crying—
but never in public. She had never been in love before either, so who knew how she would behave?

She was trying to prepare herself for the ordeal.
She had been practicing to be her normal, calm self
with Lucinda this afternoon, trying to forget she had
ever met Lord Alverston, and trying to share with her
friend all of the excitement of the day's anticipation.
She thought she had been doing a fair job of it until
Mrs. Greeley encountered them in the ballroom
where the girls were supervising the hanging of gold
bells and ribbons throughout the Hall. Her hostess,
having noted Anna's lassitude, told her that she
needed a bit of rest before the evening and that she
ought to go up to her room and lay down. Anna had
nodded her head and had slunk off quietly to re-
group and restrategize her public self in private.

Now, head upon the pillow, she was unable to sleep.
She kept running over in her mind the same images
and words that she had been thinking of all week,
but now they no longer made sense.

Previous to the Chetham ball, Lord Alverston had
been all that was gentlemanly and kind; he simply
could *not* have taken her into such instant disgust, or
even aversion. True, he had played least in sight this
week, and too Anna thought no better of her chances
with a peer of the realm this afternoon than she had
one week ago following the disastrous opera. But she
could not quite believe anymore that the earl despised
her simply because she had foolishly revealed her feelings for him.

Her earlier reaction had been extreme and had
been caused by her own pain, Anna admitted, turning
onto her side and staring out the window at the afternoon blue of the sky. Lord Alverston was most

likely simply embarrassed—for her and perhaps even for himself, for his inappropriate show of attraction for a girl of her humble social standing and birth. Besides, there was the chance that he felt deeply Lucinda's cooling of affection toward him; this might go far in explaining his reluctance to visit. These explanations suited what she knew of him somewhat better than the other. They were unsatisfying, to say the least, but made more sense. Certainly having devised them Anna felt generally less ashamed and more accepting of the state of things as they were, if not happy. He *did* seem to be avoiding *her* in particular, and one could not like, after all, being despised for one's love.

Suddenly Anna felt as if lying in bed and thinking one more minute would drive her mad. She had to be outside. Before she could think of any of the many reasons why she should not take a ride in the Park, she jumped from her bed, rushed to her wardrobe, pulled out her riding habit, and rang for her maid to have the groom ready the gray mare. She would ride a bit, feel the bright afternoon sun on her cheeks, and imagine she was home at Hedgecliff and that the most disappointing night of her life did not loom ominously before her.

SIXTEEN

Guests began arriving shortly after dinner, and Anna took her place in the greeting line at the entrance to the ballroom, in between her aunt and Lucinda. Candles sparkled on chandeliers and in sconces throughout the rooms in use for the ball. A small orchestra was nestled in one corner of the ballroom, which was sparkling with hundreds of little gold and silver bells, and fragrant with dozens upon dozens of ribbon-tied white, yellow, and gold clusters of flowers. Supper would be served in a room adjacent to the ballroom, and a card room was arranged for those who wished to escape the dancing. Terrace doors opening onto the ballroom were wide to let in the warm evening air, and the bright silver moon and the stars shone in the clear sky above. The night was perfect.

Anna felt much better than she had earlier in the day, refreshed, a glow suffusing her creamy cheeks. In leaving for her ride earlier, she had met Mr. Greeley; noticing her riding attire, he had quickly offered to accompany her. She was glad of the company, though a bit embarrassed for having been caught in the indiscretion of going out unescorted. She assured him as they cantered through the Park that she had been planning to take her maid with her, at least to the entrance of the Park, and to have the groom following her on his own horse the entire time. She could tell, though, that Mr. Greeley was glad for the excuse for an outing, and they had spurred their horses into a gallop and raced as far as Rotton Row would allow them. Mr. Greeley apologized for their hard ride on the way home, but Anna realized he was only practicing his apology to her aunt and his wife in case they should discover the outing or she herself should be found to be too exhausted for the party that night.

In fact the ride had reinvigorated her, but it was not solely the exercise that had put the color in her cheeks. Upon her return from the Park she had found waiting in her room a delicate posy of exquisitely tiny, pure white roses, tied with a gold ribbon. She had supposed they were a gift from Mr. Greeley, or perhaps her aunt, who she knew had been worried about her this past week, although they had not spoken of it.

Anna drew the small silver-embossed card out of its envelope, and she gasped; its inscription read *The Earl of Alverston*. Hands suddenly trembling, she had turned over the card and read its simple note: *Miss Tremain, I wish you great happiness for this evening and always. Yours, Valentine Monroe.* Anna had taken the roses in her hands and pressed them to her mouth, breathing in their sweet fragrance and feeling a warmth suffuse her that had nothing at all to do with the late-afternoon sunshine pouring through her bedroom window and setting the room aglow in its softness. Later she learned that the earl had also sent Lucinda a bouquet, but there was no personal note written on the other girl's card, and Anna had kept her own card's message a secret.

Now, standing at the head of the few stairs that descended into the ballroom, she greeted their guests with more warmth and genuine pleasure than she had

felt all week. She was no longer experiencing the lassitude that Mrs. Greeley had seen in her earlier in
the day, but she was not entirely cured of her ill
mood. However, she knew she would have to endure
an evening of being in the same house and room as
Lord Alverston, whatever he had intended by his gift
of the flowers, and she would have to keep a tight
rein on the emotions that he aroused in her. But she
now felt more able to take on the events of the evening than she had before. She was anxious, nervous,
and wary; but she was also confident, to a degree, of
her ability to sustain her own peace of mind.

Anna and Lucinda were excused from the greeting
line as soon as the orchestra began to tune up for its
first set. Mr. Pendleton appeared before them to claim
the hand of his betrothed for the dance, and Anna
let herself be led onto the floor by the Viscount Bramfield, who had earlier in the week requested that she
honor him with the first dance of her own ball. He
was very pleasing company, and distracting, Anna
thought gratefully as the set formed and the music
began. If only he were not such a good friend of the
earl, everything would be perfect. She sighed and
smiled up into his face, and the dance began.

From where he stood at the ballroom's entrance,
Valentine could see her every move and expression,
and his heart went with the woman who moved in
time across the parquet floor with his best friend. She
was wearing a gown of white spun silk, shimmering
with a thousand golden stars embroidered upon it in
jewel-like beads. She wore around her neck a single
pearl hanging from a simple golden chain, and her
hair was swept up gracefully, held with a gold comb
and decorated artistically with three tiny white roses.
A few golden brown tendrils gently curled down her
neck and the sides of her exquisite face. She wore
yet more miniature roses on a ribbon around her nar-

row white-gloved wrist. Valentine could not understand why there were not ten men or more on the dance floor right then, fighting Timothy for her attention—the dance and propriety be damned.

He, however, would resist the temptation of putting his imaginings into practice himself. Valentine had not been able to resist sending her the flowers; he hoped they would somehow soften her attitude toward him so that if she ever heard Drysden's rumors, she would feel less inclined to believe them. He had not expected to see the flowers adorning her already perfect beauty, and he was more gratified than he could have put into words.

He had vowed before he arrived at the Greeleys' home not to approach her this night, and certainly not to ask her to dance. He would plead war injuries or some such thing if anyone asked; after all, he still used his cane every so often. But he would not put himself through the real physical pain of getting within several yards of Anna Tremain. He was no green fool.

Dragging his eyes away from the vision of her, Valentine grabbed a glass of champagne from a passing footman and went to seek out the card room. If he could not have her in his arms, then he damn sure wasn't going to make a fool of himself *and* her by standing around and slavering over her like a sick puppy all night long, regardless of how much he wanted to. He had been obligated to come to the ball, for Lucinda and Mrs. Masterson's sake, if not as much for his own, but he did not have to suffer through every moment of it, although the prospect of doing so seemed strangely appealing to him at this very moment. The earl shook himself and quickly made his way out of the ballroom.

* * *

An hour later Valentine was yawning, bored to death with playing cards and sore in the neck from straining to keep himself from looking through the doorway to the ballroom every ten seconds to see if he could capture a glimpse of Anna. He hadn't yet, and he had looked that way aplenty, despite his good intentions. He did not know why he didn't just go out there, dance with her and then young Lucinda, and leave. He knew he should make his bows to the ladies. He was sure his hostesses would remark it if he did not, and Lucinda, bless her heart, would be hurt if he ignored her on her big evening, even though they were apparently not playing the courting game any longer. They had become friends, after all.

Miss Greeley had not sought out his company this past week, although truth be told he had not, since the Chetham's ball, frequented the places he imagined their party would be. Lucinda, he had decided, would have to fight her own losing battle. If Anna and Pendleton had come to some sort of an agreement since last week, he would not be the one to throw a rub in the way of it. He had not known quite how to put this to Miss Greeley, since he could not well tell her the truth and reveal his feelings to someone who was unlikely to keep them a secret from Anna for long. So he had avoided having to say anything at all, and in doing so had also avoided putting himself in proximity to Anna herself. He had absurdly thought this the best way to begin to forget about her.

Valentine looked around at the aged matrons and old men clustered around the card tables and sighed. He should have gone back to the country. He should have left London as soon as he had known there was no chance for him. *Blast it!* But he had stayed because he had wanted to find an excuse to see Anna again, whatever the cost to himself, and then he had spent the whole week making that impossible. Now that he had the opportunity, he was wasting it in this godforsaken card room while the woman he loved was dancing the night away in the arms of other men.

Shaking himself for the second time that night, Valentine made as if to stand and leave when his own name being spoken at the table behind him caught his attention. Steeling himself against turning to see who was speaking, he relaxed again into his chair and nodded to the dealer at his table to deal him in; she was an elderly and heavily bejeweled woman who had already this evening won a sum from him almost as great as the worth of that ruby on her finger. He had been playing with half of his attention. Valentine trained his ear on the conversation going on behind him and calmly picked up his cards.

"Why, no officer would consider such a thing!" the speaker, an older man, was saying in response to a statement that Valentine had not heard. "It is entirely dishonorable, and foolhardy to boot!"

The response was almost inaudible, but the soft, controlled voice of the speaker sent icy tendrils up Valentine's spine.

"Indeed, sir, I quite agree. It seems, however, that Captain Monroe did not find it so foolish, nor so dishonorable." He paused, and then added. "Perhaps he himself did not know better."

"Not know better! An officer in the king's army!" sputtered the old earl, whose identity as an outspoken—and, Valentine had long thought, ignorant—critic of Wellington's Spanish campaign was well known.

"Civilians! Indeed!" interposed a female voice in horror-filled accents.

The other voice, once so familiar to Valentine, came back quickly. "Or perhaps the captain was afraid." The words hung in the air, and Valentine's blood chilled within him as the cards dropped from his hand. Behind him, in smooth tones, Drysden added, "Fear, you know, my lord, can make better men than the earl do shameful things."

The frigid cold that invaded every fiber of his being forced Valentine to his feet. Barely knowing what he was doing, he turned slowly where he stood, and met the narrowed eyes of Andrew Camfield, Marquess of Drysden. The woman at Drysden's table gasped and dropped her lorgnette, and the earl beside her scowled at him openly, if in surprise. Drysden, on the other hand, looked as cool and calm as if he had just been heaping praise upon the name of the Earl of Alverston and not scorn. Valentine met his languid gaze with eyes of ice gray and lips thin with white anger and something else. He stood a moment like that, and then turned away and faced his own table-mates again. They were staring at him as if he had pulled a revolver from his waistcoat and turned it on them. Through the haze of his emotions, Valentine supposed he might very well look capable of doing just that. He glanced at the dealer, put his hand to his waistcoat, and bowed.

"I'm afraid the play tonight has become too deep for me, ma'am. Good evening, ladies, gentlemen." And he turned and walked toward the door, heading for the French doors onto the terrace, wanting only escape and forgetfulness and the undoing of a history that would never leave him be.

From where Anna stood some feet from the door and inside the card room, she saw the whole thing: saw Lord Alverston stand, saw him turn and stare at the fashionably dressed man at the table behind him with what looked to her like both fury and deep hurt, saw him bow to the people at his table and bid them good night, and then saw him depart, his face a stony mask except for the violence of hopelessness in his stormy eyes.

She felt paralyzed by that look. He had not seen her, had walked past her as if blind to everything around him, appearing as if he could actually *do* violence if not for the complete lack of animation on his face. The pain in her body was greater than any she had ever experienced before.

She turned to see what may have caused the earl to act in such a way, the shawl that her aunt had asked her to retrieve from the card room forgotten in her hands. Three persons sat at the earl's former table, all conversing quietly amongst themselves and passing brief glances at the table next to them. There Anna saw Mrs. Fletching rapidly flicking a black ostrich-feather fan. She was sitting next to the aged Earl of Worchester, who was scowling at the cards facedown on the table in front of him. Another man Anna did not recognize shared their table, but he was staring at her, with an unfathomable expression in his shining eyes, as if he were seeing both her and something entirely different from her within his mind. Mesmerized, she stared back, and his lips slowly curled into a thin smile that unaccountably sent chills up Anna's spine.

She dropped her gaze, and turned back to the door. Lord Alverston was all the way across the ballroom, and Anna saw him exiting through the French doors and onto the terrace that ran the length of the ballroom at the back of the house. Without looking back at the man behind her, she hastened out of the card room and around the dance floor.

Finding her aunt, she deposited the shawl around the woman's shoulders, pressed her hand warmly, and left to calmly make her way around the ballroom to the French doors. It would not do, she thought as she willed herself to move slowly and naturally, to have anyone take notice of her leaving the ballroom. A woman did not go unescorted onto the terrace during a ball; a young, unmarried woman did not go out there at all. Finally Anna came abreast of the open French doors, and glancing around her one last time to make sure no one was watching her, she stole out onto the terrace and into the night's darkness. From across the ballroom, Louisa Masterson thoughtfully watched her go. Then she turned attentively to the matron with whom she was speaking.

Trying to make herself unnoticeable behind a pillar against the wall, Anna allowed her eyes to become accustomed to the near darkness of the terrace. Chinese paper lanterns provided low illumination so that once Anna could, she saw that the earl was not among the few ballgoers who were taking advantage of the night's mild weather to escape the crowded ballroom. Two couples stood along the railing of the long stone terrace, and another pair strolled on the grass in the garden below, each close to a concealing potted palm or sculpture, each trying to be as inconspicuous as possible while concentrating less on the stars than on their own activities.

Gracious, so this was what she had been missing as an unwed maiden! Anna would have giggled to herself if she had not been preoccupied with looking for the earl—and worried about him. All the better, though, since her presence on the terrace was unlikely to be noticed or commented on by these particular guests.

The earl must be somewhere out here, she thought desperately, *but beyond the reach of the lantern light.* She did not question the need that drove her to find him, but quickly and with light steps stole down the terrace and past the other open doors, her slippered footfalls making no noise on the stone. When she came to a place almost at the very end of the terrace, behind a bend in the wall and out of the light of the lanterns, she stopped and her eyes quickly accommodated the dark. The stars and moon were bright enough to provide her with ample light to see by.

Before her in profile, his head in his hands and his fingers tangled in his sable locks, the Earl of Alverston sat in the silver light. He was seated on a stone bench set into the wall of the old town house. A high wall beyond him, covered with ivy, provided privacy from the garden of the house next door. The moonlight shone down onto the terrace, casting silver-blue shadows around the earl and making Anna's gown glow ethereally in the dark. Sensing her presence, the earl raised his head and looked straight at Anna. She gasped. The look on his face was that of a dead man.

"My lord, I . . ." Anna began, and took a tentative step forward. The earl stared at her with eyes devoid of emotion, as if he were looking right through her. She tried again. "I saw you leave the card room. I am afraid something is wrong." She paused, searching for words, unable to look into those empty gray eyes for more than a moment at a time. "I do not wish to pry, to know your business; I am certain it is none of mine," she said. "But I do wish to help, if I may."

While she stood there looking at him, the quiet sounds of the night and the music from the ballroom seeming very far away; his stoney expression did not change, but his dark eyes gradually took on a light until, Anna thought, they seemed to glow with a warmth banked by layers of sorrow. It was as if he were waking up, but very slowly, and even now not ready for daylight. He took a deep breath, clasped his hands in front of him, and when he spoke his voice was low and not entirely steady. He looked directly at her.

"You have already, Miss Tremain."

Anna let out a breath that she did not even know she was holding. But it was not enough, she knew suddenly. He was not free of whatever demons that were chasing him. His expression was still haunted, and his hands were clenched tightly together, as if to keep from trembling. When Anna looked more carefully, she saw that in fact they were trembling.

Anna responded to his look and demeanor and not his words. He had not moved from the sitting position he had been in when she approached. Knowing him for the gentleman he was, Anna felt this in itself to be an indication of his distraction, his total immersion in the pain he was experiencing right then.

"Lord Alverston, I fear I must retract my earlier assurance not to pry—and beg your forgiveness if you can give it." She clasped her hands in front of her tightly in her nervousness and struggled to find words. "You seem to be in great pain." He looked up at her sharply, his expression hard and white. "I— What I mean to say is, it seems as if you are for some reason bearing more than one person should bear alone." She took a deep breath and looked to him, as if expecting a reply. He continued to stare at her with his distant storm-tossed gaze.

Anna took one more step forward until she was standing right before him. Somewhere in the back of her mind she hoped that she would have the time to finish what she had begun before someone surprised them in their inappropriately private situation.

"My lord," she said, laying a hand lightly on his broad shoulder and trying to ignore the frissoning of heat throughout her body that followed the action. She felt him tense beneath her touch. "My lord," she began again, "should you wish someone to talk to, I offer my ear gladly and freely." Anna stumbled on the words as the expression in his eyes changed, and there was questioning now amidst the suffering. "I would do the same for your sister, you know," she added hurriedly but with candor, trying to infuse in her voice all of the sincerity she felt. She actually felt pain at seeing his so clearly written across face and body. Anna believed at that moment she would do anything—beyond what she would ever have done for her friend Valerie—to erase the suffering from the earl's expression.

With a movement so slow it was almost untraceable, Lord Alverston looked down at Anna's arm stretched between them. Quickly, she removed her hand, belatedly ashamed of her forwardness; but the earl reached out his own and took hers in it, and drew her down onto the stone bench beside him. He released her hand, and she clasped her hands in her lap.

"Are you cold, Miss Tremain?" His voice was quiet and very deep. Afraid to reveal her trembling through her voice, a trembling that had nothing to do with the night air, Anna shook her head. He spoke, looking out into the dark garden. "I would not have you take a chill on my account."

Anna felt as warm as she ever had before, sitting closer to the earl than she had even during carriage rides. "It is a very warm evening, my lord. In any case, I am made of stronger stuff than to take a chill on a mild summer's night." She chanced a glance at her companion and felt immediate relief at noting the scant gleam of amusement in the earl's gray eyes.

"Yes, I believe you are," he replied, this time with a voice less heavy. She watched him take a deep breath, mesmerized by the play of the blue-silver light on his sculpted cheekbones and dark hair. "I went to war a boy, Miss Tremain," he said, as if he were commenting on the weather, but Anna could hear the tension in his low voice. "They ought never to let boys go off to war."

He was silent for a moment, and then she thought she heard something like a laugh come from him, but it was a harsh sound coming from deep within his icily immobile frame. "I was twenty-one. Females that age are mothers of entire families already."

"I imagine, my lord, that war is much different from childbed," Anna responded quietly. "One destroys life; the other creates it."

Slowly, very slowly, Lord Alverston raised his hand to his face and covered his eyes, rubbing them as if to erase the images he was seeing behind them.

"I will never forget their faces, Anna. I will never be able to forget them, not as long as I live."

She was certain he was unaware of having called her by her given name. The sound of it on his tongue sent shivers through her and, unaccountably, filled her with an aching longing.

"Perhaps you are not meant to forget them, my lord."

The earl nodded his head slowly. "You are right. I am not meant to forget their faces, every one of the trusting faces that looked to me for leadership. The people I was supposed to protect." His voice was once again ravaged with pain; Anna could hear the sobs that were fighting to break free, those she was certain the earl had not in two years allowed to come forth.

"You speak of your soldiers," she said, not as a question, her tone intending to soothe. "They were trained to protect themselves, were they not, my lord?"

The earl stared into the blackness of the night. "And they did. Valiantly, to the last man," he said, clearly recalling their courage in his memory. Then he turned his head and looked at her, and his tone sent an ice into Anna's blood with which the warm evening air could not compete.

"But I speak of the villagers. The townspeople of Callanera, Spain, whom I armed so that they could defend themselves against the enemy. Who, because they carried those British arms, were each and every one of them—old men, women, children—executed one after another in the town square by the enemy for treason to the emperor."

SEVENTEEN

Anna's breath failed her as she looked to the earl with wide, confusion-filled eyes.

"But why were there not British soldiers to bear those arms, my lord, to defend the villagers? Or others? You say your own soldiers fought well."

She knew she was speaking as if to convince herself that some other events must have followed, as if what the earl had just told her could not have happened. Every fiber in her rebelled against this barbarous violation of what war was supposed to be. Even she, who through her studies understood better than many of her friends the evils of war, could not take in such a tragic series of reversals in the rules of honor.

Lord Alverston stood up and moved toward the railing. He turned around and leaned his tall frame against it. His face fell into shadow, and Anna strained to see his expression in the dark.

"My soldiers did fight well," he began. "They had been ordered to protect the village from the French regiment moving through the area, and they did so. But many were wounded in the process. If that had been the end of it, the decrease in our numbers would not have mattered." He looked away from her for a moment, and then brought his memory-clouded gaze back to her again. Anna had the sense that Lord Alverston was only with her in body, that his mind

and heart were far away in that hot, desertlike summer, with his men.

"Instead, the French returned, in greater number,"
he continued. "My scouts began to bring back reports
of enemy troops ten times our number entering the
area. The French needed to take our location. It
was"—he paused, and then his voice turned sour—"a
strategically important position. We had known that,
of course, and had long before prepared a chain of
communication with the other companies of our bri-
gade to call for help. As planned, I sent immediately
to the neighboring areas for reinforcements. Messengers returned from two of the three nearest posts re-
porting too many wounded in those companies to
come to our aid. It seems the French had been there
before they attacked us, but in fewer numbers. The
entire region was unprepared for such an outpouring
of force from Bonaparte's army. Our analysts still do
not understand why that madman considered the area
so essential." The earl pushed himself away from the
terrace's stone railing and walked to the wall of the
house somewhat behind Anna. She shifted in her seat,
and saw him running his hand along the brick of the
building as if it were an alabaster statue.

"I never heard from the third company. Oftentimes
messengers will be captured or killed." He looked to
her, but continued when he saw that her expression
was unchanged by his bald words. "I assumed the
worst, and sent another. The second and then the
third failed to return as well. I was forced to assume
that my friend's company had been entirely destroyed
or taken prisoner. Such things," he said very slowly,
"have been known to happen when the odds are very
uneven."

Anna stood up. "Your friend, my lord? Were you
close to the officer in charge of that company? I am
sorry for his death." Her voice was soft, compassion-

ate. Lord Alverston turned and looked directly into her fathomless brown eyes. He crossed to her and took her hands in his.

"He and I were very close, yes," he said, his hold on her light, yet he feared that if he let go, he would not be able to say the next words. "He did not die, though. He was alive, he and his whole company."

"But—"

"The French attacked the town, and after the first day I had twenty-five out of a hundred soldiers standing, half of whom were badly injured." Anna gasped. He released her hands and moved toward the edge of their shadowed corner of the terrace, where the light of the lanterns fell on the gray stone in silver ripples. He stopped just short of the lamplight. Anna could hear the music from the ball distantly, as if in a dream.

"Before dawn the next day, they attacked again, and then suddenly they were gone. It was then that the people of the town came to me and asked me to give them guns, sabers, anything with which to defend themselves. They had heard of how the French sometimes dealt with the local people, and they were afraid. They begged me, pleaded with me, men and women alike. It was unlike anything that my training as an officer had prepared me for." He was barely breathing, remembering the panic of the Spanish villagers in terrible detail.

Anna could not keep herself from asking the awful question, "What would the Frenchmen do to them?"

"Everything," the earl said, as if it was the easiest word in the world to speak, and Anna began to shiver, despite the warmth of the night air. "I knew this," he went on, "and I gave them guns. They were farmers—they did not have one real weapon among them. I gave them all of the arms of my dead men. I gave my own gun to a boy who barely reached my waist in height, and I fought with my saber when the French finally returned," he ground out between clenched teeth. "I gave them all of the ammunition they could use, and they killed three times their number of the enemy. They fought and they fought and still the enemy kept coming. There must have been hundreds of them to our handful. My men died around me, trying to keep the villagers from having to meet the French soldiers, and where they dropped, women and children and old men took their places, behind windows and empty barrels and wagons." Anna trembled as she watched the earl recite the events passing across his memory. He seemed entirely absent from this time and place, wrapped up in the massacre he had witnessed.

"I was captured," he said eventually. "Shot in the leg and the shoulder, I had lost a great deal of blood, and I must have lost consciousness for a moment, because suddenly behind me there were several French soldiers. I remember shouting over the roar of gunfire for the villagers to retreat, to run, but I don't think they heard me. Or perhaps they did." He was silent for a moment, thoughtful. "By the time I regained consciousness a second time, trussed and tied to a wagon, they were executing the villagers." Anna was certain he did not know she was even there as he spoke. "One by one, in front of the survivors, their mothers and children, sisters, grandfathers. The French killed them and let the bodies lay where they fell. I watched every single one of them die." The earl's voice had become a whisper. "They were proud and angry, as if their Spanish blood could not admit defeat even in the midst of their own destruction."

He looked into the starry sky, and Anna wondered what he saw, this man who had punished himself for his decision by watching the people he was responsible for being murdered one at a time. "They were good people, I think," he said finally, turning to her. "I did not know them long enough even to learn their names."

Then his shoulders began to tremble, and Anna reacted from instinct. Moving quickly to the earl, she wrapped her arms around him and drew his head down onto her shoulder, murmuring soothing sounds into his ear as his sobs began to come hard and violently.

She held him and thought of the guilt he must have suffered since that day two long years ago, and wondered that he had been able to carry it within him for so long. All at once she understood his reclusive life in the country, Valerie's veiled comments in her letters about the wounds he had carried back from the war, his sister's presence at the Hall for such an extended period of time. Anna imagined that Valerie had worked to heal her brother's wounds and that her care and generosity had been the balm that had helped him make his way back into Society. She knew, however, that he was not yet whole, that the wound he had suffered would most likely never heal. It would, though, with tending, grow smaller over time.

When it was over, and the earl drew away from her, his gray eyes glittering with the few tears he had allowed himself to shed, Anna felt herself at a loss. Holding him had seemed so natural, as if it were not the scandalous thing it actually was for an unwed girl to comfort a man in such a fashion. His gaze was on her, and she watched anxiously as his lips parted, waiting for the apology.

"But whatever happened to your friend, my lord?" she said hurriedly, grasping for something to forestall the appropriate words he would say that would only serve to embarrass her and break the magic intimacy of the moment. "The one who never responded to your call for aid."

Lord Alverston's fine lips twisted. "He chose not to come."

Anna's eyes flew open in shock.

"He decided not to put his men at risk, it was later discovered," he continued in a flat voice. "At the time, however, in order to defend his cowardice, he let it be known that I had armed the villagers out of pride. After the battle, while my release from the French was still being negotiated, he sent notice to the general that I had rejected all offers of assistance and instead had given arms to the Spanish in the arrogant belief that I could lead any soldiers, however ragtag, to victory. I suppose he counted on me dying along with all of my officers." The words fell bitterly from Lord Alverston's lips. Anna could see the fury simmering just beneath the surface of his dark eyes, but she kept her silence.

"Two of my officers did live," the earl continued. "And, as you can see," he added with a humorless, self-punishing grin, "so did I. Our release was eventually and rather miraculously negotiated with the French. Even Bonaparte admitted to the atrocity his commanding officer had ordered, and word was that other French officers considered the man a rogue, a madman even before Callanera. I suppose they, too, thought me some kind of madman or fool, and assumed my superiors would deal with me appropriately. My officers came forward then to tell the truth."

"But you took the blame, of course," Anna said in almost a whisper. "You did not let your officers share it, did you?"

The earl's lips curled in another mirthless grin. "Of course I did not let them share it. It was my mistake. I gave them the order, and they were well trained. They accepted it, despite themselves. In any case, the

tribunal judged all of the officers involved innocent
of wrongdoing, since the members of it could not
come to an agreement over who should carry the
blame."

Anna moved away from Lord Alverston, slowly going around him to approach the railing. "Naturally,"
she added as if ignoring the last information he had
offered. "Officers in the king's army are trained not
to think, only to accept their superior's orders, however mad they might be," she said calmly and quietly.
"The fault was entirely yours. There is no one to
blame but you for the massacre of those poor, innocent people, not to mention all of those noble English
boys."

Anna felt herself grabbed roughly by the shoulders
and turned around to face the earl. His eyes were
dark, angry, and filled with self-loathing. "It was my
fault! I did wrongly. I killed those people as surely as
if I had done so with my own hands."

"You did what you had to do!" she hurled back at
him, her voice shaking yet strong. His hands were
tight on her shoulders, almost painful. "You had no
choice. You say they were begging you, the villagers?
What if you had not succumbed to their wishes? What
if you had left them unarmed and the French had
taken the village, had used the women and killed the
old men as they tried to defend their daughters? What
of the children who would have been orphaned or
died, the young girls—"

"Stop!" the earl entreated with panic. "You must
not say these things! What have I done? What have I
made you hear and imagine?" His eyes were anguished, his face a battlefield of torment and confusion.

"I know what goes on in war, my lord. I am not
an ignorant woman, as so many in this Society are,"
Anna retorted with heat. "I hate war because I know

what happens to people, and I understand that there are no innocents in war, and thus the blame for the horror it creates cannot be shouldered by one man, even were he a general." She stood, trapped by his unmoving hands, and looked up directly into his stormy eyes. "What of your friend, the officer who did not respond to your summons? What of his blame, what of his cowardice? Who is this man, this friend of yours that you take the blame for, for something that very well may have been his fault?"

Anna felt the earl's hands loosen on her shoulders, felt the more gentle caress of his fingers on her arms below the fabric of her sleeves. She shivered and he dropped his hands.

"His name is Andrew Camfield. We were friends at university," he explained, "and we used to dream of going to war together, of fighting the French and coming home heroes. We were so foolish."

"You were young," Anna said.

The earl looked at her thoughtfully for a long moment, and then away again.

"Drew had inherited an Irish title from his uncle. The man was a wastrel and a gambler and a notorious thief like his father before him. The estates were deeply encumbered with debt when Drew's uncle died, and he saw no way of earning the money that would pull them out of disaster. He sold as much of his property as he could, but was still in bankruptcy. So he sold everything he had and bought a commission in the army. He thought to win glory and through it either the hand of a wealthy bride"—here the earl looked at Anna, a grim smile on his face—"or death."

Anna nodded in sober understanding. "But glory eluded him," she said thoughtfully.

"Or more accurately, he eluded glory. Or death."

"Perhaps both," Anna suggested. "If he had come

when you called, would you have defeated the French at Callanera?" The anger had gone from the earl, leaving behind it a weariness and fatalism that to Anna was almost as frightening in its grip on the man.

"Perhaps, perhaps not."

He straightened his shoulders, as if allowing all the remnants of the pain and fury he had released to slide off and away from him finally. The panoply of raw emotions that had swept over him in rapid succession since he had been in the card room seemed now to melt together and evaporate as he breathed in deeply. "It matters not any longer. The murder of those people will forever be on my conscience, but Andrew Camfield's betrayal means nothing to me anymore."

Anna looked up at the earl, her expression careful. "But it meant something to you tonight, did it not?"

The earl's expression changed from one of exhausted resignation to something that Anna could not read. She suddenly felt that with her question she had somehow altered the tone of their conversation.

"Yes, it did," he responded cautiously. Anna found herself anxious about saying the next words, but some irrepressible need urged her to do so.

"Why, my lord? After all of this time?"

"Because," he said, his eyes shimmering blue-black in the silvery moonlight, "after all of this time I was suddenly afraid that the woman I love would hear the story from his lips and that she would believe him and look upon me forever more with only disgust and disdain."

Anna felt her heartbeat stop and her courage plummet to her toes.

The woman he loved.

She did not know if she wanted to learn the identity of this lucky paragon whose opinion of him mattered beyond all else. In the agony of the aching loss sweeping over her, Anna sought for words to shift the conversation away from such a revelation when in shock she heard her own voice ask in quiet tones, "And who is this foolish woman, who would so easily dismiss the love of such a man because of the words of another?"

As if in a dream, she felt the earl take her gloved hand in both of his and raise it to his lips. They were warm, his touch gentle.

"A woman who is strong and intelligent and compassionate," he said, his suddenly tender gaze filling Anna with warmth. "A woman whom I have sorely misjudged in believing that she would be so inconstant." He drew her toward him, slipping his arms around her waist and gazing down at her with eyes the color of the night. "This woman."

His kiss was tender yet resonant with desire, and Anna felt the ground underneath her disappear as her arms slid up around his neck and he drew her yet closer to his body. Her lips parted under his gentle pressure, and she tasted the warmth of his tears and anger and love in the touch of his mouth and hands as she responded to his emotion with her own deep need. When he drew away, she opened eyes she had not realized she had closed and looked up questioningly into his smoldering gaze.

"This is not because of the things you told me to—"

"This is because I love you, and have loved you for longer than you can know," he replied, stroking her cheek with the backs of his fingers with a tenderness that robbed her of breath. He was smiling, but there was a tension to the edges of the mouth that was still so close to hers.

"You must not blame yourself for what happened," she replied softly but earnestly, interpreting his look. Her fingers twined deliciously in the curling locks of hair at the nape of his neck. "I cannot blame you, knowing the truth."

The earl's hand stilled on her face. "But there is a truth you do not yet know, Anna, and for it you may truly despise me." His voice was low and intense of a sudden. Anna looked into eyes that made her heart swim with love, and she opened her mouth to speak, but his fingers over her lips stopped her.

"I need to tell you—"

"The supper bell has just been rung, and I think it might be noted were one of the guests of honor not found when everyone thinks to look for her," came a voice from a few yards away in the lighted area of the terrace.

Anna sprang away from the earl as he released her instantly, but he retained her hand in his, holding it tightly. Louisa Masterson looked upon the couple she had caught embracing, noting the earl's straight shoulders and taut expression, her niece's bright eyes and high color, and was satisfied.

"Mrs. Masterson, I wish to—"

"Yes, yes, I'm certain you do, my lord. And you shall, undoubtedly," she said with a grin, interrupting the earl once again. "But for now you two must hurry into the ballroom before you are missed. Everything else can be discussed later." She turned and moved toward the open French doors. "Come now, Anna. His lordship will follow us directly and will take us both in to supper—if he wishes it, that is," she added, looking back to the startled couple with a chuckle.

Valentine bowed. "I could wish nothing more, ma'am," he said and released Anna's hand. She looked back at him, her smile, warm and entirely loving, filling him with desire all over again. He must speak with her tonight, he vowed as he followed the ladies into the light, before she learned to fully trust through love a man who had only deceived her from the very start.

EIGHTEEN

The engagement of Lucinda Greeley and Mr. Pendleton was announced after supper in the ball-room. The guests raised champagne-filled glasses to the blushing couple, and the two young lovers led the next set together. Pleading a needed rest from dancing, Anna excused herself from her partner and remained with her aunt and several of Mrs. Masterson's friends at the edge of the dance floor. The women conversed pleasantly, and Anna waited with impatient glee for Lord Alverston to return from the silly errand her aunt had sent him on after the announcement. She suspected that her aunt thought it would not be bad for the two to be apart for a few minutes, at least for public appearances.

As she absently watched her golden-haired friends pirouette about the dance floor together, Anna admitted to herself that her aunt might be wise after all, however much she disliked the lady's tactics. She had felt entirely unlike herself all throughout supper, sitting between the earl and her aunt, struggling to make pleasant conversation with the company around them and all the while feeling as if she wanted to jump up onto the table and dance, or alternately allow herself to swoon into a hazy dream state of happiness. She had scarcely eaten a bite.

Mrs. Greeley had commented on her odd humor

and fevered look, and had asked her if she was feeling
well enough, which had brought an even brighter
flush to Anna's already very pink cheeks. She had responded to the query with a cough and a few not
entirely coherent words. Lord Alverston—*Drat his teasing!*—gallantly offered her his handkerchief. Their
hands touched briefly in the exchange, his eyes laughing down at her, and Anna had dissolved this time
into a real fit of coughing as she choked on her lemonade. She had felt her aunt's slippered toes gently
crush her own under the table for an uncomfortable
moment, and she'd stifled a gasp.

That was when Louisa Masterson had suddenly remembered that she had forgotten to remind the butler to perform some small but essential task before
the end of the night, and would my lord be so kind
as to carry her message to the man after the dancing
resumed? The earl practically ran tame in the house,
being such a good friend of the family, after all. Mrs.
Greeley looked a bit queerly at her friend, Anna
dropped her guilty gaze to the table, and Lord Alverston replied graciously that certainly he would assist
his hostess in any way that she wished. The other
guests at the table shrugged off the odd request as a
familiarity born of the young man's long acquaintance
with Mrs. Masterson and her husband.

Anna supposed she was glad now of the momentary
respite from being in Lord Alverston's presence. Her
nerves were still singing with glee and something akin
to anticipation, but at least she had recovered some
of her sanity and was able to breathe and speak with
an aspect of normalcy. Her wits had gone quite thoroughly astray after the earl's declaration of his feelings for her and that marvelous, earth-shattering kiss
on the terrace. Part of her, a very tiny part of her,
albeit, was scolding herself for being such a ninnyhammer; the other—the lion's share—part was wish-

ing the earl would get back to them right away so she could again feel that terrible almost physical longing to be in his arms instead of standing right next to him not touching.

He loved her! Anna still could not quite believe it was true. How had it happened? How could it be real? Even in her dreams she had never imagined it could have happened this way. Why, they barely knew each other! For sure, Anna knew quite a bit *about* him from Valerie's stories of growing up, told during their girlhoods spent together, and from the bits and pieces of information that had come Anna's way this past year or so in her friend's letters. But he could know little of her, and Anna could not believe he had had the time or the inclination in the countryside to listen to his sister's stories about an old childhood friend he probably did not even remember.

Anna found it hard enough to believe that he had fallen in love with her in the short time they had known each other. It was, she supposed rather dreamily, a miracle that could only happen when two people met and looked into each other's eyes. His eyes had unarguably made their message clear to her, on the terrace and again before he had gone off to take care of her aunt's request. She believed him. However previously unimaginable it was, however unlikely or even inappropriate given their vastly different social statuses, it seemed that the earl felt for her what Anna felt for him.

Lost in contemplation of this fabulously realized impossibility, she was unaware of Lord Alverston's approach until he was standing next to her again. All at once, Anna's heart began to pound furiously, and she felt her mouth curving into an irrepressible smile. She chanced a glance up at him, and was rewarded with the tender expression in his warm gray eyes.

"Our host has requested that another dance be

added to the roster this very moment," he said, turning to the ladies around him. "It seems that the newly betrothed pair are not content with their celebratory country dance, but are insisting upon a waltz to crown their happiness together." He turned to Anna then. "May I take advantage of this unexpected boon and escort you onto the floor, Miss Tremain?"

"Thank you, my lord; I am honored." Anna put her trembling hand into Lord Alverston's outstretched one, and he swept her into his arms as the opening strains of the waltz filled the sparkling room. Anna forgot to be nervous or scatterbrained or tongue-tied as the earl drew her a bit closer to himself than was customary, and fitting his hand to the small of her back, whirled her into the dance. Unaccountably shy about meeting his eyes in this intimate position, she let her gaze roam over the rest of his face and rich, curling hair.

"You are beautiful tonight, Anna, as always," he whispered so that only she could hear, and she smiled unashamedly.

"I was just thinking the same thing, my lord, of you." Her grin was playful, her eyes sincere. His hand grasped hers more firmly yet as he guided her about the floor effortlessly.

"Perhaps you might consider changing the 'my lord' to something more familiar?" he asked hopefully. Anna looked up into his smiling eyes, the music swelling around them, her skin hot where he touched her and her body humming with sensation. She opened her mouth to speak and was halted by the intensity of his look. The earl's gaze warmed even more, and he bent his mouth to her ear for a moment.

"You must not tempt me so, Anna," he whispered. She tried to pull back to see his expression, but he held her near. "Your lips parted like that are an invitation that I—notwithstanding that I am a gentleman—cannot for long ignore." His voice was low, yet he was smiling. Anna breathed a sigh of pleasure as the thrill of his words swirled through her.

"My lor— Valentine," she responded quietly, laughing despite herself, "you are putting me to the blush quite shamelessly."

"I wish to put you to many other things shamelessly, my love," he said, his tone a mixture of teasing and intensity, and Anna's heart turned over in her breast at the glittering look in his charcoal eyes. She smiled tremulously, trying to gather her wits amidst the sudden spiraling of her own desire. "But first we must talk." His eyes held hers, and Anna nodded wordlessly, somehow suddenly afraid.

"Tonight?" she asked, feeling her joy pierced by a prick of fear.

"It is your ball . . ." Valentine let his words trail off, wishing with all of his soul that he could tell her now and have it over with, but knowing that he should not, that he could not ruin the happiness of her celebration, quench the joy he saw sparkling in her eyes, with his confession this night.

She must know as soon as possible, he vowed, and his heart clenched within him at thinking of how her trust in him would be entirely destroyed when she did finally learn of his betrayal. Valentine was torn between needing her to know immediately and knowing that he could simply not tell her during the ball. Whatever her reaction, it would not be fair to tell her the truth of the letters while she stood amidst those of Society she knew in Town, the people in this house tonight for her sake and Lucinda's. He could not know how she would react—he still did not even know if she loved him!—but he would not expose her in that way to the prying eyes and gossiping tongues of the *ton*. Putting aside his own burning emotion now, Valentine made a decision.

"Tomorrow, then. May I call upon you in the morning?" In his brief silence, Anna had watched his face turn from open and warm to worried . . . or something much worse, which she could not read. She could not imagine what it was he had to tell her, what news was so important that he could not share it with her now.

"Yes, of course, I will be waiting, my lo—" she stumbled on the unbidden word, and then raised her clear eyes fully to his, wishing with all of her heart that she could will away the disquiet in his. "My love."

She watched the sparks ignite in the earl's dark eyes as his lips curved into a wide smile and his arms drew her closer still. Anna felt his thumb caress the palm of her hand through her glove, and wondered only fleetingly whether anyone else in the crowded ballroom was taking note of their scandalously close embrace. Then she lost herself to everything but the sweet, lilting music and the man holding her closely in his beloved arms.

"Anna? Anna, are you awake? May I come in?"

The scratching at the door was Lucinda's, and the soft voice was high. Anna, who had been lying in her canopied bed in a dreaming half-sleep for hours it seemed, turned over and sat up, spilling the soft covers around her waist. Morning sunlight streamed through the tall window of her bedchamber, heralding an unusually brilliant spring day. She stretched herself luxuriously and her mouth opened in a smile filled with all of the joy and happiness that was welling up inside of her. Her dreams had been sweeter than she could ever remember.

"Yes," she said on a smiling yawn, "I am awake."

The painted paneled door opened and Lucinda entered, wearing a yellow muslin gown sprigged with

green embroidery, and followed by a maid carrying
a tray laden with toast and chocolate. There were two
cups on the tray. Lucinda's own face was bright,
though she appeared somewhat sleepy-eyed as she approached the bed and sat down on the side of it.

"I have brought breakfast for both of us, darling,"
she said, gesturing to the tray. "I could not eat when
I awoke, but Mama tells me I am not to lose any
weight due to my new sleeplessness and lack of appe-
tite." She poured out chocolate for both of them and
handed a cup to Anna, then looked at her friend over
the rim of her cup with guileless green eyes. "I told
her that since I have not yet been fitted for my bridal
gown, it does not signify in the least."

Anna chuckled and reached over to grasp Lucinda
by the hands. "I am so very glad for you and Jason,
my dear. Congratulations on your great happiness."
She looked down with little interest at the contents
of the breakfast tray, but accepted a cup of chocolate
out of courtesy. As she lifted the cup from the tray,
a letter sitting upon it and wedged underneath the
toast plate caught her eye. She reached for the envelope, but Lucinda snatched it away.

"Oh! I wanted to give this to you right away, but I
am so distracted, I almost forgot." The blond-haired
girl clasped the letter close to her for a moment,
gauging her friend's interest. "It is addressed to you,
but you will never guess where from, and I am simply
green with envy that you have received something
from such a faraway place."

Anna's brow furrowed slightly, but she could not
be provoked by Lucinda's teasing. She was so filled
with a warm, constant happiness that nothing could
alter her mood or shake her peacefulness this morning. Not even a letter from an exotic location. She
held out her hand, palm up, and waited.

Lucinda drew the letter away from her breast and

looked at it again before handing it into her friend's grasp. She could not resist saying in a breathy voice as Anna looked at the direction on the cover and the frank marks, "America!"

Perplexed, Anna turned over the letter to see if there was any clue on the outside of it as to the sender. Lucinda bounced impatiently on the bed. "Open it, for goodness sake! I must know who has written to you from America, you fortunate thing!"

Anna picked up a butter knife and gently slid the letter open, unfolding several pages of thick writing paper crossed and recrossed with a not-so-neat and rather light hand. She knew no one in America, she thought as she filed through the pages to the end. Her eyes lit on the signature and opened wide in surprise. It was signed simply *Valerie*.

Ruffling through the pages, Anna looked for a monogram on the paper, but found only an unfamiliar mark at the top of each page embossed into the stationery. Lucinda, who sat restlessly waiting, could take the suspense no longer.

"Anna! Who is it from? Do you have a relative, or perhaps an admirer in America? How exciting!" Her voice was animated.

Trust Lucinda to invest a simple letter with all the romance in her young heart, thought Anna as she shook her head and turned again to the first page.

"No, dear. Nothing so fabulous, although I am happy to have it. It is a letter from my friend, Valerie."

Lucinda eyed Anna, who looked up with doelike eyes that were not entirely focused on the present.

"Is she not the sister of Lord Alverston?" she asked in a leading tone, peering at Anna from beneath gold lashes. Anna felt her cheeks redden, and she laid the letter down onto her lap. Picking up her cup of chocolate, she took a sip, trying not to smile too broadly.

"Yes, indeed she is. She and I have been friends since we were children. I am certain I have told you about her." Anna avoided Lucinda's curiously knowing gaze.

"But you have not told me about the earl, and I am dying to hear!" Lucinda made another little sitting hop on the bed. "I may only have had eyes for Jason last night, but I am not blind." She giggled. "And neither were our guests! There was enough speculation after supper last night about the two of you to raise a balloon in Vauxhall Gardens!" Anna met the question in Lucinda's eyes, her own bright with mirrored happiness. "Do tell me, you secretive girl!"

"Secretive!" Anna said in laughing astonishment. Now that all seemed settled to everyone's mutual joy, she no longer felt any anxiety over her friend's former flirtation with the earl. "Why, I had no idea that you felt so strongly about Jason, Lucinda! I was almost as surprised as the next person when you revealed your feelings for him to us all," she countered, "although I had suspected his affection for you for some time. I knew you admired him, but I also knew you admired the earl. And you were spending quite a bit of time with the latter up until the very moment Jason declared himself, if I am not mistaken." Anna's tone was questioning.

Lucinda smiled demurely, but Anna spied a hint of guilty pleasure in her expression. The girl glanced away from her friend as if interested in what was going on outside the window.

"I do indeed admire Lord Alverston, Anna, but we are simply good friends. He has been very kind to me, and I have been glad to have his company." Then she looked again at Anna. "I love Jason, though. The feeling is an entirely different one from mere admiration. Is it not?"

Anna's face again grew warm, and she dropped her eyes, smiling. "Yes, I must agree with you on that." She looked up to see Lucinda beaming at her, a grin as wide as her rosebud lips would stretch brightening her already rosy face.

"And you will not tell me all about it?" she demanded playfully.

Anna was unaccountably reluctant to share any of the details of her newly found happiness with her friend just yet. She paused, not knowing how to tell Lucinda this gracefully, but the younger girl saved her from making the attempt.

"My darling, I can see that you are uncomfortable with my curiosity." Lucinda patted Anna's hand in an almost motherly way, and stood up from the bed. "I *am* eager to hear about whatever it is that is going on between you and the earl, and I can only surmise that it must be honorable and genuine, by the look of the two of you last night. But I will pry no further today."

She moved toward the door. "I will leave you alone with your enviable letter from America, and hope to see you soon in the parlor. I expect to be getting a visit from my betrothed this morning." She looked back significantly, a grin on her lips. "Perhaps another caller will make an appearance sometime today as well." Then she was gone.

Anna stared after her, seeing not the closed door of her room but a sensuously curved mouth, stormy eyes, and sable locks. She sighed. She still could barely believe that man, that breathtakingly handsome, warm, intelligent, thoughtful and entirely masculine man loved *her.* It seemed like a dream that she would awake from if she but opened her eyes.

But her eyes were already open, Anna thought smilingly and with deep satisfaction as she placed her cup on the silver tray before her and again took up the letter from America. She knew she must get dressed and make herself presentable soon. Her blood stirred with excitement at the thought of Lord Alverston's impending visit, despite a little tremor of concern over his soberness last night with regard to the mystery he was to reveal to her. There was little left of the morning, happily; he would undoubtedly arrive soon. But Anna could not resist the lure of Valerie's letter.

America! It was more of a surprise than it should have been, she thought as she unfolded the pages again and spread them before her. Valerie was always doing outrageous things, or at least she had been in the habit of doing them before her short Season in London two years ago and her subsequent rustication at the Hall. Anna's eyes scanned the unpretty missive, then sought the salutation, and she prepared to have her questions answered.

February
Boston, Massachusetts

Dearest Anna,

It has been so very long since I have seen you or corresponded with you—so long that I am beginning to forget even the tone of your voice and the loving smile in your pretty brown eyes. I beg your forgiveness from the very opening of this letter, because it is I who have been remiss, who have been an untrue friend, a selfish wretch. I hope that by the time you have finished reading this letter, you will understand my behavior. I can only hope you will remain my friend, even as so many others have not. You were ever constant and always forgiving of my transgressions. I pray that this two-year-long silence of mine has not been a transgression that you will find unforgivable.

Anna's brow furrowed in confusion. She looked again at the date at the top of the page and blinked her eyes as if to clear her vision.

Two-year-long silence? Her heart fluttered in apprehension. Perhaps something had happened to Valerie, maybe even to her mind, to make her imagine that they had not been corresponding this past year and more. She had heard of such things happening, after an accident or an emotional shock such as the deaths of Valerie's father and brother would have caused. Anna's eyes met the page this time timorously.

As you will see by the frank, I write to you from America. By the time you receive this letter, I will hopefully be sailing across the Atlantic on a packet bound for Dover, and will soon set foot on the shores of my beloved England.

As I write, however, I am sitting in my room in the house of my cousins Denbridge and Margaret Penbarrow, in Boston, Massachusetts. From my writing table I can hear the now familiar call of the gulls flying over the bay not too far from our house. It is a charming neighborhood, a charming if rather small city. The Americans I know are quite friendly and amusingly proud. Boston is a fine place; I am glad to have come here.

But I will not bother you with insignificant details. I will come straight to my explanation and hope my pen will prove more eloquent than ever it has before.

You may remember that my cousin Margaret served as chaperone for me during my Season two years ago in London. She and Denbridge travel back and forth across the ocean rather frequently, for business and because my mother's family still resides in Britain. They had agreed to host my come-out in Town, and Margaret took it upon herself to find me a suitable husband under the distant scrutiny of the Earl, who remained at the Hall during this time. You will likely remember all of this.

For the first few weeks I was in Town, I enjoyed it immensely. Every day that passed brought new gaieties and a new dozen faces who over the course of many activities together became friends. I wrote in my journal daily of the people I met, the conversations I had, the adventures I dreamed up with my new circle of intimates. I wrote thinking of you, Anna, imagining your reaction to my anecdotes as I put them in ink. I intended to share this journal with you during the summer; my father had intimated to me that if my time in London passed without incident, I might invite you to spend the summer with me at the Hall, and every day I wrote with our long, lazy summer in mind, excited to share with you all of the adventures I was having and the people I was meeting.

Woe that I ever imagined a happy outcome to that wretched Season!

As you warned me before I ventured into London, too soon I became bored—worse, exhausted!—with the inanity of the activities and of the people I met. I valued some few of my friendships, but these were not enough to keep my mind from dwelling on the foolishness and vanity of all the rest of it. Cousin Margaret— bless her soul!—did all in her power to amuse me, yet after a time I—spoilt girl!—could think of nothing but going home or visiting you in ____shire. I wrote to the earl and begged him to allow me to end my Season prematurely. He told me that I was acting like a child and that he expected me to behave like a lady and find myself a husband before the Season was out. So I proceeded to do so.

I met Paolo at a ball a week later. He was the vio-

linist in the ensemble, and I fancied myself in love with him from the moment he looked at me. He was really more your sort of man, Anna, if truth be told, and if you will forgive me for making light of this. Soulful dark eyes and dark hair; not at all what I usually find attractive. Quite exotic, however . . . and quite inappropriate. We made an assignation to meet at Vauxhall Gardens the very next night. I never doubted he would be there.

He was, and after being seen by not one but three *of the patronesses at Almack's (who were members of the same supper party there together) alone in his company, I eloped with him in a hired chaise. We got as far as the Great North Road before Paolo strained his bow hand repairing a broken wheel spoke, I changed my mind about marrying in such haste, and Denbridge and two of his cronies caught up with us. Paolo hastily withdrew from the scene, and I wished him a fond but not heartbroken good-bye. I was taken back to London in disgrace.*

Within days it was clear that all of the ton *knew of my escapade and that I was entirely unwelcome among the* beau monde *any longer. I did not care too much for the general censure, but when I appealed to those whom I had thought were my true friends, they also turned their backs on me. This last cut my heart sorely, Anna, but the worst was to come: The Earl wrote from the Hall that he had had enough of me. Denbridge and Margaret were shortly to return to America, and I was to go with them, in exile from not only the Society that had rejected me, but from a father who no longer had any love left in his heart for me.*

My dear Anna, I will not tell you of the wretched journey I made across the Atlantic, full of the knowledge that my parent wished no more to look on my face or even hear my name mentioned. He forbade me to contact any one from my former acquaintances. He withheld from me any correspondence that I received. He wished me dead, I think, rather than to have to think of me and remember the shame that I had caused him for so long. I believe if the ship had gone down somewhere before we reached the Back Bay, he would have mourned my cousins and shed no tears at all for me.

I was in Boston for no more than a few months before I received the news from my brother that the Earl and James had perished in a carriage accident. I was filled with remorse, Anna, and now that my behavior no longer mattered, I suffered bitterly over the years I had wasted in childishness. I could barely face what I had done to the Earl. Valentine wrote that I must come home and make our family together with him, but I refused. I wrote back to my brother telling him I wished to have nothing to do with anything from my past, and could not return. Nonetheless, he continued to write to me every few weeks, though I did not respond to any of his letters. Some I could not even open when I received them. My misery and feelings of guilt were profound.

My cousins bore with me through this new stage of childishness, were unfailingly kind, and encouraged me to go into Society again. Eventually I did so, but still with no feeling for it or for my own happiness. Almost two years passed thus.

Several months ago a time came when I began to see that in rejecting England, my brother and our family—and you, Anna, my most cherished and constant friend—I was only continuing the selfish game I had played for so long. I am not certain when I decided that I must finally grow up, but there did come a moment, or a series of moments, when I found myself longing for home and the life I had left. Margaret has been a gentle tutor during this period, and I have spent a great deal of time—you will be astounded!—in church.

I am finally ready to go home again. I wrote to Valentine just yesterday of my decision, and hesitated in writing to you only long enough to sleep.

My dearest Anna, my sister, my friend, I hope you will somehow find it in your heart to forgive me for the wrong I have done to my family and to you. As you well know, I am not rich as you are in the ability to explain what I am thinking or feeling, or why. I can only hope that my story will serve this purpose, and that your kind and generous heart will do the rest. If I am restored to your favor upon my return, and if my brother will accept me again into our home after these months of silence from me, I will have all that I can ever wish for again in this lifetime.

I will write to you when I have reached England and home. Until then, I remain always,

> *Your loving friend,*
> *Valerie*

NINETEEN

When Anna emerged back into her own world from that of the letter she read, she was standing by the empty hearth in her room, staring at the painting above it with sightless eyes. She held the pages of Valerie's letter loosely in her chilled hands. Shaking her head to restore herself, she moved away from the fireplace and sat down on a chair by her bed.

What could it all mean? This letter from her friend was genuine, must be genuine. The story was not so incredible when one knew Lady Valerie well, not in the least. Anna even found herself smiling amidst her immeasurable dismay at reading of Valerie's infatuation with the Italian violinist; it was so very much what that girl might actually do, given the opportunity, never mind that it was absolutely awful and had led to her friend's immediate banishment from England! The scenes in this farce-tragedy all fit together, but it was as if they were of another play entirely than the one Anna herself had been acting in these past two years.

She stood up and once again paced over to the fireplace, leaving the letter behind on the bedside table. An incident flickered in her memory, something that she had heard, if only she could remember . . .

Yes! Certainly! That evening not too long ago when she had overheard Lady Chetham conversing with a friend. She had wondered at their condemnation of Valerie over what Anna had then imagined must have been a minor indiscretion. They had had unkind words for the sister while extolling the virtues of the brother, as Anna recalled now. She remembered having felt irritated with Lord Alverston for allowing Valerie to remain cooped up in the countryside when she would be much happier, Anna thought, enjoying the sights and activities of Town instead.

Anna's eyes widened slowly.

The earl must certainly have known all along that his sister was in America. Indeed, Valerie had herself written so in her letter. Anna searched her memory for everything Lord Alverston had said about his sister over the course of the past few weeks in London. She was briefly comforted to recollect that he had not on any occasion actually misrepresented Valerie's location or occupation; he had always spoken of her spirits or state of mind, rather than of her situation.

Anna felt a heaviness in her middle and a creeping uneasiness stole over her. He may not have told her lies, but he had certainly not told her the truth. She could understand his decision to respect his sister's desire to be left alone in America, to be cut off entirely from her own world of English Society; but she could not necessarily like it, or agree with it.

Somehow, Anna did not know how, Lord Alverston should have done something more for Valerie. He should have forced her to return home to those who loved and cared for her, to those who could help her to regain some of her joy of life and to let go of the guilt with which she was torturing herself. Twisting her hands before her, Anna supposed that he would have, had he not been battling with his own pain and guilt. With compassion for the man she had only so recently realized she loved, Anna thought that the past two years had not been any easier for him than for his sister, after all, and perhaps worse. He had had his own healing to see to . . .

Her head turned slowly to the side, and her eyes went to the letter lying on the table by her bed. Suddenly trembling, she moved by slow steps across the room to where the pages lay and gazed down at them with wide eyes.

Words and phrases crossed and recrossed the paper in thin, unsteady characters, sentences punctuated with only the minimum of expression. Anna reached down fearfully to the table and, as if suddenly afraid to touch them, brushed aside the top pages to reveal the signature on the bottom of the final sheet. *Valerie.* The name was written out full, in tall, rounded letters.

Closing her eyes, Anna took a deep breath, filling her lungs, and let it out very slowly. Then she turned and, her dressing gown whispering against her legs, walked over to her writing table and pulled open a small drawer, revealing a stack of neatly folded letters bound with a satin ribbon. Her face a mask of blankness, she slid the top letter out of the ribbon and opened it mechanically with cold fingers. Then she let her eyes confirm again what she already knew.

The letters had not been written by the same person. They had not been written by Valerie.

Anna had let herself believe that Valerie's Town maturation had somehow miraculously improved her penmanship. She had had no reason to think otherwise. There had been no reason to imagine that the person writing to her as Valerie was not in fact that lady herself. Now, gazing down upon the neat rows of firmly written script, Anna wondered how she could have been so foolish. Valerie's handwriting had remained the same; she simply had not written to Anna in two years, as she had stated in her letter from America. Someone else had.

The knowledge that had come to her was almost

too much for Anna to bear, and she put her trembling palms on the surface of the writing table and
leaned against it, staring down at the whiteness of her
knuckles on the wood. Her breath caught. Lying on
the desk, not a finger's length from her hands, was
a calling card, the one that had been attached to the
roses the earl had sent Anna just yesterday before the
ball. She had taken it up before finally falling into
bed in the early hours of the morning, to look at it
again, to hold it to her cheek and imagine again the
magic of his kiss and the way his eyes had looked so
lovingly into hers. Now, lying face down, the note written in the earl's hand stared up at her, the script firm
yet unfamiliar. But what made her heart grow numb,
slowly and thickly, was the signature.

The earl had not taken care to disguise his own
name, it seemed. It was written exactly as it had been
in every letter she had received over the past months
from Alverston Hall, except that in her letters he had
shortened it to his nickname. Anna had heard his
friend the viscount call him thus on countless occasions: Val. Everything about those three letters was
identical between the card and the letter lying open
before her. Everything about those three letters filled
her with a coldness and, unaccountably, a fear that
took hold of her so suddenly she found herself sitting
on the floor, her entire body trembling, her hands
covering her face as if to ward away the truth.

It was impossible, unaccountable! Why would he
have done it? He had known nothing of her before;
they had not met except that one time so very many
years ago. Why would he have perpetrated this charade? Had it been some kind of joke, some terrible
prank played by a wealthy and bored young man to
rouse himself from his unhappiness after the war? It
could not be! Anna's heart and head cried out to her

in confusion. All that she knew of the earl was not consistent with this explanation.

Her eyes flew open.

But she knew so much more of him than ever she had imagined! He had written all of those letters, all of the precious letters that she had cherished so greatly these past months, that she had read over and over again until the pages were fragile with use. He had written of himself, his life at Alverston Hall. He had told her obliquely of his sadness, his grief, and eventually his healing. He had been her confidant, had read her stories, had laughed with her over so many things. He had shared with her his ideas and had encouraged her in hers. God almighty, he had read all about her infatuation with Jason Pendleton and all of her attendant foolishness!

Anna's face grew hot with shame, and she raised her hands to cover her open mouth.

How could he have done it? How could he have done such a thing and then made love to her the way he had last night? How could he have betrayed her so, before he knew her, and then afterward, when he had supposedly come to love her?

His words of only a few hours before came back to her with painful intelligence now. He had loved her for longer than she could have known, he had said. She had thought it romantic flattery, had not questioned it. He had told her that she would despise him were she to know the truth, and he had tried to tell her, had been about to tell her. . . .

Anna lifted dry eyes, unable to cry in the depth of her grief, and gazed out the window at the brilliant morning outside. How would she have reacted if he had told her last night? How would she receive him today with this knowledge already hers? What could he say that would erase the hurt and betrayal that filled her heart now, pushing out all of the new, fragile love she had been feeling? How was she to look into his dark eyes today and see not the gaze of a friend and lover, but that of a stranger instead?

For with one awful revelation he had become a stranger, a stranger who knew her soul perhaps better than anyone else in the world, but whom she knew suddenly not at all.

Valentine suspected that he did not know himself very well after all.

Walk? Why had he decided to walk to Field Street? Was he mad? He berated himself for his foolish choice of transportation this morning as his feet moved him not rapidly enough along the tree-lined streets and away from his Mayfair address.

He had thought walking would calm his nerves, work out some of the anxiousness he was feeling in anticipation of the interview he was about to have with Anna. He had not considered that it would be added agony to travel toward the Greelys' address at such a frustratingly slow pace. And where was a blasted hackney coach when a fellow needed one?

Searching up and down the street for a conveyance, Valentine did not notice the three finely dressed men strolling down the stairs of a house not far ahead of him. The trio stopped at the foot of the steps, two of them whispering to each other, and the gentleman in front moved out into the walkway. Not looking ahead of himself, Valentine almost ran into the man, but for his silver-tipped walking stick that struck the man's highly polished boot first. He looked up sharply, his expression distracted but apologetic.

"In a hurry, my lord, yet on foot?" The voice of the Marquess of Drysden was smooth, almost insolent.

Valentine did not bow, but he paused, unwilling to directly cut his onetime friend in front of the other two gentlemen. He vaguely recognized them as members of London's dandy set.

"Excuse me, gentlemen. Yes, I am," he said, and began to move around the stationary group.

"Ah, perverse as ever, I see." The words came from behind him as he moved away. "A man peculiarly fond of doing things the wrong way."

Valentine's feet came to a halt, though his mind told him to continue on. Drysden's companions were chuckling behind him, as he turned slowly to face the three men again.

"I do not understand you, sir," he said, his voice icy. "Please make yourself clear in what you mean to say, if you will." He watched as the marquess looked to his two companions and, as if he had all the time in the world to pass, took a silver snuff case out of his pocket and opened it.

"I simply mean to note that one might achieve greater success in an endeavor if one did not always choose to act alone, without the assistance of others." Drysden took a pinch of snuff between his fingers, lifted it to his nostril, and sniffed. He closed the case and dropped it casually into his coat pocket. The high-collared gentlemen on either side of him were sniggering without any attempt at subtlety. Valentine looked at the three of them, imagined Anna's face before him, and relaxed his clenched fists.

"I will not be baited, Andrew," he said in cool, even tones. "You and I know the truth. Say what you will, spread what rumors you wish. Only fools will listen to you."

"Now see here, sir," began one of the dandies, but Drysden cut him off.

"Fools, you say?" The marquess raised an eyebrow. "And what of the lovely Miss Tremain, my lord earl? Is she a fool, as you so rashly suggest?"

Valentine's spine stiffened and his mouth went dry.

"You sully her name by speaking it, Drysden," he ground out. "The lady has nothing to do with this."

"Oh, doesn't she?" The marquess brushed his fingertips on his lapel and looked down as if to study them. "Last evening it seemed she did." His voice was mocking.

"She is none of your business." A pulse beat in Valentine's temple as he sought to maintain his calm.

The marquess looked up sharply, a silken smile curled around his lips. "Since last night I have decided to make her my business, Alverston."

Valentine's control dissolved. He barely knew what he did as he hurled himself at the other man, grabbing Drysden's cravat with his left hand and driving his right fist into the marquess's jaw with all the force of the rage inside him. The marquess's head snapped back and he fell to the ground as the earl let go of him and stepped away. The other two men gaped in astonishment and then began to laugh. One of them withdrew a handkerchief from his pocket and handed it with exaggerated delicacy to the marquess, who leaned upon one elbow and bared bloody teeth to the earl.

"You will pay for this!" he spat out furiously, glancing from his mirthful companions to Valentine. "Name your second!"

Valentine did not move to assist the marquess to his feet, but looked at him in wonderment and disdain. "I will not. I have seen enough killing to never want to bear a weapon again for as long as I live."

"Coward!" Drysden spat out, climbing to his feet without the assistance of either of his friends. He took in the earl's still but ready form, his expression of thinly veiled anger, and did not move toward him. His words were, Valentine thought much later, admirably free of the tone of bravado. "You will meet me, or be counted more of a coward and fool than you already are."

"He's got that right, Alverston," spoke up one of the gentleman standing behind the marquess. He was sporting a yellow and orange-striped waistcoat and had a quizzing glass wedged in his left eye, his long finely gloved fingers wrapped daintily around its ivory and gold stem. "Heard the Duke of Manchester hi'self yesterday saying something about the like of it, if I do recall correctly."

"I couldn't care less what you recall, man," Valentine said with impatience, "nor what the entire *ton* thinks of me."

"But what about what they think of your Miss Tremain, my lord?" whispered Drysden slyly from between lips that were beginning to swell slightly. "Do you think she will remain unaffected by the censure that comes your way?" The marquess narrowed blue eyes at Valentine and saw that he had hit his mark. "She will be spurned as thoroughly as you when your cowardice is broadcast, as if she herself were equally to blame for your—"

"Enough!" Valentine said as his insides churned within him at what he was doing. "You have won, Drysden." He struggled for a breath. "To which one of these"—he paused, gesturing—"*gentle*men shall I send my envoy to arrange matters?" The earl was barely aware of the puffing-up of affront evident on the faces of both of the marquess's companions, so lost was he in grim contemplation of the task he had set himself for the morrow.

"Fostingly will attend me. He can be found at King Street," Drysden wiped gingerly at the blood on his lip, and then stilled as Valentine turned to leave. "You will not default?" he called after him.

The earl turned and stared at him with eyes gray and haunted in the shadows of the tree-lined street.

"No, Andrew. Because of you, my killing is not yet finished." He turned again, and strode quickly up the street.

Valentine stood straight before the Viscount Bramfield, awaiting his friend's reply. His dark eyes were hooded.

"Of course I will stand for you, my friend. You need not have wondered."

The earl nodded grimly. "I thank you, Tim."

Timothy Ramsay circled the desk he was standing behind and approached his friend as Valentine reached down to pick up his hat and cane from the chair on which he had left them. The morning was wasting away, first with the encounter with Drysden and now with having to detour in the opposite direction from Field Street in order to make certain his best friend would serve as second for him in the cursed duel on the morrow. He had not even left his hat with the butler when the old man had opened the door, but had strode directly into Timothy's study upon learning that his friend was there. He was in a hurry to be on his way to Anna's house finally.

"Valentine, wait!" the viscount called out. "We need to talk. There is much to be arranged."

Valentine turned, painfully impatient but controlling himself for the sake of his friend. "I am expected elsewhere, Tim. I must be going."

The viscount furrowed his brow. "You are going to Field Street, aren't you?" he said. Valentine nodded slowly and Bramfield shook his head. "You must not, my friend. You are in no condition to see her now; take my word for it." He gestured to the mirror over the hearth, and Valentine followed his friend's gaze to his own reflection. He saw the tension and distraction written clear across his face.

He resisted.

"She is expecting me, Tim. I cannot disappoint her this morning. It is nearly too late already to make a morning call." He looked at the clock on the mantel.

"And tomorrow it will be too late altogether for her *and* you if you do not stop and think about your responsibilities right now," the viscount said firmly, his fair-skinned face a handsome mask of concern.

"Do you know if you have all of your affairs in order, Val? What if Drysden kills you tomorrow, or wounds you gravely? Are you prepared for that?" he said, none too gently. "Are you certain that Valerie is provided for, and your servants, your tenants, should you not return alive from your appointment in the morning? You are a young man. Are you certain of the provisions of your will?" Seeing that his words were having an effect on his friend, he sat down in a chair and gestured for the earl to do the same.

"Have you considered what a serious thing this is that you are doing, Val, what your responsibilities are? You have no heir, and you would die on account of an illegal duel. What position will your sister and es- tates be in if that should happen?" Timothy paused. "You are not thinking straight, my friend," he said in a gentle voice, and Valentine lowered himself into a chair in front of the cold fireplace.

Finally, the earl looked at his friend with distant, smoky eyes.

"I am thinking only of her, Tim."

Timothy Ramsay felt a lump rising in his throat, and swallowed. "I know you are," he responded. "And I am here to help you think of the rest."

A few moments passed in silence. Then Valentine set his hat and cane aside and ran a hand over his face as if to clear his mind of lingering confusion and distraction. When he spoke his voice was clear, defi- nite.

"I need to write a message," he said. "May I ask one of your men to deliver it immediately to the Greeley house?"

The viscount let out a breath of air, nodded, and stood up to procure the needed paper and ink.

"She will not come out, nor will she invite me to come in. I am afraid there is something dreadfully wrong, Mama." Lucinda's voice was a near whisper as she stood in the hallway not far from Anna's door and spoke to her parent. Samantha Greeley nodded in worry and drew her fidgeting daughter down the hall to the stairs leading to the ground floor.

"And you say this began after you brought her breakfast and the letter from America?" the older woman asked in still-hushed tones, even though they were now descending the steps to the lower level.

Lucinda nodded. "She said the letter was from her friend Valerie, the earl's sister, though why Lady Valerie was writing from America she did not explain." The two stopped at the foot of the stairway. "I think, Mama, that she was expecting a call from the earl himself this morning." Her voice was tremulous, as if she herself had been jilted, not simply her friend. Mrs. Greeley touched her daughter's worried face affectionately with her hand.

"You are a kindhearted girl, my Lucy, to feel so acutely for your friend," she said fondly, but then her smile faded. "He did not come, of course," she stated. "It seemed last night as if everything was settled. Louisa said as much this morning before she went out." A near scowl crossed her elegant face. "Now why did that woman have to go and leave us here alone today when she knew something was afoot between the two of them?" she asked in frustration.

"Aunt Louisa said she had an appointment with

another breeder. Mr. Masterson had been counting
on it for months, and she could not break it, even
for . . . for—" Lucinda's voice broke off on a delicate
sob. Her mother put an arm around her and patted
her shoulder.

"Yes, yes, I know my dear. Even for an engagement." She scowled again. "She has been so certain
of the two of them almost from the moment they met
that she considered the whole thing over and done
as of last night, I suppose."

"Oh, no, Mama! Aunt Louisa would never be so
vulgar."

"Of course not, my dear," Mrs. Greeley assured her
daughter. "Perhaps, though, she did not know the
earl planned to call this morning."

Lucinda's emerald eyes brightened, and she looked
toward the hall table where a silver salver held the
day's post. "There did arrive a note for Aunt Louisa
this morning, Mama," she said, somewhat heartened.
"I was passing through the hall when it arrived by
messenger from Lord Bramfield's house."

Samantha Greeley's thin brows rose over her
straight nose, and she moved toward the table.

"From the viscount, you say? I wonder. . . ." She
took up the folded paper and turned it over. "Aha!
The seal bears the earl's signet. He must have sent it
from Bramfield House for some reason. Perhaps he
was held up this morning." The older woman put the
letter back on the tray and instructed the hall footman to be sure Mrs. Masterson received it as soon as
she returned home.

Lucinda was still uneasy. "But why did he send a
note to Aunt Louisa, Mama, and not to Anna herself?"

Mrs. Greeley linked her arm into her daughter's
and led her toward the drawing room. "Because, my
dear, an unmarried gentleman does not send letters

to an unmarried lady. It would not be considered
seemly."

From the small window of the traveling chaise,
Anna watched the sun set in a rose-violet haze. The
evening descended with brisk and brilliant clarity as
the stars began to glitter in an unusually clear early
summer night sky.

It would be a good day for travel tomorrow, she
thought, both hearing and feeling the slowing of the
coach as it pulled into the posting house. She was
almost sorry for it. Bad weather and uncomfortable
travel would have surely distracted her from the aching of her insides.

They had set out, after short preparation and much
attempted dissuading on the part of their host, quite
late in the afternoon, and had not gone far before
the coachman had told Anna and her aunt that they
would be stopping for the night. Anna was sorry they
could not travel in the dark. She was certain she
would not be able to sleep this night anyway, despite
her exhaustion and heavy head. Her aunt, though,
would need rest, and the roads were certainly safer
in the daylight.

They had left the house without saying good-bye to
Lucinda or Mrs. Greeley, for which Anna was both
immensely grateful and terribly sorry. They had become good friends, and she hoped this rudeness
would not harm what affection had grown up
amongst them. But, as she had explained to her aunt,
she could not remain in London another hour, let
alone an entire night. The Greeley ladies had gone
out in the afternoon and were not expected back until evening, just in time for supper. Anna could not
wait that long. She could not wait any longer for the
earl to arrive, for she was certain that he would not.

Somehow, during the course of her day alone, she had convinced herself that all she had thought of him was an illusion, a mirage that she had built up around her foolish hopes and wishes. She had made herself believe over the course of a frighteningly tearless day that he was not an honorable man, that he had in fact been playing with her, had invented this whole charade in order to amuse himself; now that it had come to its expected conclusion, he had tired of it and moved on to something else. Alone in her room, waiting for him to call, empty from lack of food and heartbroken over his betrayal, she had believed all of the terrible scenarios with which her fertile imagination had furnished her. Without explanation, she had begged her aunt to leave town, to set out this very day so that by sundown she could be as far as possible from the man who had caused her to feel this way.

Louisa Masterson had guessed at the reasons for her niece's desperate behavior, and had acquiesced to the scheme. She hoped that by the time they were on the road, perhaps sometime overnight, Anna would become calmer and her natural reason and levelheadedness would bring her to her senses once again. She did not know exactly what had precipitated the need for immediate flight, but her niece's unprecedented behavior had led her to act upon the girl's wishes and to hope for information to come later.

Anna's aunt had ordered the carriage to be readied, had given instructions to their maids for packing, and had sat down to write a hasty note to their hostess and her daughter, trying to explain as best she could what was happening. Louisa Masterson was certain their friends would understand; she just wished that she could have seen them to gain a better understanding of how the day had passed in her absence. She cursed the appointment that had made her leave the

house that day, and even more so the untrustworthy
lord who had, until this afternoon, had all of the trust
that Louisa could have hoped to lavish on her niece's
future husband.

She did not know why he had not called to ask for
Anna's hand today, so obvious was his intention of
doing just that the night before. She knew there must
be some explanation, but agreed silently with her
niece that it should come from him. As it had not,
she could offer no comfort to Anna, however useless
that made her. Her only real use could be in deliver-
ing Anna from the place that now offered her only
so much unhappiness. They did not belong in London, in any event. Louisa Masterson was glad to bid
it *adieu,* if even in such an unceremonious manner.

Now, gazing steadily at her niece as the carriage
pulled into the posting house yard, Louisa was not
certain she had made the right decision. The lovely
young girl looked almost as if she had seen her own
death. Her complexion was pallid, her eyes dull, with
none of the fevered anguish that had served to convince her aunt earlier that action was called for immediately. It was as if the girl had left her own heart
behind in London and was only now, a dozen or more
miles away into the countryside, discovering that she
could not live without it.

"Gone?" The earl's expression was a mask of hope-
less disbelief. He stood in the hallway of the Greeleys'
town house, hat forgotten in his hand.

"Yes, my lord, she left late today with her aunt, just
before madam and the young lady returned home for
the evening," replied the diminutive butler in his
most obsequious tone. "There is however a package
for you." The butler moved to the table in the hall
and withdrew a small paper-wrapped parcel. He

handed it to the earl, who ignored the man's obvious curiosity and opened it without hesitation. Fingers stiff, Valentine uncovered a neat stack of letters, bound with a blue satin ribbon. A folded paper lay atop the stack, and he opened it, his heart turning chill within him. In a neat, clear hand was written only: *Lord Alverston, I believe these are yours.*

The butler cleared his throat.

Valentine blinked, aware that he should say something, but unable to make any sound come out of his suddenly numb lips. He looked at the man blankly, and then his gaze swiveled to the hall table. Beside a thick stack of the post lay the note he had sent by messenger to the house so many hours earlier. It was unopened. His eyes moved back to the butler.

"A message from the Viscount Bramfield, apparently, my lord, to Mrs. Masterson," the little man said, with some diffidence in his voice. "It was covered over by the post and overlooked during the hurried preparations for the ladies' departure, I am afraid. The footman on duty has been reprimanded, of course," he added with satisfaction.

Valentine turned cold, steel-bright eyes on the butler, but his face did not otherwise betray his feelings. "Of course," he said. Then he turned and, without another word, walked out of the Greeleys' house and into the starless city night.

TWENTY

Dear Anna,

Mere hours have passed since you departed, but I must write to you of something that I fear you cannot like at all. Jason brought to the house this evening dreadful news: Lord Alverston is to fight a duel!

Jason heard the news at his club this afternoon; it seems to be quite common knowledge in the men's clubs. My betrothed even admitted that there is a betting book in which the earl's chances for—it is too terrible, Anna!—survival appear to be quite good! (Of course, my beloved did not put down a bet; he was as shocked as I!)

The earl is to meet the Marquess of Drysden tomorrow morning. Mama tells me that the Villain was at our ball last night, but I do not remember meeting him; perhaps he arrived late. It seems there exists a Quarrel of long standing, but some are saying that the earl resisted a duel and the marquess near forced him into it. I do not doubt it, darling Anna, knowing how the earl must love you so— Everyone saw how clearly he did last night! How could he agree to such a terrible thing when he is in love? If you will forgive me for

saying so, I think men fools, all of them, for forsaking
the women they love for some stupid ideal like Honor.
I cannot imagine what he could care so deeply about
that he would risk his own life. I am overset, I can
barely write for trembling with foreboding!

Dearest Anna, I will send this note by messenger, so
that you will receive it upon your return home. The
rider will likely pass you on the road, but it will be
better that you not know he bears this ill news. I will
write again tomorrow of the outcome. In the meantime,
I will be praying for our dear earl to survive the dawn's
dread.

> Your friend,
> Lucinda Greeley

* * *

> Pendleton House
> London

Dear Anna,

I have asked Lucinda to enclose this note to you in
her letter, since I am certain without reading her missive that she has painted the news we have learned of
in the most terrible colors. She is a dear, dear girl, and
I am ever grateful that you brought us together; but
she does tend to dramatize things, as you with your
levelheadedness would undoubtedly agree.

I know not how to approach the subject delicately,
and wish not to pry into your business, but you should
know that the earl will certainly come through the
morning's event with success. It is well known that he
has been maligned, that he refused the challenge honorably, and that he was given little opportunity to re-
fuse it a second time. It is also agreed that he is the

crack shot of the two, and as he has chosen pistols, apparently to his adversary's great dismay, he should come to no harm at all.

Do not fret, my friend. I will report to Lucinda what I learn on the morrow, and she will write you again to report to you the particulars. Until then, I remain

Yours,
Jason Pendleton

* * *

Field Street
London

Dearest Anna,

He has triumphed!

Jason came with the news at breakfast, and we were all so relieved and happy that Mama's stuffy butler almost suffered an apoplexy watching us cavort around the breakfast table in glee. It is such news, such happy news! I have just come from the breakfast room and left Jason and Mama and Papa there in order to write to you.

I will tell you everything that Jason reported to us, which he learned from Viscount Bramfield shortly after the duel. Jason refused to tell us where he had seen Lord Bramfield, and I am quite overset thinking that he may have attended the actual duel itself, but I did not say anything in Mama's presence, fearing that she would take it amiss of Jason were she to suspect the same thing. In any case, I shall tell you all that he told us just moments ago.

The earl and the marquess met at dawn, as planned, and the earl again stated his wish to cancel the duel. The marquess persisted and, we are told, went so far as to further insult Lord Alverston. (Jason was par-

ticularly reticent on the details of this point, I'm afraid, and I was quite upset with him for withholding important words that were spoken, but he was adamantly silent on the topic.) They took up their pistols, counted off, and fired. Oh, Anna! Can you imagine how dreadful it must have been? Even imagining that my dear, beloved Jason may have been there within hearing distance of it all makes me shiver with terror!

The earl was not hit; the marquess's hand shook so that he fired off into a tree, Jason said the viscount told him. Lord Alverston shot the marquess in the arm, it seems. The viscount told Jason that he was certain the earl meant to hit his opponent there, since the earl is accounted an excellent shot and had not wanted to kill the man in any case, even were he to be killed himself in turn. What bravery! A doctor saw to the marquess's wound, and it is believed he will not even bear a scar from the incident, so slight was the injury.

I have told you of the duel now, have discharged my duty with great joy. Oh, darling Anna! Happy Anna! How relieved you must be to hear such great tidings! I know that you love the earl. Last night I lay abed until it was light out, trying to think of the reason you left in such haste yesterday. I concluded it was because you knew of the duel and felt its wrong keenly, as any gently bred female would, and could not bear to remain longer when your beloved was going so willingly to his death and was so inconsiderate of your feelings. I fell asleep in greatest admiration for you, my good friend, and am happy that now that your reason for leaving has disappeared, you can return to the people who love you and long for your company again.

Please do come back to London, Anna. I await your return with confident hope.

Your friend,
Lucinda Greeley

* * *

Pendleton House
London

Dear Mr. Masterson,

 Information has come to my attention of which I think you and your wife should be aware. I share this with you in the hope that you will see fit to pass it on to your niece, in whose happiness I and my family-to-be are very interested.

 Knowing how very close are you and your wife to Miss Tremain, and how those in your family share each other's woes, as you do your joys, with a common heart, I must assume you have some knowledge of the duel that was fought not a sennight ago in London between the Earl of Alverston and the Marquess of Drysden. The news concerns their history of antago-nism, and serves to expiate the earl of any wrong of which he has been accused. In the absence of correspon-dence from your niece, my betrothed and Mrs. Greeley have been trying to understand the depth of feeling that could have driven Miss Tremain from Town last week. I feel that I may have some better understanding of what may be involved, being privy to information that ladies are less likely to hear in their rounds of London Society. Because of this, I wish to share with you the following.

 The accusations directed toward Lord Alverston had to do with his part in arming a village of civilians in Spain who were under attack during Wellington's Pen-insular Campaign, along with British soldiers, by a French regiment of considerable strength. Those Span-iards who were armed when the French won the ill-matched battle were executed, along with several of the remaining British soldiers. The marquess had been put-ting about this rumor, along with the information that the earl had acted out of simple arrogance. It seems that much of the story is true, but not entirely.

Shortly after the duel last week, a former officer under Wellington came forward to denounce the marquess publicly and officially. He served under Drysden during the campaign in which the village under the earl's protection was attacked by the French, and had a very different story to tell of the events that passed there. It seems that when Alverston applied to Drysden for reinforcements, which he did three times by messenger after his own company had been nearly decimated, Drysden and his unit were already occupied, but not honorably. The officer reported that he had previously been afraid to admit to the truth, fearing for himself, but when he heard of the injustice of Drysden's challenge to fight the earl, his conscience had forced him to speak out.

Drysden's company had taken up quarters, it appears, in a Spanish brothel. The messengers from Alverston at the besieged village had arrived, but Drysden and his men had been too busy with their house's former tenants to respond to the summons. Shortly, when the marquess learned what had passed at the village through another company's commander, he had quickly fabricated the lie that Alverston had not called upon him at all, and that had he done so, he and his soldiers would have been ready and willing to fight the Frenchmen. To protect himself, Drysden threatened his officers that if they divulged the truth they could be sure of retribution from both him and the Home Office. With the fear of court-martials hanging over their lives, Drysden's officers agreed to the falsification, leaving the marquess to elaborate upon the untruth with which he had begun.

It seems that the defamation of the earl undertaken here in Town over the past several weeks had much to do with Drysden's fear that somehow the truth would be found out. The marquess had learned of Lord Alverston's return to Town after a two-year hiatus, and *became concerned. He conceived of a plan to weave a web of social disgust so strong among the* ton *that the earl would be forced to abandon London and perhaps even Society altogether. It backfired on him, I am glad to report.*

As I am certain your wife has told you, Mr. Masterson, the earl is an honorable man. I could not wish for your niece's unhappiness ever, but especially not if it is sustained under false pretenses. I trust you will see fit to share this information with her, in the hope that the breach that has come between them will be that much nearer to mending.

> *Your servant,*
> *Hon. Jason Frederick Pendleton*

* * *

> *Hedgecliff*
> *_____shire*

Dear Samantha,

I am unable to provide you with encouraging news with regard to my niece. Although when she is in company with her uncle and me it is hard to detect any unhappiness in her demeanor, we know it is there nonetheless. She has kept much to herself this week that we have been home, a previous tendency that has become quite extreme since our return from London. She eats little, and her attention often wanders so that I find I must address her several times when I wish to speak to her.

You will note, of course, that these are the signs of love, but I fear that in this case they are not welcome signs. We have heard nothing from Lord Alverston . . . .

* * *

Bramfield House
London

Dear Louisa,

*I think you ought to know, I have been told by my
son Timothy that Alverston has returned to his country
seat. He received notice from his sister that she is returning to England; it seems she has been abroad in
America since her Exile from Society. The earl left for
the countryside so that he can meet her upon her arrival at their home. . . .*

Anna sat with her back to the afternoon sun, the
broad brim of her straw hat sprinkling dapples of sunlight onto her upturned face.

She was watching a hawk circling the edge of the
wood not far from her uncle's orchard. The great,
dark bird descended on broad wings toward the tree-
tops in ever-decreasing circles, gliding on the early
summer breeze as it sought its prey below. Anna
blinked, allowing her lashes to lie against her cheeks
for a moment longer than necessary, thereby resting
her eyes, and when she opened them again the bird
was gone. At this time of year the predator had not
needed long for its hunt, she thought pragmatically,
if a little sadly.

Little in her occupations and experiences of the
past two weeks had *not* struck her as melancholy. She
berated herself daily for her mood, especially when
she espied the looks of sympathy and concern in her
aunt and uncle's gazes upon her. Anna was loath to
advertise her despondency, and was doing her best to
bring herself back into spirits again, or to hide it
when she was unable to rouse herself—which seemed
to be more the usual case than not.

She tried to distract herself with reading and found

that her mind strayed too often from the page, no matter how interesting the text seemed to be. She painted and her brush strayed off the canvas and onto her skirt in her preoccupation with visions that were not of the landscape before her. She sat down to write to her friends in London and was unable to hold the pen for the strength of the memories that came flooding into her mind with an action as ordinary as the dipping of the quill into ink. She had even tried to ride away her thoughts, and had spent several wild mornings racing across the fields on her mare, hoping for forgetfulness and an exhaustion of body that would allow her to find solace in sleep when night finally came. Oblivion won this way was only temporary, however, and when her uncle made note to her after several days that he was concerned for her safety, she withdrew from the stables in shame, as much for having misused her cherished horse as for the knowledge that her attempts at stemming the flow of her unhappiness were not going unnoticed by her family.

Finally she had come to see that she could not will away her broken heart through keeping herself active. Her love had been a long time in growing, and would be an even longer time in dying. Anna recognized disconsolately that she would have to wait it out, wait for the pain to abate, for the images to grow dim, for the feelings to fade. She would be a wrinkled octogenarian before that day came, of course, but she was confident that if she made it that far, she would undoubtedly triumph.

Perhaps, she mused grimly, she would write some bad poetry. She had been reading some before she left London, for amusement and to know what her acquaintances were speaking of more than for her own personal edification. Anna was certain she could spin verses of woe and melancholy as effective as those of the latest popular poets or at least she could approximate them. Why, she had been writing for an audience for over a year already, she thought with a bitter smile; this could not be that much different, after all.

Anna let her gaze stray in the direction of her aunt's garden, and was surprised to see a footman approaching her from the house with something in his hand.

"Miss Anna, a letter has just arrived for you by messenger," the man said, holding out an envelope in his gloved hand. Anna took it and attempted a smile.

"Thank you, Thomas. It is good of you to bring it out here to me." The footman nodded and looked meaningfully at her, but Anna had already turned away, intent once again on the horizon far beyond the edge of the woods. The day was gloriously bright, the heavens blue, and the gentle hills of the pastures and farmland before her rolled one upon another until they met the sky many miles away. She took in a breath of fresh, summer-scented air, and looked down at the letter in her hand. Her heart froze.

It was from the earl.

Ever since the moment the carriage had pulled away from the Greeleys' town house two weeks ago, Anna had regretted the loss of the letters he had written to her over those many months. She castigated herself for her hasty decision to return them to him, to let him know in that dramatic gesture that she was ignorant of his charade no longer. For if she had kept them, she realized when it was too late, at least she would have something of him, something to remember him with; something to bring back to her those lovely months of happiness during their correspondence, when she had thought the letters came from his sister and felt delight at every one she received; something to hold when she imagined again what it had felt like to be held by him during those precious

hours when she had known she was in love with him
and had believed that he had felt the same for her.

Now, although she had given up those treasures,
she was still able to recognize the writing of the man
who had penned them. The bold script of the direction stared up at her with tantalizing force. Anna had
so convinced herself that with his letters she had left
Lord Alverston behind as well, it took her a moment
to bring herself to believe the letter in her hand was
truly from the earl himself.

Slowly, with thudding heart, she broke open the
wax seal and unfolded a heavy single sheet of paper.
Inside it were yet more pages, folded together and
likewise sealed, addressed to Anna at the Greeleys'
townhouse. She took the opened sheet in one hand
and the sunlight fell upon it, blurring the few lines
of black ink in brightness before her eyes adjusted.

Dear Anna,

*I send this in the hopes that you will be kind enough
to read it, even knowing from whom it comes. I know
not what else to do now but share with you this that
I had hoped you would never read; after this short time
spent out of your company, I am compelled to do something to restore myself to your graces, however futile the
effort may prove.*

*It would indeed be craven of me to wish that every-
thing could have happened differently. I pray that when
you read the enclosed you will take it into your heart
to understand, if not to forgive. I have been awarded
the treasure of your affection once before, and cannot
expect that fortune could be so generous as to allow it
to me again.*

Valentine

TWENTY-ONE

Anna swallowed down the lump that had risen in her throat and wiped her fingers across her moistened eyes.

Again? How could she give him her affection again when she had never taken it away from him?

Even the few words of the note served to prove to Anna the futility of her own will. She had not stopped loving the earl, not even when she had discovered his perfidy. She had felt anger, fear, betrayal, hurt, and finally foolishness; but she had never ceased to love him. Even to respect him. She had not been able to convince herself that he was a dishonorable man, no matter what the facts were. Her mind and heart had both rebelled at her own folly of continuing to esteem him, but neither emotion nor reason had prevailed. She had loved him for longer than she had known him and nothing, not even such a reversal, could serve to erase that so easily.

Wiping her now streaming tears on the back of her hand, Anna fumbled for the sealed letter with her other hand and opened it. She smoothed out the pages of fine writing paper with trembling fingers, her eyes seeking the salutation.

Alverston House
Mayfair

Dearest Anna,

   Tomorrow morning I shall meet the Marquess of Drysden in an ill-starred duel. There is a chance that I will not leave the field alive. It grows late, but I write this now to you in the event that I should not see you again after the morrow, and thus would leave you with no explanation as to my actions of the past year and a half.
   I am aware that I do not deserve the opportunity to explain myself, and that you have no obligation to satisfy me by hearing what I have to say. On the chance, however, that your heart is not entirely closed to me already, I must offer you this narrative, for my sake and for yours. You are, I know well, tender of conscience, and my own feeling rebels at the idea of leaving you without some justification for what I have done. Once you are in possession of the whole, I welcome you as my judge; Heaven could not provide for me one more just or compassionate.
   You know already that I was the author of the letters you received in my sister's name from Alverston Hall this past year and more. It is the greatest punishment for me to have them back, as they are a tangible marker of the wrong I have done you, a wrong which can never be erased. I will tell you, though, that despite this wrong, I could not ever wish to erase it. Your letters have meant more to me than anything that I have been given or have experienced, before or since, and I will cherish them until I die—be that day tomorrow or decades from now.
   But I should begin at the beginning.
   I returned home from Spain shortly after my release from the French prison in which I had been held, as

I told you last night. I learned of my father's and brother's death upon my release, and traveled to England immediately after the hearing at the Home Office to take up my unexpected inheritance. I then passed several unhappy months at Alverston Hall, deeply troubled by the experience of which I told you. My days I filled with drink or intense work, oftentimes both, and my nights passed in nightmares only slightly less horrible than the reality I had witnessed in Spain. I spent my time alone, unable to sleep and unfit for the company of others. My steward did what he could with me to teach me of the responsibilities of an earl, for which I had not been groomed, but I fear that at times even he despaired of me. I was barely living, and had no particular wish to continue doing even that. It tells as a pathetic story now, but at the time I truly had no notion that I would ever emerge from that living death.

Then one evening I chanced to notice the letters you had sent to my sister after her Season in London. I was quite foxed, and recalling the girl that you had been, I opened them and read them, an act unmistakably ungentlemanly. When I had, I was unable not to act upon your entreaties; I felt that by allowing my sister to maintain her silence from you, I myself was at fault for your unhappiness.

I will not try to convince you of how I did attempt to write to you in my own persona *to explain the situation. In short, I failed to do so to my satisfaction. In order to satisfy myself, and you, and to respect my sister's misguided wish to remain silent, I found myself writing to you as if I were she instead. I cannot explain to you or justify how or why I came to do this. I do not understand it myself. I do not regret, however, my unorthodox and wholly dishonorable act.*

I received your response to my letter when in a particularly wretched humor. The warmth and caring that you expressed pierced through my grief and filled me with a longing for comfort that I had not known I needed until the moment I read your letter. I wrote back to you in full knowledge that what I was doing was wrong, but needing so desperately to trust in someone, and to lose myself in someone else's unfrightful world, that I did not care.

It was only after this had continued for quite some time that I recognized how through your letters—full of joy and compassion, intelligence and humor—I was learning to feel once again at peace in the world. I began to see in my own household and the people around me the things I had always before taken such delight in, things I had not been able to see since Spain for the images and the knowledge that assailed me night and day in their place. I began to live again, and to love the world I was living in. I was nourished by your words, like a man who has been in the desert for years who, when he finally finds water, cannot stop drinking it. I drank my fill, and became whole again.

Anna, I realized that I felt something profound for the author of those letters many months before we met in Town. In London, however, I learned that what I had been feeling—based on your written words, your stories, your thoughts as you saw fit to share them on paper—could not compare to the love I treasured once I came to know the entire woman. I have heard of how when a man recovers from a serious illness he is liable to fancy himself enamored of his nurse, and I admit I feared such a thing to some extent. But after only a short time in your presence I knew that this was not the case for me. You are a woman of spirit and peacefulness, animation and contemplation, passion and laughter. I found healing in your compassion and courage, delight in your wit and irreverence. My heart met its desire.

I cannot bring myself to regret the false hand I have played you. For if I had not, I may never have known *you, only the lovely package that your heart and spirit are wrapped in. I have seen that you keep these well guarded from most others; indeed, I took courage in the fact that with me you did not do so. I imagined— convinced myself—that if you came to care for me, you would not so easily despise me for what I had done when you learned of it. I was wrong.*

When last night I saw in your eyes the trust that you offered to me, that I had taken from you, I despised myself more than ever I had before. Even the emptiness I lived through for so many months after Callanera did not compare to the terrible mixture of pleasure and pain I felt last night when I was holding you in my arms, knowing that this time I had been the one who had brought on my own destruction.

I will not ask your forgiveness, for I cannot expect you to give it to me. As I have said, I write only so that you can understand better why I have done what I did, and so you will know that should I not survive the morning I have loved you with a heart scarred and imperfect, but entirely and eternally yours.

Valentine Monroe

A warm breeze stirred the pages lying across Anna's lap, and a few stray tendrils of golden brown hair escaped from her hat and whispered over her cheeks and eyes. She raised her hand absently to push them back, feeling an unmistakable, marvelous rush of joy slowly welling up inside of her.

Messenger? Had Thomas said that a messenger had brought the letter? It had not come with the regular post? She must catch him! Perhaps he was waiting at the house. She must not let him leave without sending a reply.

Anna quickly gathered the pages of the letter into her hands and stood up. She turned toward the house, her face radiant with what she imagined was ill-advised happiness, but which nonetheless she could not deny, and met the dark gaze of the earl.

She gasped. He stood not five yards away from her, his back against the peach tree under which she had read and written so many letters from and to him over those many months. As she watched in amazement, her heart pounding in her breast, he straightened and began to walk slowly toward her. His expression was enigmatic, unreadable in the bright midday sunshine. His eyes, though, glowed richly gray. Anna was mesmerized. She stood, unmoving, until he was standing just before her. If she reached out, she could have touched him.

"I knew the time it would take for the post to return a letter to me coming from this house," he began, his voice low and not entirely even. "If, that is, I should be so fortunate," he added and paused. "I could not wait that long."

Anna stared up at him, once again speechless in his presence, her heart beating rapidly within her. During the past two weeks, she had thought missing him was the most awful thing she would ever have to bear in her life. Now, with him standing before her and looking impossibly handsome and vulnerable, she knew that she had sincerely underestimated the depth of her feelings.

Sunlight played in the locks of his dark hair, the breeze causing an unruly curl to stray across his brow. She imagined herself reaching up to smooth away the creases forming there as the earl's expression changed.

"Have I done wrong, Anna?" he asked softly, tentatively. "Should I have remained at home and waited? Have I again been overly confident?" He paused. "Would a reply ever have come?"

With these words her voice came back to her, and

she did reach out with her empty hand. The earl took it in both of his and carried it to his lips. The brush of his kiss on her upturned palm caused her own words to quiver.

"Yes, a reply would have come," she said. "I have become so accustomed to writing to you, you see, that I do not think I could do otherwise now."

His eyes showed unease as she removed her hand from his and touched his cheek with the barest caress. His skin was smooth along the cheekbone, roughening toward his jaw. She reveled in the sensations against her fingers.

His hand came up and stilled hers. "You cannot be happy with this correspondence, then? You do it out of habit or some sort of pity for me?" His suddenly aching eyes bore into hers, his hand clasped hers tightly, and Anna felt her breath quit her for a moment. A tear escaped her eye and ran down her cheek.

"You are mistaken, my lord," she said as evenly as she could. "I have done it, and would do it now still, out of love."

The transformation of his expression was rapid, but not entirely complete either. Anna felt herself holding firmly onto his hand, trying to express to him through her touch the truth of her words. A smile trembled at the corners of her mouth as she watched his eyes take on a glow that warmed her from head to toe.

Valentine reached up and drew her broad-brimmed hat back from her head, dropping it on the bench behind her. Still holding her hand, with his other one, he gently touched her clear brow and ran his fingers through her long, silken hair.

"You will not tell me you have forgiven me?" he asked, more of a statement than a question, his eyes roaming her face.

"You said you would not ask forgiveness of me. How can I give it if it is not requested?" she said. "You must remember, my lord, that I am a lady. It would not *become* me to give away something unsolicited."

Her voice was not entirely even, and he looked down into her eyes sharply. Anna stared up into his, her own glowing now with love and, amazingly, mischief. Valentine felt the fear and apprehension and guilt he had been carrying with him melt away as her lips curved into an inviting smile.

"I have forgotten my breeding entirely, I fear," he said, drawing her close and wrapping an arm around her. She fit against him with delicious ease, her free hand resting on the front of his dark coat. "And if I were to request forgiveness, in an uncharacteristically gentlemanly manner?" He gazed into her eyes, not inches away from his, and Anna's heart turned over.

"I would not wish you to step out of character for me, my lord," she replied on a smile. "For it is that very character that I have come to love." She felt his arm tighten, and her fingers played at the lapel of his coat. "But I would still offer my forgiveness, nonetheless." Her eyes rose from his cravat to look into his smoky gaze. "And with my forgiveness, would you accept also my censure?"

The earl's look turned confused and he began to move away from her as he sought for words, but Anna held onto his lapel and pulled him close again. She looked directly at him, eyes suddenly alight with sparks.

"How could you—you foolish man!—fight a duel?" she demanded angrily, shakily. Her hands went to his shoulders, his face, as if she was just now realizing that she had almost lost the chance to ever touch him like this. "I could kill you myself for doing such a senseless, foolhardy thing!" She gestured to the pages that she had let fall to the ground beside them. "If you had been killed, or arrested and thrown in gaol, a thousand letters would not have served to comfort me," she said with fervor.

Valentine took her frantically moving hands in his and drew them again to his mouth.

"My love, again I am sorry," he said, drawing her then into his arms. "I knew how foolish I was to accept the challenge, and I promise you that I made every attempt to stop it." He cradled her head against his broad chest, and Anna's hands curved up around his neck. She looked up at him.

"Why did you not simply cry off?" Her eyes were bright. "Was it that you could not bear to have your honor further injured?" she asked, and her voice held an unmistakable tone of regret.

"It was not my honor that Drysden was threatening," Valentine said after a pause, "but yours, my love." Anna gasped softly, seeing in his eyes the reluctance he felt to speak of it. "I could not stand by and allow it to happen," he added. "I am sorry to have done what I did, but I could see no other way out of it."

Valentine looked off at the horizon and then back at Anna's wondering face. A rueful grin creased his lips.

"I seem to be using that as an excuse rather frequently as of late," he said, not ill-humoredly. Anna's lips curved into a smile in response, and Valentine felt her fingers curl in the hair at the nape of his neck.

"And given your present *situation*, my lord," she said, her voice suddenly low, her eyes shimmering with something he had not seen in them before, "what options can you see now upon which to base your actions?" Her face tilted up to his, and her full, rose pink lips parted slightly in a tantalizing smile.

"I am not an inventive man, my love," he whispered huskily. "I can see only one."

His lips met hers in a gentle caress that quickly turned hungry as the earl pulled her tightly against him. Anna's arms encircled his neck, her body thrumming with sensation, and she met his kisses with a passion she had not known she was capable of. She drank in the wondrous feeling of his mouth moving atop hers, his hard body pressed against her, his hands beginning to move over her back in sensuous rhythm; and desire surged within her until she could barely stand it.

Valentine drew back, for the first time in his life fully regretful of having to do so. His dark eyes reflected the passion in hers, and he felt himself trembling with the force of his hunger for the woman in his arms. Her lips, reddened and damp, drew his gaze, and he closed his eyes for a moment, setting his forehead against hers. Anna sighed.

"I am glad," she said.

"Glad of what, my love?" Valentine asked, his hand underneath the fall of hair behind her neck caressing her skin tantalizingly.

"Oh, of a great many things, actually," she responded, "but especially that you are uninventive."

Lord Alverston pulled away a bit and looked at her in curious amusement. Gazing at the expression of incipient mischief on her beautiful face, he was amazed to feel his blood racing. With a deep breath, he took her hand in his and drew her away from the house, toward the path that wound through the orchard and out onto the hills beyond. "And why is that?" he asked as she fell into step beside him. Her hand was tucked in his arm snugly, as they walked along closely.

"Well, because if you had been really creative I might have been writing letters for over a year to your

estate lawyer, or your Aunt Broomhilda, for all I
know." She looked up at him, her eyes dancing.
"Really, Valentine, you could have thought up something much more outrageous." Anna could not repress the laughter in her voice. "As it was, you
learned of the side of me that hoped to entertain
your sister in particular, and that really is a rather
tame side, after all."

Valentine laughed. "Tame! I beg to differ," he pro-
tested "I would wager that the two of you have not
spent a tame day together in your lives. Why, when I
was younger I felt positively green with envy at the
stories I used to hear from my father of your esca-
pades here during the summertime. My friends and
I never thought up such outrageous capers, at school
or afterward."

They were walking through the rows of peach trees,
the fresh green of the new buds lustrous in the summer sunlight. Anna broke off a bloom from a tree
and twirled it around in her fingers. Valentine drew
her hand to his mouth and breathed in the fragrance
of the white blossom, then kissed the fingers that held
it. He lingered on the last and gazed over Anna's
hand into her slightly flushed face. The warmth in
his eyes took her breath away. She let her gaze drop,
and she chuckled as they resumed walking.

"They were all Valerie's ideas," she said, shaking
her head. "She dreamed up all of our most dangerous and shocking adventures. I went along because
she wanted me to, and because I could never say no
to her." Anna's voice had grown reflective. "She was
the sister I never had."

The two had arrived at the edge of the hill and
the end of the orchard, and rolling hills of farmland
stretched out before them for miles. Valentine turned
to Anna, his expression sober.

"You have been very hurt by her silence," he said,

knowing the truth of the words he spoke. "I regret having made you believe something of her that was false."

Anna gazed down at their joined hands, and let her thumbs run over the roughened skin of his strong hands. She brought her gaze back to his.

"You must not regret it. Each action serves a purpose, however wrong it may be to begin with." She touched his face with her fingers, and he leaned his cheek into her palm, closing his dark eyes. "Your actions brought us to each other," she said wonderingly, and then put her hand in his again and looked away. "I feel sorrow only that she did not come to us for comfort." Anna's gaze sought Valentine's. "We could have given it to her, but she did not seek it from us. Why?"

Valentine shook his head. "I do not know, Anna. I wrote to her every month," he said, "but she never responded. Until now, that is."

"Yes, and now she will return to find things much changed in her absence," Anna said somewhat shyly, beginning again to smile. She looked up at him through lowered lashes.

"So much changed that she will truly have a sister when she comes home?" Valentine's voice was hopeful yet unsure. "Can you marry me, after all that has passed, all that I have done?"

She gazed at him in wonderment, drinking in every line and detail of his beloved face, wishing that she could wipe away the memories, the pain still weighing on his spirit, but knowing that what remnants there were would take a lifetime to heal.

"What have you done but love others and try to protect them?" she asked gently, and watched his expression alter again until his eyes shone.

"Will you marry me, my love?" His voice was again husky, taking Anna by surprise, and his gaze held hers so firmly that she was mesmerized by its intensity. She tried to think of something to say, something that would convince him of her feelings, her constancy, but she could not. There were no words to express what she felt, what she had found in him.

Valentine drew her toward him again finally, as he had been wanting to do since they had begun walking. His arms circled her waist, and Anna felt a tingling in her everywhere that he touched her. She wrapped her arms around him, wanting to feel every inch of his broad, masculine body with her own, and for once in her life not knowing how to express with words what she was feeling so powerfully with her entire being.

"Anna, I love you," Valentine said softly as he brought his mouth down on hers. The kiss, long and deep, left them both breathless, yearning for more.

"And I love you, Valentine, my lord," Anna said, losing herself in the longing in his storm-gray eyes. "I do so with all of my heart and soul."

The next time their lips met, Valentine had no doubt as to the answer to his question.

More Zebra Regency Romances